# *What the critics are saying...*

৪৩

### THE CAKE BABE

**4 Hearts** "THE CAKE BABE was full of humor and lots of hot sex. This quickie is enough story to make your icing drip. This reviewer really enjoyed this story." ~ *Love Romances and More*

**5 Angels** "This was a good summer wedding read. It's not very often that I fall in love with a couple who have just met but with these two I did. […] This story draws you into the book, and you cannot wait for Jason and Marissa to be the ones getting married. Great job M. A. Ellis for a book that was very well written, and I'll be looking for more books from this author." ~ *Fallen Angels Reviews*

### HALLOW'S EVE HUNK

**5 Lips and Reviewer's Choice Award** "I simply loved this delicious little story. Reading *Hallow's Eve Hunk* by M.E. Ellis is like eating the entire bowl of Kandy Korn on Halloween; very, very naughty, but oh so pleasurable! […] Halloween is such a fun holiday; my advice is skip the high calorie candy and reward yourself with reading this delightful story instead. I guarantee you'll wish for your own 'Hallow's Eve Hunk!" ~ *Two Lips Reviews*

**5 Angels** "M. A. Ellis is a fantastic writer and hooked me on her books […] This book did something that I don't think an Ellora's Cave book has ever done for me and that was to bring tears to my eyes at the end of the book. The emotion was very in your face and impossible to ignore. I'm counting the days for the next Henderson brother's book. Great job, Ms. Ellis!" ~ *Fallen Angels Reviews*

## LOVE'S ALLY

**5 Angels** "This book was hot, hot and hot! […] The thing about the book that hooked it for me was the very end, I dare you to read it and not laugh yourself silly because it shows that these two people are absolutely perfect for each other."

~ *Fallen Angels Reviews*

**4 Lips** "The verbal sparring and clever exchanges in *Love's Ally* add a nice flavor to this smoking-hot erotic novella from M.A. Ellis. […] Overall this was a very enjoyable read."

~ *Two Lips Reviews*

# HARD
## AS *Nails*
# M.A. ELLIS

ELLORA'S CAVE
ROMANTICA PUBLISHING

An Ellora's Cave Romantica Publication

www.ellorascave.com

Hard as Nails

# HARD AS NAILS

ઝ

# THE CAKE BABE

&

# Dedication

## ❧

*For Elliott,*

*Your belief was the foundation. Your encouragement built the stairway. Your strength pulled me back on the treads when I threatened to careen over the side. I cherish each and every day I've been blessed with you by my side and love you with all my heart.*


# Acknowledgements

## ❧

*My heartfelt thanks to Jaynie Ritchie, editor extraordinaire. You have helped me reach that final step and I will forever be grateful.*


# Trademarks Acknowledgement

## ❧

The author acknowledges the trademarked status and trademark owners of the following wordmarks mentioned in this work of fiction:

Godiva: Godiva Brands, Inc.

Ritz: The Ritz-Carlton Hotel Company, L.L.C.

# Chapter One

### ∞

Marissa Hughes heard the commotion in the distance and chose to ignore it. She rotated the turntable another two inches and pulled the spatula upward with a final flourish. *Ta-da.*

"Now that's what I'm talking about," a boyish voice echoed from the doorway of the private kitchen.

"Hey, Randy." She offered a quick smile to the shamelessly beautiful brother of the bride-to-be. He, like the rest of his siblings, was proof that perfection ran through the gene pool of the McLaughlin clan.

"Sissy's *chatting* with the caterer right now. She's already reduced the florist to tears. I was worried you might be next."

"No chance," Marissa replied confidently. She did excellent work. Her wedding cakes had become the talk of Grand Harbor and the surrounding enclaves.

"You're pretty confident, gorgeous."

"Gotta be, and save your flirting for the mindless horde of adoring females at the reception. Those smooth lines don't work on me, buddy."

"Geez. Talk about cutting a guy off at the knees." He walked behind her as she rinsed her utensils off in the sink.

"I'm sure your ego will survive." She adored Randy. He was as equally spoiled, and privileged as the rest of his siblings. Yet, in stark contrast, he was genuinely kind. His mother and Marissa's sister were best friends. She'd known Randy since the day he was born, all red and wrinkly. At fourteen she had found a surrogate baby brother. She smiled at the memory. He wrapped his arms around her waist and rested his chin on her shoulder.

11

"There's leftover iiii-ciiiing," he singsonged next to her ear, and she had to laugh. "Come on, Auntie M. Just one teeny taste?"

Jay turned the corner into the country club's guest kitchen and halted mid-stride. When the "Wicked Bride of the West" had issued her order, he'd been more than happy to oblige. He heard that laugh and quickened his pace. He never expected to find her, *the cake babe*, wrapped in a pair of lanky, teenage arms.

He'd caught glimpses of her all morning as she worked, seemingly impervious to the flurry of activity that was striving for a *Grand Harbor Packet* headline proclaiming this the wedding of the season. She'd been focused on her work. This was a giant plus for him. He didn't have to worry about her noticing him staring a little too long at the hint of lush curves under her white chef's jacket. She had a great ass. He noticed that when she bent over a large plastic storage bin on the kitchen floor. He nearly dropped the case of beer he'd been holding. The loose, striped pants had stretched taut over her roundness and his mouth had actually gone dry. Much like it was now.

He cleared his throat and they turned as one. The McLaughlin brat apparently felt no need to release her. She looked pretty comfy there too. Shit. Maybe she liked them young and pliant in her tiny hands. Or perfectly formed mouth. *Who wouldn't want to be pressed against those full lips?* His cock twitched in response.

"The bride wants a bottled water." His words came out harsh and both pairs of eyes widened.

"I'll get it," the kid offered with a laugh and Jay didn't miss the little squeeze he gave the cake babe. Mental images of her interrupted his work more than a few times that morning. She was fantasy material for sure, all in a neat "hi, I'm your neighbor" package.

"See you guys later."

He barely heard the kid as he closed the distance between them. A few tendrils of chestnut colored curls had broken free from her ponytail and Jay couldn't resist the urge. He reached out and rubbed the silkiness between his fingers before brushing the strands behind her ear.

"So. You offering free tastes?"

The breath Marissa was holding hitched. From his touch, from his words, she wasn't sure which. *Wouldn't it just suck to faint when things were suddenly getting interesting?* She'd seen him that morning when he slid a case of beer into the industrial refrigerator. She pretended not to notice, but anyone with half a pulse would have responded. Now he loomed before her in all his yumminess. Sandy blond hair framed his chiseled face. Eyes the color of warm maple syrup bore into her. His chest was wide, the muscles corded under the worn damp t-shirt that proclaimed *Tattooed In Places You'd Love To Lick*. If only he knew.

"Are you?" His voice was low, utterly seductive. Marissa gripped the sink and eased her legs together against a rush of unfamiliar warmth.

"Am I what?" Heat was creeping slowing into each and every pore.

"Giving out free tastes?" He looked ready to devour her.

*Oh, yeah!* "No," she replied, trying to get her heartbeat under control. He had the nicest lips. Her fingers itched to trace them.

"No?" He sounded disappointed, but the corner of his mouth rose.

"I can't waste any. I need to make sure I have enough." How could a supposedly mundane conversation about frosting make a person so damn hot? She knew the answer, of course. It had nothing to do with talk and everything to do with timing. The girls had predicted just last Tuesday over margaritas she was due. According to Tarot-reading Tessa, the cards told it all. Eleven months of self-imposed celibacy was too long.

"And when will you know if you have enough?" His lips parted to reveal straight, white teeth.

Concentrate. Focus. So hard to do when she could feel the heat rolling off his big body.

"Later. After I get the latticework and edging on." *Good job, Marissa. That sounded pretty normal.* "When all the flowers are done. I'll be here the rest of the day."

"Maybe even into the night?"

*Oh, lord.* Need reached lazily outward in a big, giant yawn. "Maybe," she whispered.

"So, not even a little taste now?"

The amber gaze bore into her and she licked her dry lips. He gave her a sexy grin that made her belly clench and her heart stumble.

"I'm a patient guy; I'll see you later."

Body thrumming, Marissa watched him walk away, enjoying the way the faded denim hugged his ass. He didn't turn and wave when he reached the door. *Why would he?* Hot guys didn't wave bu-bye. Hot guys caused nothing but pain where she was involved. To be fair, so did the not-so-hot ones. Her relationships had been few, usually short-lived and always disastrous. She had sworn off men and it had worked.

Her business had grown rapidly and she pushed relationships to the back far right burner, the one for extra low simmer. She didn't need to date. That was the mantra she repeated most evenings and every weekend. Her friends believed all she needed was a quickie—a little mindless sex to take the edge off her periodic loneliness. That wasn't, as the saying went, how she rolled. But damn. She might just reconsider if it was Mr. Tall, Ripped and Gorgeous for just one night.

The thought sifted in and out of her mind all day. She worked steadily on the wedding cake, the intricate details failing to keep her as focused as she wished. Her nerves were strung so tight she literally jumped when the pizza guy popped his head in the door and asked where the delivery went.

A fragile petal crumbled in her hand. *Fifth one today.* She was having serious trouble concentrating with each passing half hour. Her back ached, the pressure between her thighs had never truly abated and she was starving.

"They must belong out back, in the tent. I didn't order," she said, tossing the ruined flower in the trash. The wafting smell of pepperoni made her stomach growl.

No sooner had the guy left than another man walked in.

"'Scuse me. Do you know where Jason put the beer?"

Jason. *Nice.* But it became apparent with each passing minute there really wasn't going to be time for the "I'll wait 'til later" moment she'd been picturing all afternoon. *Get a grip, girl.*

"I think he put it in the walk-in cooler," she replied.

"Wow. Pretty cake," he said on his way past. "All those flowers made from icing? They look real."

"All edible," she smiled. "The bride wanted roses, lilies and forget-me-nots."

"Yeah," he snorted. "What Sissy wants, Sissy gets." He pulled open the cooler and retrieved the beer. "Want one?"

"No thanks, I'm almost done. Have a nice night."

"You too. It's gotta be better than the day," he mumbled on his way out.

Marissa smiled. She'd been spared Sissy's prenuptial wrath. In true bridezilla fashion, the woman had turned into a profanity-breathing dragon and cut a swath through the ranks that afternoon. It wouldn't have mattered if Sissy's ire had come in her direction; Marissa would have tuned her out and kept all thoughts on him. *Jason*. It was nice to put a name to the man behind the daydreams. The very wet daydreams.

It was one lewd image after another, some of which had Marissa appalled at her depraved train of thoughts. Ever devoted to her craft, most of those fantasies involved melted dark chocolate, a pastry brush and double sifted powdered sugar. She looked down at the royal icing she had just formed into the final perfectly shaped lily petal and relaxed her tightening fingers.

She placed it carefully with the others that had survived her total lack of concentration and unbuttoned her jacket. There was only the small bowl of butter cream icing to put away. *He's not coming.* The five layers of red velvet cake were completely iced, reinforced and ready for assembly tomorrow. *No hot cocoa fantasy.* Then she'd attach the flowers, stack the tiers and wait for the oohs and aahs. *No oohs and aahs for you.*

"I. Am. Tired," She stretched her neck with each word.

"But are you hungry?"

Marissa spun around and her jaw slacked. He was back, as promised, his hair damp, slicked back from the fine planes of his face. He had on a fresh t-shirt and jeans and the sporty scent of body wash enveloped him and he held out a paper plate.

"Have a seat." He hooked a metal stool with his toe and pulled it out. "You look exhausted."

That brought her out of her stupor. "Thanks," she grimaced. "I bet you say that to all the girls." Self consciously she rewrapped her ponytail, walked to the island and plopped down on the tall stool.

He laughed. "Yeah. I do. But usually not until a lot later in the night."

Images that had swirled all day slammed into her.

"Want a beer?" he asked, waving the two bottles he carried in his other hand.

She shook her head. He put the pizza down and slid it toward her. "Start eating, I'll get you some wine. You want white or red?"

"White, please." There. Her voice was back. She picked up a slice of pepperoni and took a bite while he rummaged in the industrial refrigerator. It was delicious and her stomach rumbled. He looked up and gave her a playful grin. She could barely swallow. "Should you be stealing the alcohol?"

"I don't think anyone will miss it." He wiggled the cork from an already opened bottle. "The chef's a lush; he's not going to tell anyone since he's probably pilfering it himself." He grabbed a plastic cup from a pantry shelf then stopped before he poured. "You want me to go to the bar, get you a real glass?"

"No, that's fine." Her hands weren't too steady. She needed that wine.

He poured a generous amount. His hand brushed hers as he set it down and a jolt shot up her arm.

"What's your name?" He pulled the other stool out from beneath the counter and twisted the cap off his beer. He took a long swallow and she watched the muscles in his throat work.

"Marissa." She sipped the cold wine, felt its path down her throat and into the hotness of her belly.

"Nice to meet you, Marissa." He touched the tip of his bottle to her cup.

"You, too. Jason."

His brows rose, just a little. "You know my name." He rolled the bottle between his fingers. "What else do you know about me?"

She chewed thoughtfully. She might be out of practice, but she knew the first steps of the game he wanted to play. *Go Marissa, go Marissa! It's your birthday!* Well, not really. But boy if it was, she knew what she'd wish for.

"I know you work hard," she looked down at his huge arms and hid a smile when his biceps jumped. She'd imagined how they would flex when his weight was propped onto them and he was rocking into her.

She finished the first piece of pizza and moved onto the second—four cheese, her favorite. *Forget about the calories, this is refueling.* In those fantasies, she needed all her strength.

"I know you like pepperoni and *quattro formaggi.*"

"Pretty insightful," he smiled, taking another sip of beer, handing her a paper napkin and tapping the corner of his mouth.

Marissa licked away a bit of sauce with the tip of her tongue, ignoring the napkin, but not the way his smile faltered. She could be brazen. That's what the girls would tell her to do. She took a final bite, pulled the cheese away from the crust and wrapped her tongue around the long, gooey string repeatedly until she worked her way back to the crust. She bit the cheese free. He quickly drained the beer and stood up.

"I know," she said, looking at him over the rim of the cup, "you're probably going to kiss me sometime within the next ten seconds."

"Well, see," he moved behind her stool and bent down next to her ear. His warm breath tickled her neck. "That's where you're wrong."

She felt his hands grab the edge of the stool, his thumbs brushing her hips a second before he pulled her back from the counter. The sound of metal against the floor startled her and her heart began a quickening pace.

His warm fingers reached beneath the collar of her jacket and slowly pulled the garment down her arms. He tossed it on the counter and then his hands were on her shoulders, scorching her flesh.

She knew he could feel her pulse thrumming. One long finger trailed a path up and down the side of her neck. The stroking felt so good, she arched back.

"Oh no you don't." He ran his hands halfway down her spine, applying pressure on the way back up. "Relax your body, lean forward." He circled around her shoulders before running just his fingertips down her arms. He grasped her elbows and moved them outward then retraced his path and pressed her torso forward firmly.

"What you don't know is I'm one of the best stress relievers in the tri-state."

*Oh, baaaby!* She rested her forehead on her hands while his thumbs worked methodically around her top vertebrae then slowly moved lower. He worked his way up and down her spine for what seemed like hours.

"Aren't your hands getting tired?" Her voice muffled against the countertop and she hoped she wasn't drooling.

"I work with them all day. They're pretty strong."

"Mmmmm." Her bones felt like warm molasses.

He moved across her shoulder blades, worked up and down her ribs, stretching his hands wide. He stopped a third of the way down and simply rubbed his thumbs back and forth and she couldn't help but moan. With each swipe he moved his hands closer to her sides.

He leaned forward and nuzzled her, his hands never stopping. He placed his lips against the exposed column of her neck. She wanted that coolness against her heated skin. *I'm gonna take control again in just…one…second.* Her breasts began aching, swelling beneath the fabric of her tank. His hands were too far away. She wanted them on her.

She squirmed on the seat, clenched her fingers. She felt his lips open and stretch across her skin. He nipped her neck as his hands moved forward to cup her breasts. His tongue swirled against the skin he held between his teeth. He sucked gently as his thumbs brushed her nipples. The sensation brought her up and off the seat, her hands splaying flat against the counter.

"Oh god," she moaned.

"You got that right," he whispered against her neck as his hands left her breasts and skittered downward across her flat belly, coming to rest on the waistband of her pants. He shifted and she felt his hardness press into her.

"I've been praying all morning and afternoon for this." His fingers worked on the drawstring and if Marissa thought her legs alone might hold her up she would have helped him. He was draped over her back, his power unmistakable. "It's not fair that a man has to dream about what's under these oversized clothes you cake babes wear."

"Cake babes?" Marissa gasped through the lust that assailed every inch of her body. His fingers worked the ties loose and snaked their way over her bare stomach, around her navel and downward, barely slipping under the edge of her panties.

"I didn't know your name. I had to call you something when I was in the stall, eyes shut, pumping off like there was no tomorrow."

Him fondling himself while he thought of her hadn't been one of her fantasies. The thought caused a tiny ripple and her juices dripped.

"Mmmm, cotton. Are they white, too?" His fingers rubbed the fabric slowly. The tip of his thumb brushed the top of her curls. She nodded her head and he groaned. "Nothin' hotter."

He pulled one hand from under the thin material and moved it down to cup her mound. "No, this is hotter and so damp."

Marissa couldn't stand it. She ground against him and whimpered. It had been too long. So, so long.

"Shhh," he said against her hair, moving his hand slowly, fingers just missing her swollen clit. "Easy, babe."

She spun around in his arms and pressed herself against the length of his rock-hard body. She rose up on her toes, wrapped her arms around his shoulders and stared boldly into his eyes. She saw desire reflecting back.

"I don't want to take it easy," she said, pressing against the firm bulge of denim that proved he was definitely as wanting as she was.

"Do you always get what you want?" His hands rested lightly on her ass.

*Grab it. Press me closer.* "Rarely. It's been a while since I've gotten anything," she admitted, pulling herself higher. That revelation was rewarded with a purely masculine smile that made her catch her breath.

He leaned forward and pressed his forehead against hers. "Then let's see if we can't remedy that."

In the space of a heartbeat he hauled her off the floor, spun her around, planted her ass firmly atop the opposite counter and wedged himself between her thighs.

"I've been waiting all day to taste you," he said huskily. His lips brushed gently then firmed to envelop hers. He murmured something about honey, trailing a line of feathery kisses to the shell of her ear, licked his way down her neck, finally resting at the sensitive hollow at the base of her throat. "Sweet, sweet, sweet."

"And here I thought it was my famous butter cream you were after," she said through the haze that clouded her vision. She dropped her head backward to allow better access, but his lips abruptly vanished. Calloused thumbs took their place, tracing lazy circles up, down. Up, down. Up, down.

"I'd love to taste your cream," he rasped. The pulsing between her thighs intensified.

His hands slid down her shoulders and hooked the material of her tank top. He grinned like a wolf as he eased the fabric down her breasts. Her nipples were achingly tight. He stopped, pulled the edge of the fabric back and forth over the distended tips and Marissa couldn't repress a cry. She tried to press her legs together but his body blocked her progress.

He took a step back and simply stared at her. "Christ. Lean back, babe," he said, voice strained.

Marissa placed her arms behind her. The movement caused the already taut material to push her breasts upward. She felt completely wild. Half naked, pussy ready to explode, gorgeous guy unbuttoning his jeans.

"So how good's that icing?"

"W-what?" *What kind of question was that?* She watched his hand reach under the waistband of his boxers. He shifted, repositioned himself and brought his hand out empty. *Not fair. So, so, so not fair.*

"Where is it?"

"What?"

He tipped her chin upward. "The icing," he purred.

"In that bowl," she motioned with her head. "I didn't have a chance to put it away."

"My lucky day," he reached for the bowl, his heated gaze never leaving her. With one finger he scooped a small amount and stuck it in his mouth. His eyes drifted shut and he hummed when he pulled his finger away clean. Marissa's mouth relaxed. She wanted a taste.

As if reading her mind, he dug in again and brought a sample to her lips but stopped short.

"What tastes better, babe? You or the icing?"

"I-I don't know," she said. "I've never tasted myself." His eyes darkened, and her face flamed.

"Then I guess I get to be the judge."

His finger traced a path around the outside of one nipple and she gasped. He reached back in the bowl and she braced herself for the sensation of him touching the turgid peak. It never came. He repeated the process slowly on the other side, avoiding the center once again.

"Do you think that's enough?"

She stared at the smooth, ivory-colored frosting surrounding the dark pink tips, waiting. Wanting. She'd never done anything so daring, but it felt so right.

"No, "Marissa boldly stated, "you missed a spot."

"Here?" He asked, touching her nipple again, tracing an elongated figure eight up and around. Her muscles began to tighten.

"Not there," she breathed, anticipation building as he dipped his finger into the bowl again.

"Then here?" The rich icing was responding to her body heat. The first layer had softened. It caused a silky smooth friction as his fingers teased the other nipple, purposely ignoring the aching bud.

"The centers. Please," she pleaded. "Touch me there." Her thighs began to quiver.

"I will. I'm gonna touch your very center," he promised, "but not yet. I've waited too long for this."

Marissa's back arched as his tongue licked under then over. He licked his lips clean before he turned his attention to her other breast and laved it in a similar manner.

"Jason! Oh god. That feels so good." Her breathing became labored.

"All I can taste is the icing, I want to taste you." She watched, transfixed. He opened his mouth wide and covered her breast. His tongue swirled as he sucked hard. He looked up into her eyes, long lashes dropping as he slowly pulled away, letting go completely just before he reached the peak.

"No," she cried, shaking.

"I need to try the other one." He moved his arm behind her and pushed her hips to the edge of the counter. His other hand lifted her breast and brought it to his lips. She closed her eyes and flung her head back, threading her fingers through his hair to press him closer. He twisted, his free hand inching its way under her waistband, into her panties. The sensations were swirling, building. The pressure between her thighs, his kneading lips.

Just as his fingers began to snake through her damp curls he pressed his lips hard around one dark tip and she crested, the orgasm rocking her backward.


*What the hell just happened?* Well, he knew what happened but *shit* he couldn't believe it. Her hand had his wrist is a tight grip and her breathing was still erratic. It wasn't a giant screaming orgasm, but just like that, she came. He hadn't even made it to her pussy. "Holy fuck."

"Yeah," she said, her eyes blinking open slowly. "Ditto."

He stared into their deep blue depth, still clouded with desire, and reached for his remaining buttons when her grip tightened.

"We can't do this."

"*What,*" he croaked, gently tugging his hand free.

"Health issues," she said, her eyes clearing more rapidly than Jay would have thought possible.

"Jesus. Not a problem. I'm clean," he offered, "and it's been awhile for you, I take it." If she shut him down now, he might actually cry. She was hot and sweet and her essence hung in the air between them.

"That was pretty evident," she blushed. "I don't mean we can't do *this,*" she made a little back and forth motion between them. "I mean we can't do it here. This is so not up to code. I can't have my worksite contaminated." A weight lifted from his shoulders, but not from his balls. He'd never wanted a woman more.

"Oh no. Do you think there are security cameras here?" she looked quickly around the room, panic filling her voice.

He pushed his fingers into her hair and brought his lips down in a silencing kiss. He expected her to break free and argue, but she wrapped her arms and legs around him. He picked her up and deepened the kiss. When the tip of her tongue touched his bottom lip he pulled her tight against his rock-hard cock, which was probably a mistake since he was trying to think where they could go.

The locker rooms were out since people were still golfing. They couldn't use any of the offices in the clubhouse, there'd be too many workers around. There were banquettes in the adjoining lounge, but what if Sissy and the bridal party showed up to store more shit for tomorrow? *Think!*

What was he doing, anyway? Anyone could have walked in on them. He wasn't some horny teenager, for fuck's sake. Wouldn't it have been grand if one of his brother's had strolled in —

"Come on," he said lowering her slowly down his body. "You up for a quick run?"

She glanced down at his boxer-clad erection pressing through the vee of his jeans. "You can run with *that*?"

Jay chuckled, grabbed her hand and pulled her toward the door. "It'll hurt like hell but for you, babe, I think it'll be worth it."

# Chapter Two

**ℬ**

Marissa looked over her shoulder, waiting for someone to catch them as she followed Jason down the stairs. She felt like a very naughty schoolgirl sneaking out of the house to meet a boy her parents didn't like. She'd have had a lot happier childhood if there had been a boy who could have made her come like that without even getting into her pants. She grinned and promptly bumped into Jason's back. She peeked around his shoulder as he fished a small key ring out of his pocket and opened a door.

"It's not the Ritz but private enough that no one will hear me scream." He held the door open to let her pass.

"You're a screamer?" The storeroom was large with tall shelving. An old leather couch sat in a corner. There was a desk next to it, piles of invoices neatly stacked on top.

"Well, I bet I can't hold a candle to you when you really let go," he teased. He turned on the small desk lamp then flipped a switch. The harsh fluorescent ceiling lights went off.

"That was…unexpected," She placed her palms against heated cheeks.

He pulled her hands away. "It doesn't happen all the time?" His voice was low, his eyes searching hers.

"*It* rarely happens at all. And never from just—touching." She saw his surprise, but his brow furrowed.

"What kind of assholes have you dated?" he asked incredulously.

"The usual," she said, only half joking. "You're going to find out soon enough I'm pretty hometown white."

"Hometown white?"

"Yes, as in bread. You know. The ordinary, the predictable." She looked away but he grabbed her chin and forced her back around.

"You think what happened upstairs was *predictable*?"

She bit her lip in response. He scooped her off the ground and tossed her on the couch. Her bottom hit with a long whoooooosh.

"Hell, babe. There's nothing ordinary about that *or* you." He reached behind his neck and pulled his shirt over his head, tossing it aside. "Don't you know how beautiful you are? Sure, you've got great breasts," he winked. He had her tank top up and over her head before she knew what happened. "And I'm pretty certain when I *finally* get to see this ass," he punctuated his words by sliding his hands between her and the cushion and grabbing tightly, "it'll bring tears to my eyes. You're not ordinary, Marissa. No where near it."

She raised her fingers to his chest, circling his small nipples before trailing a path over stony abs to the fine line of hair leading downward.

"I want to lick every inch of you." The tone of his voice made her shiver. Strong hands moved to her sides. He yanked her pants and underwear off her hips. The cool leather shocked her.

"I want to know every taste, every smell," he growled and slid the fabric down her legs, pulling the clothes and her work clogs off together until all that remained were her socks.

His hands pressed at her knees and a purely feminine response made her resist. His hands moved higher, to her thighs. He rubbed methodically upward until she relented. It wasn't a great sacrifice. She'd wanted him with a need that was all too consuming.

"I want to hear each and every one of your cries when I drive you over the edge, Marissa, and I want you to hear mine." He pressed his thumb against the very bottom of her slit and she shuddered at the single, teasing trail it followed.

He licked her dampness off his thumb and rose to his feet, looking deep into her eyes. "What do you want?"

She lay back on the cool leather and opened her arms.

Her chestnut hair was tousled, her nipples dark little peaks and her pussy gleamed. But it was the tiny white socks that did Jay in. He pushed his jeans and shorts down over his erection in one smooth move and went into her arms praying, seriously praying, that he could last. He pushed the thought and everything else aside the minute she clutched his back.

He drove his tongue into her mouth, licking and stroking. She tasted like wine and pure sugar. Her tongue met his, dancing, and she squirmed beneath him. His cock was throbbing and with each movement Marissa made, he was slicked with her juices. He placed a firm hand on her hip and stilled her.

"Babe, you've gotta stop that or I'm going come all over you."

"Would that be so bad?" she asked, eyes tempting him. But she hadn't moved.

"Hell, no," he laughed, the conversation giving him the time to grasp some control. "But not being the world's best planner, I've got one condom at my disposal." His elbows rested on either side of her shoulders and he brushed her hair off her forehead. "We can play. But this first time, I want to be inside you when you come."

"Too late."

"There's coming," he grinned wickedly, "then there's *coming*." He emphasized that point by rolling his hips.

Her blue eyes twinkled and her lush lips, moist from their kisses, turned upward. "Let me look at you," she said.

He pushed himself up and onto his knees and her smile wavered.

"Good, lord," she whispered.

Here it comes, he thought. *It's too big. It's never going to fit.* There were times it hadn't, but it couldn't be that way with Marissa. He closed his eyes, willing things to be all right.

"Can I touch it?"

His eyes shot open. *Can I get an amen?* He rolled back on the couch and stacked his hands beneath his head. "It's all yours."

Her hand hovered then cool fingers wrapped around him. His loud groan echoed through the room.

"Smooth and silky, and sooo thick." Her fingers didn't meet and her grip was far too loose for his liking. She worked him up and down, never touching the darkened head. She exhaled, the rush of breath caressing the taut skin and his cock jumped. "It's beautiful. I've never had the chance to be this close and really look before."

"You're kidding," he asked and she laughed. Her soft breath hit him again.

"I *have* sucked cock," she smiled up at him. "But it was always pretty straightforward. No *playing*." She stressed her point by rubbing her thumb across his cleft. A drop of pre-cum oozed out. She turned her head to study it and her hair tickled his thigh. Her tongue reached out and touched the tiny bead. He clutched at the leather and closed his eyes.

"Mmmmm. Not as good as Godiva, but awfully close." Her hands gripped him tighter and he shifted toward her. "But I'm a little disappointed, Jason. No tattoos."

He opened his eyes in time to see her lips part and take his tip into her hot mouth. She swirled her tongue and he nearly cried when she let the swollen head pop out. "Anywhere."

She pursed her lips then ran them down the side of his shaft. "I want to lick." She pressed her tongue flat against him and ran from base to head, flicking lightly at the top.

Tattoos? What the fuck was she talking about? Where she wanted to lick? Then it hit him. The shirt. The latest wager.

"I lost a bet. My brother's idea of a joke." He saw her lips a fraction from where he wanted them and replied desperately. "Look, babe. I'll get inked tomorrow if you'll just please quit talking and put your mouth back on me."

She chuckled just as she slid over and pulled him in. The vibration made his balls tighten. She sucked the long path down to his root. Once. Twice. A third time. It was soft, warm velvet up and down his shaft and he touched her hair gently. She picked up the pace, rotating her head every so often until he was twirling right out of control. He cradled her head firmly.

"Marissa, stop. I-I'm a little shaky here."

"That happen a lot?" she asked teasingly, a small thread of throat lube stretching from her lip to his shaft as she pulled away.

"Never," he replied honestly. He never lost control. Ever.

"I don't mind if we do this first." She stroked his thighs, close to his balls, her smile catlike.

"Well I do," Jay said, easing away from the attraction of her lips and tongue and soft fingers. *Liar, liar, liar.* "I'm going to make this special for you."

"You already have," she whispered and leaned back into a reclining position. "I'm ready for you."

"You're *ready* for me," he snorted.

She looked at his cock and scooted back a little more.

"You're nowhere near ready for me," he said with a devilish grin. He grabbed her ankle firmly and moved her foot to the floor.

"I am," she said, her hand drifting to the damp brown hair between her thighs. "I'm wet."

He spread one leg wide and looked her straight in the eye. "If you're still able to form cohesive sentences, babe, you're nowhere near ready." He rolled off the couch and crawled toward her. "But you will be soon."

Marissa felt the cool air on her pussy and let her eyes drift shut. His finger inched up her leg, tickled behind her knee before resting in the sensitive crease of her thigh. His thumb stroked through her pubic hair softly and her skin prickled.

He wasn't in a hurry, although his cock was plastered against his stomach. He was taking his time and she marveled at his control.

"Remember what I told you? I want every feel, every taste. Are you ready?"

He palmed her, rubbing gently before spreading her pussy lips with thumb and forefinger.

"You have to speak, babe."

He spread her lips wider and with the other hand slid one long finger inside. "Ohhhhh." Her inner muscles clenched around him.

"Just what I wanted to hear. You're so snug, Marissa. Open your eyes. I want you to see."

She watched him pull one finger out then let his middle finger take its place, higher and deeper than before. He worked it around, slow and steady. Never picking up the pace and soon she had no control as her legs opened farther, her hips moving on their own.

"No way, babe. None of that yet," Jay ordered, withdrawing his finger completely.

"Nooooo," Was that a whimper?

"You want it back in?"

She nodded quickly but he shook his head.

"You have to talk to play the game."

"I don't want to play any game," she said, a note of pleading in her voice. "I don't play games."

"You sure as hell do," he said, rubbing his finger around her opening. "You played a hell of a game with my cock a few minutes ago."

She ignored his words, but not the sight of the creamy wetness that seeped out of her. "I want you to fuck me."

"And I want to fuck you," He pushed two fingers into her pussy as his thumb slid upward toward her clit. "Bad."

"Then do it," she pleaded. "Now." She pushed her hips forward only to have him move his thumb away.

"Soon, baby. Soon. Promise you won't move."

"You're crazy," she groaned. He was sitting there, his fingers buried inside her, her juice dripping down his hand and he wanted her promise to keep still.

"I want you to lie there and let me fuck you with everything but my cock," he said softly. "Let me."

Had he been rough and demanding she could have easily told him to screw himself. But here he was, a total stranger more attentive to her than anyone had ever been. *Don't read anything into it, Marissa.* Right.

"I'll try." It was the best she could do, as promises went. His determined smile told her she'd made a delicious choice.

"I know you love when I suck you here," he said, lowering his head to draw one nipple into his mouth. She slapped her hands against the cushions, his lips a pleasant torture, but she didn't move.

"Your pussy just hugged me again. Will it do that if I squeeze like this?" He rolled the peak between his fingers and pinched gently, forcing her inner shell to bear down.

"God, Marissa. You're so tight. I'm taking these away before you break them in two," he said removing his fingers.

"Look. Look how wet they are with your sweet lube. It'd be a shame to waste it. One for me."

She watched him lick his finger, more thoroughly than he had upstairs when he'd sucked the butter cream, and she felt another hot trickle of liquid seep out.

"And one for you," he moved his finger forward and for one heart-stopping moment she thought he was going to offer her a taste, but then his finger dropped. Its slick wetness encircled her clitoris and she cried out, fighting the urge to grind into him.

"You like that too." His breath was a hot whisper against her thigh. "Now what if we lift right here," he gently pulled back her hood.

Marissa tensed. Ready. So ready. But not for the quick stab of his tongue. Repeatedly. She gave up trying not to move and fought to breathe. The heat was rising, stoking flames that couldn't break free. Just when she was about to tell him she could take no more he changed tack. His full mouth was everywhere. Sucking. Licking. He wouldn't stop. He held her hips firmly in place slanting his mouth this way then that before he thrust his tongue inside her.

"Please," she sobbed, "No more. I can't. I want."

"What, baby?" He flicked his tongue back and forth between open-mouthed kisses. "Tell me."

"You," she panted, reaching for him. "I want you!"

He pulled his lips away and her vision blurred. She clamped her eyes shut. Her pussy throbbed like never before. She heard the tear of foil and prayed he'd get the condom on quick.

"I want to see your eyes, babe. I want you to come when I'm pushing in," his voice was hoarse as he slid the tip of his penis up, down, around her swollen slit, his saliva and her desire the perfect lube.

"No! I want you inside me," she cried. "It's never happened inside."

"We can have both," he promised, snaking two fingers alongside her clit as he pushed into her. She wrapped her legs around his hips, her inner thighs tightening.

"I won't be able to." Her head thrashed from side to side. "Don't. Please. I can't come twice," she cried, and he brought her over the edge.

"Bullshit." His cock slid in to the hilt as the tremors that rocked her massaged him.

"You can," he said, pushing her knees up to her shoulders, rolling his hips steadily. She was sobbing and he wasn't sure if it was from her orgasm or him pounding into her, but he couldn't stop. Her muscles had softened for about a half second before they clamped his cock tighter than his own fist. "You'll go again, baby. Trust me." He'd make it happen by sheer will if he had to.

"Oh god," she said, and he pressed his knees tight against her ass and changed the angle. "Oh, *Jason!*" Her eyes shot open in disbelief and he smiled through clenched teeth down at her. The freight train in his head roared louder as the contractions around his cock drew him to the peak.

"Marissa," he shouted as he fell over the edge. "Come with me." And she did.

\* \* \* \* \*

Somewhere, in the back of Jay's mind that damn phone just wouldn't stop ringing. He felt a soft hand rub across his stomach and smiled, despite the fact when he tried to turn into her warmth his body stuck to the leather. *That's what a couch covered in wild monkey love juice will do to a guy.*

"Is that your phone?" Marissa asked sleepily, running her hand over his hip and down the leg he had thrown over her. The caress was soft, featherlike. He kissed her nose in response.

He reached around for his pants and dug the phone out of his back pocket as it stopped ringing.

"Not important?" She looked up, snuggled into him and his cock took it as a personal greeting.

"My brother, Tom," he said, flipping the phone open and pressing a few buttons. "I put it on vibrate. If he continues to call back, maybe we can put this to good use."

He wiggled his eyebrows and she laughed, stretching in his embrace.

"Please. I'm completely wiped out."

She said it offhandedly, but he saw her flinch when she shifted her hips.

"You're sore," he stated, brushing her hair behind her ear.

"A little," she said. "But I wouldn't have changed a minute. Thank you."

"Hah. That's a laugh. Thank *me*."

"Hey." She propped her chin on top his chest. "This might have been just another page in your sexual sagas, but I've never, *ever* experienced anything like that. So when I say thank you, I mean it. Just accept my gratitude."

"Okay. You're welcome." He placed his hands behind his head and stared her down. Her love life must have been a crying shame. He watched her eyes get all glassy and wondered if she was thinking the same thing. "God, who knew you hot cake babes were so ridiculously stupid."

"Thanks," she said softly. "Nice pillow talk."

He urged her on top of him until they were touching chest to toe and wrapped his arms around her back. "If you're going lie there and tell me you don't have any idea what you did to me, than you're an idiot, babe. I don't want your thanks. I just want you."

Her grin was dazzling and when the buzzing vibration of his phone went off, he answered it with a smile of his own.

"Hey, bro. What can I do for you?"

"You can get your fornicating ass out of my storeroom. There's a distinct aroma reminiscent of a Bangkok brothel."

Marissa's eyes widened. She heard every word his brother said.

"I didn't know you were there when I came in earlier. You were both sound asleep."

Marissa tried to scramble off him, but he held her firmly in place with one large hand splayed across her bottom.

"Hey, nice boobs, by the way. Well, nice boob. I only saw one; your damn Popeye arm was blocking the other."

This time Jason let her up when she struggled. Her cheeks were flushed and she crossed her arms over her breasts, looking for her tank top.

"Where are you?" Jason asked.

"In the hall, jerkwad. I need to get in there and get the frosted bulbs we ordered. I'll go get another cup of coffee. You've got ten minutes to clear Miss Tasty Tits out of there."

"Wait. Why are you working so late? Can't you do the bulb thing in the morning?"

"Damn, Jay. She must have screwed you senseless. It's 8:30."

"I know," he said, sitting up quickly.

"Saturday morning."

"Fuck." He snapped the phone shut and shot to his feet.

Marissa heard it all and any mortification of being found naked in Jay's arms evaporated when she learned she had less than three hours to get the cake done, grab a shower and get back for the ceremony.

"I'm sorry," he said, pulling on his jeans and hurrying to close them. "Can I do something to help you?"

She looked at his big hands fumbling with his buttons and laughed. She bent over and grabbed her panties, looked at them angrily, and stuffed them in her purse.

"You're brother's right," she finally said. "It does smell like a whorehouse in here." She pulled her pants on and yanked the drawstrings into a bow with trembling fingers.

"Hey," he wrapped one arm across her chest and the other around her belly, pulling her tight against his bare chest. "Just breathe. Everything's going to be fine." She was beyond skittish, but who could blame her? And when was the last time he'd come so hard he thought he was taking a minute to catch his breath, only to find he'd slept for hours. He kissed her temple and felt her relax. "You'll be at the wedding, right?"

"I'll be there," she said, turning to kiss his jaw. "How about you?"

"Absolutely. On the groom's side."

"I'll be on the bride's," she said, nibbling her way to his lips.

"Thought you were in a hurry?" He caressed her ass and hauled her against his semihard cock.

"I am."

"Then go, you tease," he gave her a quick, open hand swat on the bottom and pushed her away. "You're driving me crazy."

She just smiled over her shoulder and ran.

# Chapter Three

### ✂

Marissa sat next to her sister on a pristine white folding chair and tried very hard to concentrate on the ceremony and not the second groomsman from the right. He hadn't been untruthful when he said he'd be on the groom's side. If she bothered to ask him what he did for a living she'd have learned his family owned the most successful home contracting firm in the county. As a wedding gift they had done the outdoor setup. Had she asked his last name instead of simply letting him screw her witless, she'd have known he was the groom's cousin.

If she had known any of it she might have shown a little prudence. *Maybe*. Probably not. She was hot just staring at his profile, at the way the tux stretched across his back, the way he kept nervously rubbing his fingers, remembering all the things those fingers had done to her.

"Quit fidgeting," her sister, Amy, scolded in a whisper.

"These chairs suck," Marissa whispered back. It wasn't a lie. An elderly gentleman in front of them turned around and gave her a thumbs-up.

"It'll be over soon."

"Not soon enough," the old man whispered, getting an elbow in his ribs from the woman he was with.

The abbreviated receiving line consisted of the bride, groom and their parents so Marissa had to endure the idle chitchat of her tablemates, the toasts and the bridal dances before Jay made his way to her side.

"You look beautiful," he whispered from behind, his breath sending shivers through her. Her breasts swelled beneath the deep brown lace-over-satin sheath she wore.

"Thanks. You too."

"Men don't look beautiful." He laughed, taking a seat next to her.

"Don't tell that to ninety-five percent of the testosterone here. You're all gorgeous. It's criminal." Her gaze drifted over him from head to toe and back again. "And you know it," she added. He looked just as edible dressed to the nines as he did in those faded jeans and skintight tees and she moistened her lips with the tip of her tongue.

"All I know is I'm getting harder by the second and if you don't stop looking at me like that you're going to have to drop to your knees right here and let me run something a little bigger than that tongue against your mouth."

Her eyes widened when he leaned forward, grabbed her hand and brought it to his lap. *Thank goodness for tablecloths.* She fought the urge to stroke him through the fabric of his pants.

"Or I can inch that skirt up and—"

"Stop it," she whispered. His arm moved to the back of her chair, his fingers stroked her shoulder. The touch sent a jolt straight to the spot that had grown moist the minute he'd walked over. "Don't. Say. Another. Word. I'm trying to behave myself."

"That doesn't sound like fun," he said, his fingers slipping under the narrow shoulder strap. "You're shaking. Are you cold? I can warm you up," he whispered against her ear, as he wrapped her fingers around his length.

"Real original, Mr. Smooth," she said, pulling her hand away. "If things go bad with the family business you have a promising career at phone sex."

He chuckled, rubbed the upper curve of her breast with his finger and moved closer.

"Am I making you as hot as you make me? I'd like to hug those breasts as close as that dress does. Have those hard nipples pressing against me like they are through that lace."

She looked down and gasped. The lining was doing nothing to keep his effect on her from showing. She hunched her shoulders and pulled at the low, scooped neckline. Her gaze met his with more worry than lust.

"Don't fuss, Marissa. No one can tell but me."

*Oh, lord.* All she wanted to do was kiss him.

"Auntie M, there you are. I've been looking for you everywhere. They're getting ready to do the cake."

"I'll be right there, Randy. Go on, I'll catch up."

"O-kaaay," he said, looking at them closely before walking away.

"I'm going to have to do something about that kid getting in the way," Jason said. "I was just getting ready to tell you how much I wanted to pull your panties down those hot little legs."

"Good thing he stopped you then, fantasy boy," she said with a wicked grin, patting his cheek as she rose. He stood up and pulled out her chair. "That wouldn't have worked this time."

"You don't think?" He leaned on the back of the chair, his grin sure. "Why's that?"

She straightened her shoulders and whispered, "'Cause I'm not wearing any."

The good news was, he hadn't spurted right there in the rented tux. The bad news was he'd taken a long walk, made a beeline for the men's room to douse his face in cold water and he was still aroused. *No panties.* His cock jumped. *Focus on something else.* His phone vibrated in his pocket. He looked at the number and flipped it open.

"Where the hell are you, Jay?"

"I'm in the bathroom. Did I forget my hall pass?"

"Har, har. Get out on the veranda. Mom wants a picture of all of us and she's corralled everyone but you."

That bit of news made his balls loosen up. The last thing he wanted was his mother pointing out the fact he had a boner and could he "please do something with it, sweetie" so it didn't ruin the photo. He guessed having a husband and six sons made a woman fearless.

"Then we got to do that dumbass garter bit."

"Not me," Jay said, wiping his face with a towel and tossing it in the basket.

"Yes you are. Vin said Sissy wants the entire wedding party on board for the flowers and garter since everyone's single. If we have to do it, you have to do it. Get your ass out here. Mom's already straightening ties."

Marissa was happy. And horny. But right now, more happy. She heard the comments from the servers on how great the cake was as they refilled their trays and hit the tables again. The sense of accomplishment she felt when creating something everyone loved was indescribable. She never got tired of those Sally Field "you really like me" moments. She wondered if Jay had got a piece, and immediately tried to divert her thoughts.

Granted, she hadn't had sex in forever, but last night blew all other memories off the map. She'd never had a reaction to a man like she did to him. Her other lovers had never looked at her with such raw desire she felt the need to throw herself down on the closest flat surface and scream for them to take her.

It was a bit frightening, the feeling there might be more to it than sexy talk and smoldering looks. She would not become one of the huddled female masses who thought she'd found her soul mate during a bout of great sex, despite the fact Jason had taken her to the elusive pinnacle of her first ever multiple orgasm. There had been none of that next day awkwardness she sometimes felt when she'd done something a little bold in the sex department. What happened yesterday went beyond bold. She grabbed a piece of cake and went to find a seat and the man who took her to that bold beyond.

She saw him and two other groomsmen walk into the tent. His brothers, she assumed. There were enough similarities that a person couldn't mistake they were related. Nor were the older couple and three other men who stood behind them. The two youngest jostled shoulders and headed toward the dance floor. She watched Jason take his place with the other eligible males as his gaze swept the room. She wiggled her fingers in greeting when he found her. He gave a halfhearted grin and shook his head. She ate slowly, laughing at the sheer relief Jay and three of his siblings displayed when one of Randy's friends snagged the garter. The two youngest looked thoroughly dejected.

His groomsman duties done she knew he would work his way to her side. He'd want to pick up where his teasing left off, and she wanted him to. This time she wanted to be the one to make him hot. Make him so beside himself with need he'd beg her to leave. She forked another bite of cake in her mouth and closed her eyes. Was she ever going to be able to eat icing again without a flood of memories? *Mmmm.* She scraped up the remaining red velvet crumbs and licked the fork clean before turning to place her plate on the table. She turned back around and a soft, solid object whacked her square in the chest and slid onto her lap. Through all her daydreaming, she thought she missed the damn toss.

Marissa pushed the small lily and tea rose bouquet at her sister who was all but pulling her onto the floor. "Take it, Amy. I don't want it."

"You caught it. What is *wrong* with you? Do not make a scene," she warned. Her sister's idea of a scene was filing your nails in public. "Sit down and let them take a picture."

"I'm too old for this shit."

"Watch your language, for heaven's sake."

*Gawd!* Marissa heard as her sister prodded her past a group of young girls, *It's the old maid patrol.*

"Hey," Marissa called over her shoulder, "Blondie. Here — it's yours." She tossed the nosegay at the girl, who looked at it as if it were a bushel of snakes and threw it back. *Ouch!* Her bottom landed firmly on a folding chair.

She planted on a strained smile and searched the crowd for Jason, assuming he'd be laughing right along with most of the others but when she saw him he was wearing a look that was far from humorous. *It must be worse than I thought.* A nearly thirty-five-year-old with a young Adonis at her feet.

"Hey, you're the cake lady. Randy's aunt, right?"

"I'm Marissa," she smiled. "I'm so sorry about this. I didn't mean to catch the stupid thing."

"No problem. I'm Ben," he said and put out his hand while the photographer positioned them. "The cake was great, by the way."

"Thanks." She smiled and shook his hand. *Flash!*

"That one will be great," he said turning and giving his group of friends a big grin. "My girlfriend is going to be so mad."

Marissa laughed when he picked up her foot and rested it on his thigh. It reminded her of shoe salesmen of old. *Flash!*

"She didn't want to get in line for the bouquet," he said, waiting for the traditional strains of *The Stripper* to start before he inched the silk over her toes and around her ankle. *Flash!*

"She said it was stupid, but she's really shy. She left before the garter toss. I think she didn't want some old fart catching it and feelin' her up. She has no confidence in me." He stopped at mid calf to twist a finger around each side of the garter and wiggled the elastic back and forth and up and down. *Flash! Flash!*

"I told her I'd get it," he winked at her. *Flash!*

"I'm varsity basketball at Prep," he added, as if that said it all.

"Her loss," Marissa said, smile never faltering.

Chants of *high-er, high-er* echoed from the crowd. They both blushed.

"You're pretty hot for an old la— I mean, for a being so mature."

"Thank you, Ben. You're pretty hot yourself," she said, looking up to find Jay at the edge of the crowd, his face fierce. It startled her enough she flinched.

"Wow. Sensitive knees, huh?" *Flash!*

As Ben's fingers pushed the material of her skirt upward, as he slowly worked the garter over her knee she knew exactly what Jason was thinking. In that moment she remembered. *I did it for you,* she wanted to scream. His lips thinned into a line.

"Holy shit."

She'd be fine. As long as she looked at Jason, she'd be fine. Breathe. She could almost hear his voice. Breathe, babe.

"Lord god, heavenly queen," Ben's voice quavered. She felt his fingers trembling as he slowed his progress to a snail's pace. She heard young, male voices egging him on. *Use-your-teeth. Use-your-teeth.*

Marissa blinked, saw Jason narrow his eyes, and watched his brothers grab his arms. She looked down and into Ben's glazed, green eyes.

"You're not wearing any panties," he whispered reverently, his hands suddenly still.

She was saved a response as his friends took his lack of motion as a sign he wasn't going any higher and ran up and tackled him over backward. He hung onto the garter for dear life and it caught her heel on its way down. Suddenly, Jason was there, holding her calf to keep her from being pulled off the chair, disentangling the thin strip of silk and offering her his hand.

She heard "you're not gonna believe this" from the bottom of the pile and saw one of Jason's brother's haul Ben to his feet and drag him away from the group. She clutched Jason's hand like a lifeline and with as much dignity as she could muster, walked coolly by his side off the floor.

Without speaking, Jay traced a route through the clubhouse to an older section of the building where no one should have been. He pushed the door to the ladies lounge open so hard it cracked into the wall, eliciting a shriek from two elderly women at the sink.

"Good, heavens!"

"Miss Winthur. Miss Grady."

"Oh it's that lovely Henderson boy. How are you, Thomas?"

"I'm Jason, Miss Grady, and I'm fine but my friend's not feeling well."

"I should say not, she's as pale as a sheet," Miss Winthur said.

"Should we get help, dear?"

"No. No, she'll be fine. We're just going to go in here," Jay said pulling the door to the handicap stall open quickly. "Splash some water on her face. She's a little queasy. It's really hot under those tents."

He shut the stall door and they stood there, staring at each other, waiting for the ladies to leave, a frisson running between them. They heard the shuffle of feet, the outer door open then swish closed. He was still upset, she could tell by his harsh breathing. He pushed his fingers through his hair with such force she thought he might pull it out at the roots. She clenched the stupid bouquet she still held tight, a tiny rosebud snapped off and fell to the floor. She loosened her grip and tossed the flowers in the sink.

"I'm so sor—"

He cut her apology off with a scorching kiss, pulling her against him with such force her momentum pushed him back and into the stall door. The metal partition rattled loudly before he righted them again.

"Oh, Jason," she moaned when he released her lips to plant hot, wet kisses straight down her neck and over her breasts. His hand moved roughly down her back, found her zipper and yanked it downward. The material loosened over her chest and he cupped her breasts, pushing them out of the dress. His mouth tugged at one, his teeth grazing her nipple. "Oh please," she grabbed his head but didn't try to pull him away. "Don't be mad at me."

He stopped. His hand, his lips. Everything. Marissa held her breath. His arms wrapped around her back and soon she was engulfed in his warm embrace. He slid down her body, kneeling, and pressed his head against her stomach. He didn't move. "Say something," she finally whispered. "Please."

He took a deep breath and slowly exhaled.

"I'm an ass. I'm not mad at you," he admitted, hugging her tighter. "I'm mad at myself." He tilted his head and looked up at her through dark lashes. "That's the second time in two days I've been so envious I wanted to pummel someone."

She smiled and ran her fingernails over his temple. "Of someone young enough to be my child," she asked, terribly relieved.

"Please, make it sound more pathetic than it already is," he snorted. "And FYI, Randy and his pals are nowhere near young enough to be considered childlike anymore."

"Randy! Ewww, you are ridiculous," she laughed, tugging on his head to get him to stand up. "He's like a brother."

She kissed him softly. "No one's ever been jealous for me before. I think I like it," she said, boldly reaching between them to run her hands over his fly. "You deserve a reward for saving me."

"No, I don't," he said, leaning back anyway to give her easier access. "It's a sign of weakness, a complete loss of control." She unsnapped his waistband and pulled his zipper down.

"It's sounding better all the time," she purred, easing into his shorts and grasping him lightly. "You're not hard yet."

He snorted, knowing he'd be completely hard in about ten seconds. "Watching while some punk runs his hands up your leg and nearly falls into your lap in adoration has that effect on me. What about you," he countered, pulling the back of her skirt up and easing her onto the edge of the sink. "Are you drenched yet?"

"I'm afraid the imminent danger of a room full of total strangers sharing in my first Sharon Stone moment dried me up. This freezing cold porcelain isn't helping either."

They stared at each other for seconds then broke out laughing. But then the twinkling in Jason's amber eyes began to change and her nerves sang.

"Not into the exhibitionism, huh? I'm glad." He pushed the front of her skirt up to her waist slowly. "It's become suddenly clear I don't want to share." He crouched down in front of her exposed pussy and blew. "We'll warm everything up in no time."

"But I can't touch you from up here," she sighed, waiting for his fingers like a true wanton.

"Later," he said. "My reward. I get to touch you first."

She waited in anticipation and it was his tongue that touched her. He started at her very base and licked back and forth and he moved upward to bypass her clit and sweep into her curls. "Only me," he said, as if he were marking her for himself.

He retraced the path down one side and up the other, never touching her center or the tiny nub that silently screamed for him. She squirmed forward, the fullness rising.

Shamelessly, she spread her legs wider and gripped the sides of the sink.

"You can't be ready so soon." He stood up, brushed his lips against her parted mouth, sucking her tongue lightly.

"I am," she whispered, catching his bottom lip between her teeth. "Use your cock and feel." She looked down at his him, hard and ready against his stomach. He gripped it, ran his fist up and down, and then slowly pressed the head to her clit, moving left and right.

"Ooooh. I love when you do that."

He kept the light, steady pressure and within seconds her juices were dripping down the gentle slope of the sink to tickle her ass. He grabbed her hips and tugged forward, parted her inner lips and moved his shaft up and down until she was begging.

"Now please. I want you in me," she panted.

"Shit," he swore, breathing ragged as he slowed to a near stop and shut his eyes.

"What's wrong" She cradled his face between her hands.

"I-I don't have protection." He couldn't stop his hips rocking, it felt so good. He never thought he'd need to be in her at the wedding, for chrissake. Afterward, hell yes. He'd restocked his supply on the way home that morning because he knew he had to have her again. It wouldn't be just one night with Marissa.

"We don't need it."

She grabbed his cock and he stopped moving.

"Yes. We do." He hadn't been reckless since he was sixteen, and thank god that hadn't turned out to be the disaster it could have been. That day-by-day wait he'd endured had taught him a valuable lesson, one he never hesitated to share with anybody with a dick who would listen.

"I want you, Jason." She pulled him closer and slid his tip into her drenched lips. He pulled back as if he were burned.

She was hot and wet and he closed his eyes, imaging what feeling her flesh to flesh would be like.

"It's okay. I'm on the Pill."

His eyes flew open and he looked at her long and hard. Was she lying? *She'd never do that.* Yeah, but there was still a chance he could get her pregnant. *Slim.* She said she hadn't been with anyone for awhile. *How long?* He suddenly needed to know.

"When were you last with someone?" He thought she'd refuse to answer. It was none of his business. If he pissed her off, maybe she'd change her mind.

"Nearly a year, and if you're going to ask, I didn't stay on it because I planned on sleeping around—

"I never thought that," he interrupted.

"I never got off it. I thought I should, but I kept hoping I'd meet someone." She hooked her legs around his hips and inched him forward. "Even before, *all* the times before, I never let anyone go in bare. I never wanted to. I loved when you were inside me yesterday, stretching me. Filling me like no one has. I want every inch of you touching me. I want to be able to feel it all. And when you shoot into me, I want to feel that too."

His resolve caved like a house of cards. To feel her, touch her soft folds, barrier free?

"One time," he told her, lowering his mouth to her lips, but not touching. "One time then it's back to the extra protection. And if you're offering me the chance of a lifetime, I want to take you the way I want."

"Any way you want," she said pressing her lips to his. "As long as you take me."

# Chapter Four

**ΒΟ**

Jay's hands were shaking when he lifted her off the sink and let her legs fall to the floor. This should *not* be happening in a bathroom, but he wasn't turning back now. He rubbed his thumbs below her hipbones, soothing the muscles that had been stretched tight when she spread herself before him. *What have I done to deserve this?* She was offering a fantasy and he was going to live it.

"Turn around," he ordered.

Her eyebrows rose, but she obeyed.

He met her eyes in the mirror and reached around to cup her breasts and her eyes fluttered closed.

"Watch me," he ordered. Her blue gaze met his.

He kneaded, tugged the firm little peaks through the lace of her dress. Eventually, when he was no longer able to ignore the restless shifting of her hips, he pulled the neckline of her dress down and eased her arms out. Her breasts were full and high and he watched them rise and fall. He pressed his cock against her back and she inched back, raised her arms behind her head and laid her knuckles trustingly against his chest. *Why the fuck did he still have his shirt on?* He wanted to feel her bare skin.

He leaned back, pulled frantically at the ascot that suddenly blocked all his air. He saw her hide a smile before she turned and helped. The tie was gone, his jacket tossed over the top of the stall. She pulled his suspenders down and studs went flying as he ripped his shirt apart. She started to press her breasts against him, but he spun her back around.

"Marissa. If you touch me, this won't last."

He expected her to tell him to take her. Right then. But she didn't.

"Then make it last, Jason." Those blue eyes dared him. "Make me never forget it."

"Put your hands on the sink. Close to the wall."

Her breasts hung forward and he reached around to fondle them, keeping his cock as far away as he could. He'd love to make her come like that again, just playing with those nipples until she screamed.

"I like that," she said, licking her lips.

She was making it difficult for him to focus. "No talking," he ordered. "Understand?" He pinched one firm peak, then the other. She nodded, saying nothing, but she shifted her legs tightly together. He let go of her breasts and ran his hands down her sides. He hit a ticklish spot and she squirmed. When he reached her hips he inched the silky fabric of her skirt up, one side at a time to bunch high around her waist.

"Your ass is so pale and smooth." He ran just his fingertips over the fullness and watched her shiver. "Like marble." He moved one finger down between her cheeks and saw her body tighten. He looked back to the mirror. "Open your legs."

There was a hint of worry, and he softened his tone while sliding his fingers to her inner thighs and tapping lightly. "Open up, babe. I'm not going to hurt you." He saw the worry change to faith and an ache shot through his chest. "The memories are about to start."

Marissa was fully exposed. Vulnerable. All she wanted was for him to touch her. The dull ache that persisted between her thighs was trying to rise, with her legs spread it wouldn't appease. She needed him. *Him!* He moved to the side and the four fingers of his left hand dipped between her cheeks, each one touching a little closer to her anus before they traveled further and lightly ruffled her curls. *Ohhhh.* She would not cry out. She would keep quiet and then when she got him home, she'd make him pay. The same four fingers followed the same path but this time they brushed her clit.

"Wider," he said and she immediately distanced her stance.

When he repeated the movement again, the last two digits brushed her puckered rim and her eyelids dropped. When he snaked his fingers over her clit, he stayed there, slowly caressing around and around.

"I want to lick you here so bad. I know you want it too." She squirmed in response.

"Not this time, babe. But I have to look." She felt his knees brush her legs, the fabric of his pants rough as he squatted down.

"You're so pink," he said, pulling her lips apart and she groaned. "No airbrushing, no touch ups, just perfectly pink."

She was close to coming just listening to him. She felt moisture rolling down one thigh. He brushed it away before he stood, his fingers prickling her skin. He pulled his jacket off the stall and folded it in half, then half again.

"Lift your arms." He placed the jacket across the sink and lowered her elbows back down. He held her like that for a minute, staring at her in the mirror, his look silent but telling. He lowered his back and let her feel his heat, moving forward to press his erection against her spine before pulling back, letting it slide down over her ass before nudging his engorged tip into her slick wetness.

"Ready, babe?" He pushed steadily forward. It felt bigger, thicker. She could feel his muscles tense with control as he slowly stretched her. It seemed like an eternity of sweet unrelenting pressure.

"I'm not in yet," he rasped next to her ear. "One big push then I'll stop."

She'd barely nodded before he rammed himself forward so fast his balls slapped her and she gasped. As promised, he stopped.

"Marissa, baby. You're like a fucking vise."

She stood there, trying to adapt, listening to his breathing along with hers. If he had taken her this way before she'd have never let him near her again. It felt like a hot steel rod was buried inside her.

"Can I move?" he asked.

She nodded and he gave a little laugh. It caused his cock to leap and she bit her lip. "What was I thinking, telling you I didn't want to hear that voice? Hear all the little noises you make. How you scream my name. Talk to me, baby. Tell me how it feels?"

"Full. I'm so full," she moaned. "It feels too tight."

He pulled out a fraction of an inch and pushed back slowly. He waited a few seconds and did it again. Then again. "Better?"

"That's nice," she admitted. It was still stretching, but oh-so pleasantly now. He kept the pace and it went from being nice to something altogether different. She knew he felt it too, and when he reached around her front she stopped him.

"Don't," she said, grabbing his arm "I want to come from inside."

"Tall order," he said, his thrusts increasing. "I'm gonna feel like shit if I go off like a rocket and leave you behind." He watched the rhythmic swing of her breasts in the mirror.

"You won't."

"I'm not so sure," he said, moving his gaze to hers.

"I am," she said simply. "I trust you."

*Lost, sucker. Lost, lost, lost.* "Bring your legs together, baby."

The minute she did the sensation changed. His cock started bouncing against a hidden spot that had her clutching the sink.

"Oh god, Jason." Her legs couldn't have trembled more if she was standing in three feet of arctic snow.

He kept brushing the spot faster and faster and she hung her head, her breath coming in shallow pants.

"Come on, babe. Come on." His voice sounded far away. She felt him cover her completely and grab her lower belly with one arm. He moved the other next to hers on the sink to entwine their fingers.

He pulled her hips back just as he thrust higher and the white-hot tightness that had twisted her insides shattered. In the distance she heard him call her name as he pumped, his seed scorching into her, hips still moving long after she milked him dry.

He was still in her, shrinking slowly, but still there when she finally got herself under control and raised her head. His eyes were closed, his head resting against hers, his breathing more even than his pounding heartbeat against her back.

"You've ruined me for life," he said, placing a kiss on her shoulder before opening his eyes. "I didn't get to see you come."

He squeezed her hand and she smiled, clenching her sore pussy muscles as hard as she could in return. "Me either."

She was about to tell him how magnificent it was when the bathroom door pushed open forcefully.

"Henderson? You in here? Old lady Winthur hunted me down. Said someone's sick and needs help."

The voice made her stiffen. She quickly reached for the top of her dress, trying to find the arm holes.

"Not a problem. Everything's fine."

The stall door rattled and Jason guided one arm then the next into her sleeves, pulling the material over her breasts. She felt Jay ease out of her and step back. He pulled her hem down and the zipper up just as the stall door popped open. She felt him fumble behind her, hoped he was able to get himself back in his pants before Sissy's brother saw.

"Do you mind, asshole?" Jason said, placing his hand on her hip possessively. She could tell by his voice he hadn't turned around to face Maxwell McLaughlin the Third.

"Whoa! This is primo." Max laughed. "Just like the old days, weeding out the bridal party once again."

"Jay!" She heard a new voice and the sound of shoes sliding on tile. "Jesus, man. I'm sorry. I tried to stop him but the old ladies cornered me."

"It's fine, Andy. Can you two just leave?"

She heard the edge to Jason's voice and wondered if anyone else had noticed.

"Come on, dickhead," Andy said. "Let's get the hell outta here."

"Easy, junior. Aren't you interested to know who the lucky lady is who got to be on the receiving end of your brother's legendary cock?"

"Not really. I figure anyone thinking about another guy's cock has got some major issues. Let's go."

"Look at your brother's face, Andy. He's p-i-s-s-e-d. Let me guess who it is. There are tons of babes in heat out there. He's probably fucked over half of them already, so that really narrows it down. And that's no bridesmaid dress clinging to that fine ass."

"Get. Out." Jay's voice was low and menacing and she wasn't sure why Max didn't turn and run. She would have.

"Ignore him, Jay, he's drunk," Andy said.

"You never wanted the virgins, always liked them a little older. A little more experienced, right? Didn't want the bluebloods either, although they all panted for you while we stood there holding our cocks. So, let's see. Who do we have to choose from? The Wilson girls, the Anderson triplets—heard your brother Luke nailed them. That spoiled bitch Bridget Fenn. The two Hughes sisters. That older one is a fuckin' shrew but the baker—"

"Shut up." Her voice was shrill as it echoed off the walls. She picked up her head and glared at Max through the mirror's reflection.

"Holy shit! *Hometown white.*" Silence filled the room, but not for long. "I guess not so much anymore, huh?"

She turned her back to the mirror and looked into Jason's eyes grabbing the open sides of his shirt in her hands.

"Him?" His voice was soft, for her only. There was no use lying. She wouldn't have anyhow.

She nodded and the corner of his lips raised.

"Wow. Would you have thought it possible, young Andrew," Max said his tone caustic. "Doubled over a bathroom sink."

"You're a dumbass," Andy said softly.

"How the pinnacle of prudishness has taken a giant leap off her pedestal."

"What the hell," Jason shrugged. He kissed her forehead, untangling her fingers from his shirt. "Andy?"

Marissa covered her mouth with shaking hands.

Max crossed his arms over his chest. "You must really be something, Henderson. I couldn't even get her to swall—"

Fist crushing bone reverberated through the tiny space and Andy caught Max before he hit the ground.

Jason turned and met her stunned expression.

"Third time's a charm."

* * * * *

Marissa snuggled into Jay's side. He rolled over, propped up on one elbow and pressed a gentle kiss to her temple.

"You hungry?"

"Mmmm," she said, reaching to push his still damp, sticky cock aside to fondle his balls. "Always."

"I don't think I have much of anything here."

"Riiiight. You with the legendary cock," she said, squeezing his softness.

"Marissa, please," he chuckled. "Do you want me to take you someplace?"

"You've already taken me someplace. All kinds of places," She rolled onto her back and ticked them off on her fingers. "An industrial kitchen, a janitor's closet, the ladies room, the easy chair in the living room—"

"That doesn't count," he said capturing her hands and kissing each finger, "my cock wasn't involved."

"It most certainly did count," she said with a blush and the aforementioned appendage pushed against her hip. "You take me to all the best places, Jason. Places I've never been," she smiled.

"I can't help myself, but from now on, no quick fucks in public places. It's you splayed out on this bed with your hair a wild mess and those blue eyes begging me to make love to you the way you deserve."

She wasn't touching that *make love* comment, not now. She wanted whatever he was willing to give. If she secretly hoped for more and he delivered. So be it.

"But I liked those quickies," she said, pushing out her lower lip like a spoiled child. She loved that she could tease him, that he teased her.

"Insatiable," he said, rolling out of bed and pulling a pair of old cut off sweats from a drawer. She followed him and wrapped her arms around his waist from behind, pressing her cheek against his muscular back.

"Only because you make me that way." She hugged him tighter surprised when the doorbell rang. She glanced at the clock. "Company? At 9:42?"

"I can only imagine," he sighed. "There's a robe behind the bathroom door."

"Don't you want me to stay in here?"

"Marissa, I'm pretty certain whoever's at the door knows you're here."

"Where's my dress?"

"On the living room floor with my shirt, pants and boxers." He heard her groan, and laughed. "Come out when you're decent."

Jason strode through the condo and opened the door to his brothers. "What do you want?" he asked, happy there were only two of them.

"Is she here?" Luke asked. "Can we come in for a minute?"

He looked at Andy, who remained silent and totally perturbed.

"Come on in. She's in the bathroom. She'll be out in a minute and we can do introductions, how's that. Then you can report back to Mom. I'm sure she sent you."

"She didn't send us. She's got no clue. We brought the coat and buttons back from your tux," Luke said. "Andy kindly retrieved them."

"Thanks, man," Jay said, taking the coat and small sealed plastic bag of black studs and rolled up ascot. "Don't you think this could have waited 'til tomorrow, though?"

"No." Andy finally spoke. "It took me awhile to find everything you flung off in a hurry. Got it all. Everything except the condom."

Jay didn't say a word.

"Did you fuck her without protection?" Luke demanded in a harsh whisper.

"Watch your mouth," Jay threatened, pushing two fingers into Luke's chest before turning on Andy. "And who the hell are you all of a sudden? Fucking Sherlock Holmes?"

"You *did*," Luke accused.

"It's none of your damn business. Neither one of you."

"What the hell is that suppose to mean? Haven't you always looked out for us? Haven't we looked out for each other?" Luke said. "You're the one always telling us about stupid actions and repercussions."

"You don't understand," Jay said, combing his fingers through his hair.

"Hypocrite," Andy said.

Marissa chose that moment to walk into the room.

"Hi." She stopped in the archway and waved. Jay groaned. She *waved*. Who did that?

"Hey," Andy said softly.

"Come in Tokyo," Luke said under his breath, walking forward to meet her.

Jay should have scrounged up a heavy sweatshirt for her. Her nipples were poking against the light cotton of the robe. If his fist didn't hurt so badly, he'd have knocked his brother out.

"This is my brother, Luke," Jay said. "He's a degenerate. Please avoid him at all costs."

"It's so nice to meet you," she said, shaking his hand when he offered it. "I've heard some very nice things about you."

"Really? Like what?"

"I hear you're a firm believer that everything comes in threes."

Jay howled and Andy snorted.

"I don't get it," Luke said, puzzled.

"Andy, right?" Her smile was blinding. "Thanks for your help. We never really were properly introduced earlier." She stuck out her hand. "I'm Marissa."

He stared at it dubiously. "Where's the last place you had that?"

"I've washed it since I last saw you." She laughed.

He shook his head and took her hand. "Yeah? How many times?"

"Wouldn't you just like to know?"

Jay pushed them aside and wrapped an arm around her shoulders. He met his brother's eyes, over her head. *Now do you understand?* He knew by the silly ass looks on their faces they just might.

"Would you guys like something to eat?" she asked.

"Yeah."

"Sure."

"They were just leaving."

"Well, I'm starving," she said, ducking under Jay's arm and walking into the kitchen.

All three watched the way her robe swished from side to side as she walked away. When she opened the fridge and bent over to check out the bottom shelf Jay grabbed his brothers by their arms and ushered them to the front door.

"You're a lucky bastard," Luke said, wrapping him in a playful chokehold.

"Yeah, a *hypocritical* lucky bastard," Andy corrected, punching his arm lightly. "Be careful, bro."

"I will," Jay promised.

"Too late," Luke said from the sidewalk. "He's already gone."

Jay shut the door firmly and locked it. He hurried back to the kitchen, took Marissa in his arms and kissed her long and hard.

"Please don't tell me that was because you're jealous of your brothers."

"Hell, no. They're the jealous ones," he said leaning back against the dishwasher.

"Really? And why's that," she asked coming to stand between his legs.

"Because I'm the one that ended up with you," he said pulling her into his embrace. "Everyone wants the cake babe," he said seductively.

"Well, don't be too smug," Marissa said. "You know that old adage—you can't have your cake babe and eat her too."

"No," he said, scooping her into his arms. "But I'll have fun trying."

# HALLOW'S EVE HUNK

෨

# Dedication

෩

*To my buddy Lisa, who can wield a riding crop with great aplomb. You're an inspiration, woman! Seriously, it's an honor to call you my friend.*

# Trademarks Acknowledgement

෩

The author acknowledges the trademarked status and trademark owners of the following wordmarks mentioned in this work of fiction:

Aunt Jemima: Quaker Oats Company

Darth Vader: Lucasfilm, Ltd.

Light Saber: Lucas Licensing Ltd.

Jack Daniels: Jack Daniels Properties, Inc.

Miss Hawaiian Tropic: Tanning Research Laboratories, Inc.

Powerade: Coca-Cola Corporation

Q-tip: Chesebrough-Pond's Inc.

Reddi-Wip: ConAgra Brands, Inc.

Southern Living: Southern Living Inc.

Uncle Penneybags: Hasbro, Inc. Corporation

# Chapter One

**ଚ**

Darth Vader had the smallest penis Vicky had ever seen but that didn't stop Thumbelina from going down on him like there was no tomorrow. His Light Saber beat a steady rhythm against the wall as he thrust in and out, one black-gloved hand buried in the golden-haired wig, urging the fairy princess deeper.

Vicky shook her head as she walked around them on her way to the bathroom.

"All the Stormtroopers on the Death Star won't save your ass if you put a hole in Bobby's wall," Vicky said before shutting the door and leaning against it.

The pounding increased until suddenly…ah, blessed silence. What a total disaster the night had turned out to be and it was far from over. She pushed away from the door and looked at her reflection above the sink.

"Mirror, mirror on the wall, who's the biggest ass of all?" *Why you are, Victoria, for allowing your cousin and Billie his bimbo bride to coerce you into attending Halloween Lifestyles of the Rich and Debauched.* Who would have thought Bobby, director of the area's largest medical center, and his numerous well-heeled friends were practitioners of partner swaps and daisy chains? After what she'd seen downstairs, she'd never be able to eat Reddi-Wip again. Thanksgiving was officially shot to hell.

When he had mentioned hosting a Halloween party, her initial reaction had been one of excitement. She'd always embraced Halloween, loved dressing up and looked forward to all the werewolf and vampire movies that accompanied the holiday. The promise of attractive single men attending Bobby's party made this year's festivities all the better. Four of them had approached her downstairs. And then made it quite clear they wanted to welcome her to town by playing a friendly game of doctor. *En masse.*

Gee, some girls might want to get a proctology probe, a three finger vaginal exam and an all-encompassing breast check in tandem but that was a little over the top. Even for her. The ears, nose and throat doc definitely wanted to swab for strep but Vicky was pretty certain he wasn't planning on using a giant Q-tip for *that.*

She looked at her reflection, grimacing at the splattering of faux freckles across her nose. She grabbed a washcloth and rubbed them off. Thank god she had refused to wear the Elvira costume Billie had picked out for her. She'd opted for fresh-faced equestrian, a sort of *National Velvet* with curves, which turned out to be just as big a mistake. She gazed down at the expanse of cleavage and worked the buttons of her pristine white shirt closed.

"Vic? You in there?"

"You rat bastard," Vicky swore, turning around and pulling the door open.

"Come, on. Don't be such a prude," Bobby said, his gray eyes narrowing beneath the feathered mask he wore. "There are some very eligible men down there who want to get to know you better."

"You little shit," she whispered, hitting him hard in the chest with both hands. "I'm not sure when you became king of the pervs. Thanks a lot for including me in your sick pastimes. What kind of welcome home is this?"

"A pretty nice one for somebody who gives her family the old 'fuck you' as she's leaving town, only to roll back a decade later like nothing's happened."

"Oh, so this is some sort of punishment?" Vicky raised her voice. "Because I had the balls to leave and you had to stay. It's not my fault you screwed the most fertile member of the junior class, Bobby. I'm surprised that didn't work out for you, Casanova."

"You should talk. Rumor has it your march through Atlanta rivaled Sherman's, sweetheart. He chose fire—you used your cunt. I hear both were pretty damn hot and achieved the desired result."

She stared him down. Word got around a small town and she certainly remembered how gossip weaved the truth into something dark and ugly. She never thought Bobby, who had been like a brother to her while they were growing up, would be the first one to wage the attack. She wasn't about to defend herself to anyone, especially him.

"You know what, Bobby? Go down to the buffet line, get one of those big rubber dildos you have strewn around for party favors and go screw yourself," Vicky said calmly, shouldering him out of her way. "You don't know a damn thing."

"I know you want to start over. Open a shop. Those people downstairs are your target audience. I can help you."

God, it was tempting to accept his assistance. She knew there was a market in Grand Harbor for her skills. She had honed her craft for years. Her work had been showcased in numerous magazines. Southern Living had done a four-page spread earlier in the year. That was before the proverbial shit had hit the fan.

"All you have to do is play nice for a change," Bobby said.

"I don't need you or your twisted cronies," she said, rushing down the staircase, pausing at the front door to look up at him. "I quit playing games long ago."

Andy shifted on the barstool and systematically peeled the label off his empty beer bottle. "Can I get another one, Pat?"

The bartender nodded and Andy spun around, surveying the crowd. *The Rusty Angler* was lucky to have a couple dozen patrons each night. This was exactly why Andy liked it, that and the fact it was directly around the corner from his apartment. Apparently a holiday weekend didn't improve business. The place was far from hopping.

There were several couples in costume but the bulk of the customers were dressed like Andy — in blue jeans and tees, refusing to succumb to ghoulish attire. A handful of off-duty state troopers were playing pool. He watched the shooter glance toward the door then totally muff an easy shot. The quick echo of shoes against composition tile caught Andy's attention.

A beauty was striding toward the bar. Her tall boots beat a steady path directly toward him and his mouth went dry. God, she was *hot*. Tight, buff-colored knit pants encased very fit legs. Her white shirt was buttoned clear to her neck but her breasts bounced teasingly with each step. Her lips were compressed in a thin line and as she came closer he admitted she looked more like an avenging angel than a mere sexy mortal.

One of the cops said something and she stopped and turned. Andy tried to concentrate on what they were saying but the way the fabric hugged the curves of her ass had his mind reeling and his fingers tingling. The sharp crack of leather hitting leather when she whacked the riding crop down against her boot brought his mind and his cock to attention. She closed the distance and stopped one seat away before tossing the crop onto the bar.

"I'd like a double shot of Jack Daniels, please." Her voice was soft and polite, a direct contrast to her demeanor.

Andy turned in his seat and watched her pull at her leather gloves. She had a delicate silhouette, high cheekbones. She kept her head forward and he couldn't discern the color of her eyes. Deep auburn hair was pulled back in a fancy braid, a silky black bow holding it together at the ends. The shell of her ear was perfect and without thought he leaned forward. *Just one little lick.*

"If you're about to make some lame-ass comment about me riding you, save it, buster. I've totally had enough for one night." She didn't look at him, just picked up the glass, threw the shot back and succumbed to that little shiver that good bourbon prompts.

Andy chuckled and reached for his beer. She'd had enough, huh? As tight as she was wound, he doubted it. With the assumption he was like everyone else, she had thrown down the gauntlet. It would be ungentlemanly not to accept the challenge and prove her wrong.

Vicky had still been wired from her flight from Bobby's when she'd found the neighborhood bar. The fact it wasn't a dive was a plus but she was so cold from walking that it wouldn't have mattered. She'd dodged the guys at the pool table, having tolerated enough innuendo for one night, making that fact verbally clear to them and the attractive man beside her.

His soft, sexy laugh sent a frisson of heat through her. *Don't be so hasty, Victoria. Better decide just what it is you've had enough of.* She watched his reflection in the mirror behind the bar. He raised the beer and tilted his head back, arching an eyebrow in acknowledgment. She felt her cheeks flame and blamed it on the distilling skills of those fine folks from Tennessee.

In the muted lighting she could see he was more than simply attractive. Broad shoulders, dark eyes, close-cropped honey-colored hair, long fingers that traced a tiny circle round and round and round over a spot on the flare of his beer bottle. Her breasts swelled and when he wrapped his hand full around the bottle she nearly groaned.

"I'd like to think I can be a bit more imaginative than simply asking to mount you," he said, his voice deep and husky.

Vicky didn't answer but met his gaze in the mirror.

"It's Halloween," he smiled, teeth straight and white against his tanned skin. "Isn't this the night when imaginations are allowed to run wild?"

*C'mon, Vicky, say something. Be witty. Show him your sex drive is immune to that voice.* He turned and slid onto the stool next to her and her heartbeat kicked as one well-developed forearm moved across the edge of the polished bar. If she leaned forward just a little, she could all but place her aching breast in his palm. Her nipples tightened and a jolt of desire shot directly to her pussy. She crossed her legs in an attempt to stop the pulsing and sucked in her breath when his other hand grabbed her knee and slowly rotated her around.

Lord! He was gorgeous, his face all strong angles, and his eyes? Heaven help her. They were deep brown with tiny golden flecks. And they were boring into her with something more than simple interest. His fingers suddenly caressed the underside of her knee and she couldn't contain her gasp.

"What're you imagining right now, sugar?" he asked, his thumb rubbing a half circle back and forth against the top of her kneecap.

Moisture pooled with unexpected urgency between her thighs. *Libido be damned, Vic. Tell him what those eyes remind you of. Go for a good, long-standing fantasy. Like he said, it's Halloween. Go wild and maybe one of the things to go bump in the night will be your butt against his thighs.* The thought that he might be some sort of psycho madman crossed her mind. Could he be any worse than the crazies she had just run away from? He dipped his thumb to the inside of her knee and she said breathily, "Vampire."

"Vampire?" he repeated, brows furrowed.

"Your eyes are so different. They're beautiful," she added quickly. "Mesmerizing. I'm thinking if I stare into them too long they'll begin to change. Glow red."

"Mmm. Devil's eyes. I like that," he crooned, moving closer. "Then what happens?"

Her heart was drumming in her ears. The hand against the bar brushed lazily up her arm, leaving a tingling trail. His fingers danced along the side of her neck and those bewitching eyes bore into hers harder, waiting for an answer.

"I don't know."

"You don't?" he asked, his gaze drifting to her lips. She should have ordered a beer, her mouth felt as if it were on fire.

She pulled her lips together to moisten them and both his hands, the one on her neck and the one holding her knee, flexed. She shook her head in answer.

"I can feel your pulse against my palm," he whispered, his thumb tracing down the front of her throat before dipping beneath the fabric of her shirt to rest in the hollow. He brought his lips close to her ear. "I can smell your apprehension. Your excitement."

*God, he's good at this. Or maybe he's serious.* She was so damn wet she wouldn't doubt his words.

"You hoped you'd meet me tonight. You wore that high collar on purpose, thought it would protect you. You knew I'd want to taste you." His warm breath tickled her ear and she shivered with delight. "But you know it won't stop me. There are other places I can sink my teeth into you."

He eased himself back, just far enough to look at her chest, and her nipples contracted, their tight centers pressing uncomfortably against the lace of her bra.

"Your skin's like ivory. But I'll bet it's paler under that shirt, so pale I'll be able to see those tiny turquoise veins running from here," he rotated his thumb, the roughness teasing her collarbone, "all the way down to each perfect little bud. I'll have to decide which side I'll take. Maybe I'll let you choose. Let you guide me to one of those soft pillows, hold my head while I lick the spot over and over, making you hot before I place my sharp teeth against your flesh—"

"Stop," she whispered, gripping his steely biceps and uncrossing her legs. She was ready to come. Just like that.

Maybe the earlier visit to Orgy Central had subliminally whetted her somewhat dormant sexual appetite but he had to stop.

"Ah, but I can't sugar," he said softly, leaning forward until his lips teased her earlobe. "You know all the tales. Once my teeth break that sweet skin, I'm going to want to sink something else into you."

"Shit, Henderson," a disgusted voice sounded behind Vicky. She recognized it as one of the pool players and stiffened. "Open lewdness is a third degree misdemeanor. Get a freakin' room, already."

She tried to turn but his fingers held her still. He ignored the man, met her eyes and gave her a sinful smile. Her breath caught and in that second she knew if he were indeed some supernatural creature she'd have given him her soul and anything else he asked for.

"How 'bout it?" he pushed the stool back and rose. "Feel like following me over to the dark side?"

Andy's dick leaped for joy when she nodded—at least as much as it could behind the suddenly tight zipper of his jeans. He'd done a little sexual role playing before but never with a total stranger. Never in public. Never with anyone so spectacular. He threw a twenty on the bar, grabbed her hand and headed toward the door. He was not letting this opportunity slide by. No way. He pulled his leather jacket off a peg and held it open. She looked up at him as she slid her arms inside and he sucked in his breath.

God*damn* she was beautiful. Her soft blue eyes were half closed and when she placed her hands against his chest, they were trembling. All he could think of was how she'd look spread out before him. If she got this hot from a little fantasy talk, who knew where things would end up once they were skin to skin. He closed his eyes as her hands brushed over his nipples, images swirling through his mind. *Oh, yeah. Aren't* *there are all sorts of things a vampire can do with his will-bending powers?*

"Wait," he said, easing her hands away.

He rushed to the bar and grabbed her gloves and crop, ignoring the catcalls from the commonwealth's finest on his way back to the door. He wrapped his arm around her shoulder and ushered her into the night.

Typically October, the temperature had dropped while they were inside, yet he barely felt the cold. He was hot and hard and they made it as far as the corner before he backed her up against the brick wall of Rex's Pharmacy.

"One kiss," he said, lowering his lips. He brushed back and forth before settling to gently suck her lower lip. She tasted like Jack and vanilla and when the tip of her tongue met his, fire shot straight to his balls. He pushed his thigh between her legs and ground lightly, lifting her to her toes. She wiggled against him and he pulled his mouth away.

"You're so hot. If you were wearing a dress I'd take you right here," he admitted, shocking himself with the truth of the statement.

"Guess I should have gone for Elvira after all," she replied, grabbing his shoulders to inch higher until they were nearly eye to eye. "Get me wherever we're going quickly, before I do something totally inappropriate in the middle of this sidewalk."

"Like shimmy out of those britches and wrap your legs around me?"

"No," she said with a catlike grin, fingers creeping over his chest toward his crotch. "Like sliding down and tasting every inch of that vampiric erection," she whispered, rubbing her thumb against his navel.

"Whose fantasy is it now?" he said with a throaty chuckle, backing away quickly.

Her laughter drifted on the breeze as Andy entwined their fingers and forced her into an easy jog. In less than a minute they stood before the large metal door of the old warehouse.

"Keys," he said, pointing to the top pocket of his coat. He could fish them out himself but that would bring his fingers way too close to her breast and the only place that would lead was to him pulling her into the foyer and driving into her on the stairs. *Definitely not a stairwell fuck for her, Andrew.*

He took the keys, opened the door and motioned her in, pulling the heavy metal closed behind him until it clicked.

"Stairs or elevator?"

"You're kidding?" she asked, breathless. "Since you're not using your powers and whisking us skyward—elevator," she said, pushing the up arrow.

*Shit.* He was actually hoping she'd pick the stairs. That would give him time to gather some control. He'd read enough sci-fi to know Dracula never came in his pants. The doors opened and they stepped inside the metal cab. He stuck his key into the panel, turned it and pressed the button for his floor before pulling her backward into his embrace.

"It's going to be a slow ride," he said, placing a feathery kiss below her ear.

"God, I hope so," she sighed, pushing her ass against him.

He grinned, nipped her neck playfully. When was the last time he'd run across a woman who was sexy *and* lighthearted? The local girls had turned more serious with each passing year, telling him what they thought he wanted to hear. The tourists weren't interested in conversation. They wanted a non-trust-fund stud with an adequate cock for a little weekend sex. And their actions were never authentic, not like those of the woman before him who had just dropped her head to the side to give him better access to the column of her throat.

"We're not going to go at it in here," he said, swirling his tongue around at the base of her neck.

"We're not?" Her tone was disappointed but as she looked over her shoulder he saw her smile before it drifted into a luscious pout.

*Uh-oh, Andy. Get a grip, moron. It's a game, remember?* His finger replaced his tongue and he twisted the damp hairs tightly and then pulled free, leaving a little ringlet.

"I want you," she said, turning in his arms. She shrugged the jacket down to her elbows, pressing her breasts close but not quite touching him.

Her nipples were hard, straining against the fabric of her shirt and his hands grasped her small waist as the elevator stopped and jostled all those soft curves against him.

"I've man-eep-ulated your vants and needs," he said, wagging his eyebrows while they waited for the doors to open.

"You don't have to pretend anymore," she giggled.

"Are you shitting me?" he asked seriously. "I haven't been this hard since the Miss Hawaiian Tropic bus had a flat outside my university's gates." The doors slid open and he walked her backward into his apartment. "I think my dick's received some sort of preternatural power and I'm milking it for all it's worth, sugar. Well actually, *you'll* be milking it for all it's worth. We're gonna go at it all night long and if I turn to dust in the morning, I'll meet the sun with a smile on my face."

Vicky was about to laugh but the elevator door opened directly into his apartment and then whished shut, plunging them into darkness, and the mood rapidly changed. She could hear their varied breathing and neither was steady. She had a second to consider she might truly be the loose woman her cousin accused her of being, and for once, she didn't care. The man in front of her was warm and funny and sexy as all get-out. His fingers moved to the placket of her shirt, trailing between her breasts and then over her stomach until he reached the high waist of her pants. One by one he pushed the shirt buttons free, working his way upward. His fingers pushed the stiff cotton aside, the brief contact ratcheting her want a little tighter.

Her eyes adjusted and she watched his dark form, saw his head drift downward. She'd almost grabbed it and pulled it to the valley between her breasts as he'd suggested at the bar, certain that's where he was headed anyway.

She wasn't prepared when his mouth latched onto the side of her neck, running a heated path up, down, back and front, never breaking contact even when he found the spot—the one that had her throaty moan echoing through the room. He sucked gently, then licked, opened his mouth wide and licked some more.

Vicky shook her arms and his coat hit the floor. She was burning up, a fever running from the top of her head to her toes. She pressed against him and he bent her backward at the waist, one hand supporting her head, silently refusing to release her as the whole series of caresses started anew. Over and over, the pace slow and steady until she swore she could feel every nerve in her body charged in delight. She shifted her legs, imagining that same sucking and licking across the swollen nub that lay neglected and throbbing between her thighs.

He straightened, kept her secure with suction, teeth and lips, then moved behind her and began again. The sensation was completely different, more intense. He ran his hands up and down her sides and then his fingers hooked the lace of her bra and pulled the flimsy cups down to expose her fully. His thumbs brushed provocatively against the outer fullness of her breasts before creeping slowly to her nipples. He rubbed, barely touching the underside of each distended tip, and she groaned loudly.

"Please," she begged, only to be rewarded with a long, slow pinch that had her whimpering and her pussy silently pleading for more.

"So eager," he said against her neck, one hand drifting downward.

Vicky rose up on her toes to get him to where she was hurting.

His fingers drifted the final inches and cupped her sex. "You're soaked clear through, sugar."

He shifted his hand and she gave up thinking of a response. The heel of his hand moved just above her pubic bone, rotating back and forth lightly. When the thick part at the base of his thumb pressed over her clit her hips started moving on their own accord.

"Mmmm. That's it," he hummed against her ear. "Show me what you like."

She groaned and pressed harder against him. In seconds the tension was building, stretching her nerves taut as heat poured through her body. She rubbed against his hand, not caring what he might think of her wanton display. Release was eluding her and she dropped her head to her chest.

He nipped her earlobe and his warm breath caressed her. "Come on, baby."

"Unh. Oh…oooh," she panted, switching to a rocking motion. "I can't. I can't get there."

"Yes you can. I'll help. You just say when."

"When," she demanded. "When. *When!*"

His other hand shifted from her breast and gripped the hand already wedged between her thighs. The extra pressure rocked her, pushed her upward and completely over the edge. She flung her head back against his shoulder and screamed, covering his hands with hers as the darkness exploded in an array of blinding light.

# Chapter Two

**ௐ**

*Do vampires do it doggie style?* Andy sure as fuck hoped they did because with her little tremors still vibrating against his palm all he wanted to do was bend her over, rip off her pants and bury his dick deep inside. He looked across the living room at the opening to the bedroom. *When the hell did it get so far away?*

"Oh. God. Oh. *Shit*," her awestruck gasps interrupted his thoughts. "It feels like…"

She started rotating her hips again and grabbed his forearms.

*Screw it.* They weren't going to make it to the bedroom. He ignored her whimper as he pulled his hands away and forcefully tugged at the waistband of her pants. They wouldn't budge.

"There's a zipper," she pushed at his hands.

"Get it," he ground out, unsnapping his jeans with one hand, reaching for his wallet with the other. He pulled the condom out, tossed the wallet aside then worked his zipper down the exact second hers slid free. The synchronicity of it all should have boggled his mind—would have scored a perfect ten if disrobing was an Olympic sport.

The fact that she had worked the tight pants over her hips and down her legs as far as the boots would allow had the blood pulsing to his cock and pounding in his ears. He toed off his shoes, shucked jeans and boxer briefs in one quick motion, ripped open the packet and covered his dick. He pushed her shirt up and his mouth went dry. Her pale ass seemed to glow like an inverted heart in the darkness of the room and he squeezed the globes gently, then a bit harder when her muscles tightened under his hands.

"There," he rasped, picking her up and walking a few steps before placing her hands on the narrow table behind the sofa. Using his foot he pushed her feet as wide as they would go.

"Hurry," she pleaded, lowering her elbows.

He grabbed his cock, stroked it one time from tip to base, making sure they were both protected. He spread her cheeks, dipped his thumbs and stroked her wetness. Her pussy was drenched, so hot it burned and he tried to concentrate. *Nice and slow, Andrew.* His fingers felt cool against her moist heat as he spread her inner folds and slid his cock slowly downward, pressing only the head into her tightness. Then he did something he was sure no vampire would ever do. He closed his eyes and prayed for strength.


Vicky's fear that the second wave of orgasmic delight might have dissolved during the frantic rush to get out of their clothes was dispelled the second he touched her. Strong fingers gripped her ass, their heat branding her, kneading the flesh before his thumbs pulled her cheeks apart then moved lower. They brushed her swollen labia once before delving to open her and she bit her lip.

Then she felt the heat of his broad cock head as he moved into her. She held her breath, waiting for him to fill her with his length but he stood completely motionless behind her, his fingers still stretching her silky lips. Heartbeat after heartbeat, the silence stretched to the point where time seemed to stand still. It was the most erotic thing she had ever experienced. It was anticipation, tenfold, a seductive lesson in expectance. But patience had never been one of her virtues.

"What are you waiting for?" she asked, pushing back onto his erection. "Impale me, Vlad."

She heard his curse, thought he actually might have laughed but then his hands found her hips and he started to move in shallow strokes and she was suddenly glad he'd taken his time. He was bigger than she'd imagined and worked himself carefully in and out, a little deeper each time until waves of desire tightened her belly, her breasts, her very core.

"Faster," she said, reaching back to place a hand on his hip.

"I don't want to hurt you," he groaned.

"You won't." It was probably a lie but she didn't care.

"You're so damn tiny," he said, covering her back with the warmth of his chest as he changed motion.

She gripped the edge of the table, the tug in her pussy so strong it caused her to set a pace of her own.

"Jesus, sugar. Can you let me lead?" he asked, nibbling a path to her shoulder. He punctuated each tiny bite with a hard thrust that had her fingers digging into the edge of the table for support.

"Sorry. It's just," her breath caught as he secured her with one arm around her belly and began pounding in earnest. "Oh, god. It feels too good," she cried as his sac slapped teasingly against her.

"Never too good," he said, his finger zeroing in on her clit, flicking each time his balls swung away.

It was too much. His cock, his lips. His balls, his teeth. He worked her until swirls of light danced behind her eyelids. She felt his cock grow as she began to crest.

"I can't believe. I'm gonna...again," she cried, as the light began to shatter.

"Ladies before vampires," he groaned, his release far outlasting her own.

Eventually, Andy found the wherewithal to ease out of her but refused to let go. He pulled the condom off, tossed it into the trash can beside the sofa and lowered them both to a seated position on the hardwood floor, her soft bottom resting provocatively across his thighs. *Un-fucking-believable.*

He felt around with his hand for the toe switch to the floor lamp and slid it on to a dim shine.

"Wow," she whispered, eyes still closed.

Her cheeks were tinged an adorable shade of pink, her mouth parted on a long, slow sigh. With a finger, he tipped her chin toward him and her eyes blinked open, desire slowly clearing. She smiled seductively and wrapped her arms around his neck. He shifted, giving his dick a little room to maneuver once it got its second wind.

She rested her forehead against his and the corner of her eyes crinkled. "Your creature of the night is pretty impressive."

He laughed aloud, reaching for the heel of her boot and pulling until it slid off. "You think so?" he asked, removing the other boot.

"Mmm-hmm. Very talented," she purred, bringing her knees to her chest so he could remove her pants. He pushed the fabric down the inside of one silky calf, wrapping his hand behind her heel, tickling her arch as one leg came free. She squirmed against his lap, her damp pussy bathing his thighs, and the skin surrounding his balls rolled taut. He couldn't wait to see her, taste her. The tails of her shirt kept everything hidden but he could feel her heat and…*damn*! His dick seemed to be breaking all previous rates of recovery records.

He quickly untangled her other leg, snaked his hands up her arms and threaded his fingers through hers, where they rested against his neck.

"That was nothing." He grinned. "Wait until you meet my human servant."

She looked puzzled for a second and then nodded her head. "What's his name? Not Renfield, I hope."

"No. It's Andy."

"Andy?"

"Henderson."

"And this Andy Henderson?" she asked, moving their hands down to rest on his chest. "How's he different from you, Prince of Darkness?"

Andy tried to pull his hands free but she tightened her grip and stared into his eyes.

"Well, he's never taken a lady home without asking her name first." *Right. You haven't brought anyone here since you hooked up with that new waitress from the diner the night of Vinny's wedding.*

"So, he would have asked my name?" She leaned forward and kissed him softly on the lips.

"Definitely. What would you have told him?" he asked, wondering if she could feel his heart accelerate from just one kiss.

"Victoria. Wallis. Vicky." She smiled, her gaze drifting to his lips. "And once he knew my name, would he have done anything else differently?"

"He would have kissed you for more than two seconds before making you run a mini marathon because he couldn't wait to — "

"Fuck me," she interrupted.

He sucked in a breath as she swiveled and swung a leg over to straddle him and then moved quickly forward to keep his cock from springing up between them.

"Would he have let me grind against his hand because he made me so hot I couldn't wait to come?"

"No," Andy said, pulling his hands free because he had to touch her. He gripped her ass and hauled her lower body up against him. "He'd have made sure you were grinding against his mouth. All that sweet cream covering his tongue while he licked and licked and you came and came."

His dick was engorged, pressing proudly between her ass cheeks and the only thing keeping him from lifting her up, then down, was the fact he wanted to see what she'd say next.

"Then he would have had his way with me," she said, leaning back, resting her hands above his knees so she was propped at a seductive angle and still that mother-loving shirt was in the way. "Hard and deep, just like you did?" she asked, eyes twinkling.

He dipped his hands under the tails of the shirt and inched his fingers upward into the crease of her thighs and shook his head. "No. It would have been deeper." He moved his fingers across the soft skin.

"Liar, liar. Penis on fire," she said, rotating her hips in a tiny circle as she sat up and eased first one breast and then the other back into her bra.

"No lie, sugar," he chuckled, his dick bumping against her as he narrowed his eyes and offered the truth. "I had a couple more inches left to bury in you."

He watched her eyes widen, her mouth forming a little "o" before she spoke again.

"Are those the only ways you two differ?"

"Not really," he said, pulling her hand away before she set him off. "He hates wearing black. He's not a fan of sleeping in confined spaces. And there's no way he could put up with those three brides of mine seducing every man in sight. He doesn't have a tolerance for infidelity."

"He sounds more than a little interesting."

"So, Victoria Wallis. You want to heave that pretty ass off me and meet Andy? I think he's more than a little anxious to assist you."

"I can believe that," she said, placing her hands lightly on his shoulders and scooting backward. "I think I feel his presence."

Andy watched Vicky slowly stand up, appreciating every inch of her long, toned legs. It took a great deal of willpower but he resisted the urge to lean forward and peek under her shirt to see if she was as perfect as he imagined. She offered her hand and he took it, surprised when she actually helped him to his feet. He used his toe and adjusted the brightness of the floor lamp.

"This is really nice," she said walking around the couch, surveying the room.

"My brother Tom did all the renovations. He lives on the opposite side of the building on the top floor." He watched her move, suddenly feeling a little bereft. God, he wanted her back in his arms, tight against him. And he wanted her out of that fucking shirt. Unbuttoned to her waist, the glimpses of cleavage and bare midriff were driving him wild. She turned to study a print on the far wall and he stalked across the rug.

"I love the colors."

"You want something before I take you to bed?" he asked, bringing his body flush against hers. He tugged the ribbon from her braid, carefully un-wrapping the elastic band beneath it before flipping the bottom of her shirt aside and stepping into her. He slid his cock between her slightly parted thighs.

"I...um. I..."

"Want a drink?" He moved slowly, lubing himself with her juice as he unplaited her hair. He delved into the silky mass and was rewarded with her low groan and negative shake of her head.

"Are you hungry?"

"Hell yes," she whispered, pressing back against him.

"What can I get you," he chuckled, continuing his slow teasing.

"If I were the queen of cheesiness, this is where I'd say I have a hankering for some salami, right?"

"Cheesy you are not, sugar," he said with a smile. He reluctantly pulled back and swung her into his arms. Her little squeal echoed in the tall room as he carried her into the open kitchen and stopped before the fridge.

"What are you doing?" she laughed. "Put me down."

"No way. Open the door and see what you want."

"I know what I want," she said, looking deeply into his eyes with enough desire that his balls buried themselves against the base of his cock.

"Grab me the Powerade, sugar. And whatever you need."

She grabbed the bottle and nothing else then pushed the door shut. He turned and headed toward the bedroom.

"Ooooh. Wait. Over there, human servant," she said pointing to the end of the counter. "I looove peanut butter. Put me down, Andy. Where are the spoons?"

He eased her to the floor and pulled open the silverware drawer. "Do you want some bread at least?"

She had already twisted the lid off and dug a heaping tablespoon out of the jar. Her mouth engulfed the spoon then pulled it away half empty.

"Want some?" she asked, offering the spoon to him. She was smacking her lips, trying to swallow, and he couldn't refuse. She went back for seconds and he opened the drink and took a long swallow, handed her the bottle and grinned like a fiend.

He was standing stark naked in his kitchen with the biggest boner known to man, eating peanut butter from the jar with the most beautiful woman he'd ever seen, watching dribbles of energy drink slip out the sides of her mouth, down her chin and into the valley of her breasts as she chugged away. Christ, this was too good to be true. *Happy Halloween, buddy!*

Vicky silently admitted it might not be the best food and beverage pairing but as far as protein and electrolyte replenishing went, it was genius. And if the way Andy was looking at her, as if he wanted nothing more than to devour her from head to toe for hours on end, was any indication of things to come, she'd need her energy. She felt the tiny drops of liquid sliding down her chest, watched his eyes darken as he followed their trail. *Oh, yeah. This was going to be goood.* He took the bottle out of her hand and backed her up against the counter.

"I've had it with this shirt," he said, grabbing a tail in each hand. He ripped the material open, buttons flying across the tile floor. A second later her breasts tumbled forward as her bra met a similar fate.

Vicky would have been shocked if his voice, deep with desire, hadn't washed over her like a soothing hand.

"You take my breath away, sugar."

Her breasts, full and ripe, rose on an intake of breath. His gaze roamed over her and she winced as her nipples tightened, then she eased her legs together against a rush of blazing desire. His tongue, hot and flat, reached out and licked away the moisture suspended in her cleavage. She waited for him to shift his mouth to one side, to take either of her breasts and shower it with attention and when he didn't she shifted her body.

"You want me to taste?" he asked, looking up at her through thick lashes.

"Yes," she whispered, disappointed when he stood and took a step back.

"Then I suggest we take it into the bedroom. I wasn't joking about wanting all night with you, Victoria. I'm harder than a schoolboy just looking at you." He reached down and grabbed his cock, stroking it lightly as she watched.

"Well, *Andrew*," she said, reluctantly drawing her eyes away and taking his free hand. She gave him a saucy wink. "Quit playing with yourself and let's go."

He turned on a lamp and whipped the down comforter off the bed and tossed it onto the floor. "We're doing this nice and slow. You deserve more than a quickie in the foyer."

"Promises, promises," she teased, crawling across the cool sheets and flopping back onto the pillows.

"That's the second time you've challenged me tonight," he said, moving beside her until his body warmed her entire length.

"You're clearly rising to meet it," she conceded, brushing her knuckles against his erection which was prodding into her hip.

"Where you're concerned? Always," he whispered, capturing her lips in a thorough and leisurely kiss. When he pulled away, her bottom lip was throbbing from the gentle assault.

"You're a great kisser," she said with a sigh. The tingling that started in her lips shot a course right to her nipples and she arched her back in a silent plea. He rained kisses along her throat, across the swell of one breast and she wrapped her fingers around his hard cock.

"Thank you. Your nipples are gorgeous. Such a nice little dusky shade of pink. So tight and hard, they're just begging for me. They are begging for me, aren't they Vicky?"

"God, yes," she said, stroking his length as his breath heated one puckered tip. She cried out when he finally took her into his mouth and her hand tightened around his shaft. He laved and nibbled and grazed, first one then the other, until her breathing turned shallow and her hand worked him rapidly.

"Stop that, sugar," he warned, grabbing her wrist firmly.

"Andy, please. I want you. Right now." She flexed her fingers and he pulled her hand away.

"I can't," he said, his lips splitting in a pained grin. "Not now."

"Why?" She whined like a child denied her favorite toy. *Please, please don't put it away. I promise to behave.*

"I'm about two pumps away from exploding and that's entirely your fault. So," he said, kissing his way over her flat stomach before tickling her navel with the tip of his tongue. "I'm going to have to find something else to concentrate on until I get a little more control."

Vicky watched him work his way down her torso, anticipation rocketing through each and every nerve. His fingers grazed along her hip bones before drifting downward to her inner thighs. He brushed the inside of her legs lightly then delved behind her knees. Ticklish there beyond all reason, she squirmed against the mattress, legs flailing until he grabbed one in each of his big hands and spread her wide.

She quit struggling, the pressure of his hands under her knees, his thumbs tracing invisible patterns on her soft skin all but stopping her heart. She was open to his hot gaze and he boldly stared, golden eyes drifting over every private crevice she possessed. She felt a rush of liquid ooze from her slit, roll toward her anus and she turned her head to one side and closed her eyes, certain he hadn't missed the effect he was having on her.

She felt his muscular shoulders work their way along the underside of each leg and held her breath. *Soon.* Any second now he'd touch the wild throbbing of her clit. Instead, he pressed his thumb just below the unbearable ache and with excruciating slowness slid downward against her wetness.

"You're so wet," he said, rubbing his cheek against one thigh and then the other like a cat scenting its territory. "Just for me," he added, easing his thumb into her pussy as his mouth covered the swollen flesh surrounding her clit.

Her hips arched off the bed. *Just for you...just for you...just for you.*

His lips held her with the lightest suction, pulling and releasing but never completely freeing her. Over and over and over, never actually touching her throbbing nub. Twice she imagined he nearly pulled her against his teeth and each time she felt another wave of wetness leak from her folds. Her hands slapped the mattress when his tongue finally brushed against her and then just as quickly it vanished.

"Make room for me, sugar," he said, replacing his thumb with first one long finger, then a second. "I want all of you this time."

*All of him.* She really wanted to roll that thought through her brain but his fingers were moving so slowly they demanded her undivided attention. He eased into her in a rhythm all his own, one that had her taking the stairs of desire two at a time. Every so often he worked in a little twist that had her lurching to the top but then he would pull back, resorting to those long, lazy strokes that forced tiny grunts from her parted lips every time he pushed high inside her. She felt added pressure, assumed he was about slip another finger in.

Her head and shoulders jerked off the mattress when his tongue joined his fingers, dipped into her pussy and then moved to lave between her folds. She stared down at his head and clenched her teeth.

"You taste like sugar, sugar," he met her gaze and winked and then quickly lowered his head and took her aching clit between his lips.

Vicky wanted to throw herself back on the sheets and moan in abandon but she couldn't pull her eyes away. He was well and truly devouring her, his mouth moving as if she were the sustenance of life and he couldn't get enough. She hadn't been the recipient of such an oral feast in...well...forever.

She bucked against him, suddenly remembering his earlier words about her coming against his lips. He pulled his fingers from her and she swore on a loud moan and then called his name beseechingly a moment later when he shifted his hands under her ass and angled her more firmly against his mouth. In some far recess of her mind a hidden voice demanded she realize how special this moment was. How truly special *he* was.

It took every ounce of willpower—something she sorely lacked even when she wasn't in the throes of a mind-blowing orgasm—for her to dig her fingers into his hair and tug him away before it was too late.

"Don't make me come without you, Andy," she pleaded with heavy breaths, meeting his surprised amber gaze.

Andy looked into her crystal blue eyes and his heart tumbled. Maybe he needed to do a little more cardio. *Maybe you need to admit she's doing a little more than rockin' your cock, pal.*

"Together," he said, quickly moving from between her thighs to the end of the bed. When his feet hit the carpet he grabbed her ankles and pulled her ass to the edge, rested her soles on the low, wooden footboard. Her pussy was gleaming from her own lube and his saliva and he rubbed his cock against her silky folds. A brief image of him spurting over her flat stomach was enough to propel his cock toward her welcoming warmth.

"Andy! Condom?"

"Shit." What the hell was wrong with him? He hurried to the nightstand, pulled the drawer open. What the fuck had he been thinking? He never went in bare. He rushed back to her spread thighs and quickly covered himself. "Sorry."

He pushed slowly into her tight heat and groaned. "You've put some sort of spell on me."

"It's Halloween, remember?" He watched her forehead wrinkle as he pressed higher, not stopping until he was snug against her.

"Are you okay?" he asked. There was an excellent chance he couldn't stop if she said she wasn't. The allure of her heat was more than his will could stand.

"Fine," she said at last. "That's so much deeper than before. Can you go slow?"

"Sure," he said in a strangled voice and she chuckled. "For shit's sake, Vicky, don't laugh. You have no idea what that does to my dick."

"Sorry." She propped up on her elbows and gave him a less than contrite look. "Kiss me, Andy."

He shook his head, smiled before their lips met. *What the fuck is happening here?*

She wrapped a hand around his neck and pulled him close. Her mouth was a delight and he sampled it fully as he rolled his hips slowly. She scooted closer to the edge of the mattress and he picked up the tempo. Her inner muscles formed around him like a new skin. One that was suddenly aflame.

She broke the kiss, closed her eyes for a second and then stared down at their joined bodies. Andy followed her line of vision, watched her pink lips surround his dick, draw him into her warmth and slowly release him. It was beyond seductive and his balls began to prickle. The warmth spreading up his shaft didn't bode well for extended play. Her muscles contracted around his cock and he gritted his teeth.

"Harder," she said, fingers clutching the sheet.

He looked at her face, found her still staring at their joining as if in a trance and slowed to a near stop that brought her attention back to him.

"Harder?" he asked. She met his eyes and nodded.

"Harder. Now. *Please*!"

He shifted his feet farther back, widened his stance and placed his hands next to her elbows, leaning in until they were nearly touching, chest to breast. He stared at her eyes—so deep and trusting—and then he began the dance, gaining momentum with each thrust. He glanced down at the tempting sight of her rocking bosom but only for a moment. She was staring at him, eyes wide and filled with naked desire.

It felt too good. Damn it all, he couldn't remember wanting anything more than being inside her, rocking against her, hearing the little noises that were whispering from her mouth. Her cunt was on fire, spasming against him slowly at first and then with an urgency that matched each of his thrusts.

"Andy..." she panted, closing her eyes.

"Stay with me, sugar. This time," he pleaded grabbing her elbows, fighting to hold back his release. "Stay with me."

She opened her eyes and he knew the look of pain that twisted her features was a mirror of his own, a precursor to the pleasure about to overtake them both.

She dug her nails into his forearms. Their gazes locked and then mingled cries of release echoed through the room.

# Chapter Three

ॐ

In a perfect world Vicky could snuggle deeper into his embrace and smile at the events of the previous evening. But she'd learned long ago that nothing, least of all her world, was perfect. When she walked out Andy's door she'd leave with some great memories. She would get a cab back to Bobby's, have the driver wait until she went inside and got some cash to pay him. Maybe Andy hadn't realized she had showed up at the bar without a purse. If he had, she didn't want to think about what his opinion of her might be. Unlike other men she'd slept with, she actually cared what he thought. Now that the sexual euphoria had finally subsided, his off-handed brides-of-Dracula comment about untrustworthy women and infidelity wormed its way into her thoughts.

The hand cupping her breast flexed and she held her breath.

"Your heart's racing," he said groggily. "What's the matter?"

"Nothing." She wiggled back against him and felt his cock twitch, unable to believe he was ready again.

"Victoria," he said, rising up on one elbow as he rolled her onto her back. "Tell me."

She didn't want to look at him and focused on the tin ceiling, studying the intricate pattern as the first rays of dawn illuminated the room. His fingers left her breast and crept over her stomach until he was rubbing her pubic curls between his fingers.

"I'm not going to make love to you again until you tell me what's wrong."

Her eyes snapped to his. *He doesn't mean anything by that.* Her heart drummed against her ribs. *That was fucking. Nothing more, Vicky. Nothing. More.*

She looked up into his dark eyes and bit her lip. How much should she divulge? There was kindness reflected there and she watched the tiny creases at the corners of his eyes deepen. God, maybe he'd find her tales amusing. Or maybe he'd find them and her truly pitiable. That would be worse.

"I came to the bar last night without a purse."

"Okaaay," he said puzzled.

"All my money is at my cousin's house. I'm staying with him and his wife."

His gaze drifted over her features and she tried to stay focused. Just one look and all she wanted to do was kiss him.

"He had a party last night but it turned out to be a little more kinky than I expected and I had to get out of there and I didn't think to grab my purse or a coat and..."

"And?" he asked, tracing her lips with one large finger.

She closed her eyes against the urge to suck him into her mouth and pressed on.

"I don't want you to think I'm the type of person who would purposely set out to have a guy pay my way and then jump into bed with him as a means of thanking him. You know how small this town is. It won't take long for my past to catch up with me, especially if my cousin has anything to say about it."

"And why would your cousin feel compelled to say anything about your past, which is something, might I point out, we all have?"

"I might have pissed him off last evening when I told him to shove a large sex toy up his ass." She felt the vibration of his silent laughter but couldn't smile.

"Some party. Look." He cupped her face and turned her head toward him, waiting until she opened her eyes and met his gaze. "I really don't give a flying fuck what other people have to say. I like to think I'm a pretty astute guy. I can draw my own conclusions where people are concerned. Now, tell me everything you think is going to have me running from this bed."

She searched his face for some sign he was teasing. Some indication that he didn't really care.

"The abridged version if possible," he added. "My dick gets hard just looking at your mouth. I want to be back inside you so bad it hurts."

Her pussy should have been exhausted from their all-nighter but it twisted all the same.

She so wanted to have a fresh start. *Not necessarily with him. Who are you kidding? You want him. Start, middle and end.* She took a deep breath and hoped when it was all said and done he wouldn't brand a big red "A" on her chest and tell her to get the hell out.

"I'm an interior designer. I left here ten years ago, went to school, worked hard, moved to Atlanta, became pretty successful."

"That's a real black mark in my book," he teased, leaning forward to kiss her.

"Andy," she stopped him, placing her hand against his lips. "This isn't as easy for me as you think but I want to tell you everything." It surprised her but she really did want to tell him all of it.

He immediately stopped and gave her his full attention.

"I've had more than a few relationships but they've never lasted long. I tend to scare men away, for some reason. I think it's because I really, really like sex."

"Thank you, Jesus," he whispered under his breath, looking skyward for a brief moment before returning his concentration to her and she fought back a smile.

"Or it might be the fact I generally tell people exactly what I think. Anyhow, I had a great business in Atlanta. My work was well known. It was featured in a national magazine, which was unbelievable from a personal standpoint. I was a pro at juggling a successful career and a not-so-successful personal life.

"I had a very influential client who hired me to design his mountain retreat. During the course of the job we became involved, which was a first for me. I broke one of my personal credos. I never date clients. Never. Long story short, he didn't mention a wife. If he had, believe me, there would have been no involvement whatsoever. No one had met her or even seemed to realize she existed. She was in Greece visiting family. She showed up one day out of the blue and threatened me. Threatened my business."

"Because you wouldn't cut off the affair?"

"No," she laughed bitterly. "She had no problem with my involvement with her husband. She was incensed that I didn't want to continue the relationship and include her. Within three weeks my phone quit ringing. Builders stopped recommending me. Clients I'd had for years snubbed me, which really hurt."

"What about the guy?"

She was a little surprised by that question and shrugged. "He basically told me to ditch the rose-colored glasses and grow up. He'd been looking for a diversion while she was away. They apparently have a very open relationship."

He was quiet for a long time and Vicky gnawed at her lip, waiting for him to say something.

"And your cousin's being a dickhead why?"

"His associates are the people I need to target if my business has a prayer of a chance of succeeding. I know my skills will appeal to the seasonal owners, the ones who redecorate nearly as often as I change my panties. But I need off-season clientele as well. He offered to help me but I had to refuse." She watched his eyebrow arch and decided to tell him why, knowing he was about to ask. "He wanted me to have sex with four of his friends. Preferably as a group."

Andy tried to push down the surge of rage that rolled through him. It wasn't Vicky's fault her cousin was a cocksucker. He hoped his voice was steadier than he felt. "Fuck four guys and he'd help you get your foot in the door?"

"Yep. That pretty much sums it up," she said softly.

"Come here," he said, rolling onto his back and opening his arms. She came to him with a heavy sigh and he wrapped one arm around her waist and buried the other in her silky hair, pulling it away from one temple to place a soft kiss there. "As of this minute you can forget about your shithead of a cousin. You don't need him. I know someone who's much more influential."

"You do?" she asked, rubbing her nose lightly against his nipple. The little gesture shot an unexpected stream of pure want to his groin.

"Yeah. My mom takes care of liaisons with interior designers for our business. She'd be more than happy to take a look at your portfolio."

"Your mom? What business?" He felt her entire body tense beside him and looked down to see her staring at him with a look of panic on her face.

"Henderson Building and Design. Quality builders since 1969."

She tried to struggle out of his grasp but he held tight.

"Oh, shit. Andy. Honestly, I didn't know."

"Calm down. I know you didn't. How could you?"

"I'm mortified," she admitted, burying her face in his shoulder.

"Why?"

"*Why?*" her incredulous reply was muffled against his flesh. "Because I picked you up at a bar, had earth-shattering sex with you, told you my current tale of woe and suddenly find out you're in the exact line of work that would prove quite beneficial for me."

"Technically, I picked you up," he said, hauling her on top of his body and taking her head in his hands. He brushed her hair away from her flushed face. "Lighten up, Vicky. Don't you believe things happen for a reason?"

He watched her gaze slip away and her eyes blink rapidly.

"I never used to either but I do now," he admitted, thinking how his brother Jason's romance with Marissa had materialized out of thin air and had him and his remaining siblings considering new and revised opinions on lust and love.

"Maybe it was all that Halloween mojo floatin' through the air. Or maybe it's the fact you're so freakin' irresistible. Either way, I don't have a single doubt we were destined to meet. And just for your own personal info, I don't make a regular habit of bringing strange women home. And I don't believe for a minute you're some prick tease who's looking for a one-night bang before you move on to bigger and better cocks. Ones that might be attached to guys who can help move your life and career forward."

"Andy..."

He skimmed his thumbs over her cheekbones and brought them to rest against her lips.

"Shhh. Let me help you. We'll get your stuff from your cousin's. Tom has a loft that's vacant on the second floor or you can talk to him about other apartments he has available. He's like Uncle Pennybags—he's got properties all over town. He'll give you a good deal." She looked at him and the moisture in the corners of her eyes welled. He swallowed against a sudden ache in his throat. "You'll let my mom see if she can help you. She's been asked bigger favors than this over the years."

"She's not going to think I'm some enterprising slut out to seduce her son as a means to an end?"

He gave her his sternest look and refused to answer.

"Sorry," she whispered.

"I'm pretty certain she won't make you participate in any gang bangs," he teased and was rewarded by her shaky smile.

"So your mom's not some master pimp, huh?"

"Not that I know of," he laughed. "Although, she might demand you engage in illicit behavior with one guy in return for her help.

"Just one?" she asked, her eyes clearing to a deep shade of blue as she shifted up his body. "Anyone I know?"

His dick was trapped between them, tapping a somewhat restrained beat against her abdomen. He grabbed her ass and yanked her upward until her moist heat was pressed against him.

"Oh yeah, sugar. You two have met."


He was staring at her with an intensity that took Vicky's breath away and at the same time left her deeply worried. She generally needed the safety net of knowing she could walk away when things went bad. Right now, all she wanted to do was get as close to him as humanly possible. All her pre-set rules of hooking up had flown right out his fourth floor window. Everything they had shared seemed undeniably right. She'd known him less than twelve hours and trusted him more than any man she'd ever met. He was more than just some heart-stoppingly sexy hunk. She'd known that from the second he'd pushed her up against that brick wall and kissed her senseless.

"What's your choice of lubricant when you're polishing the ol' newel post, Mr. Henderson?" she asked, sliding off him to sit back on her heels.

"*What*?" he croaked.

She loved the way his jaw hung open in shock.

"Come on, Andy," she said, her gaze drifting down his body to his erection—proud and heavy against his abdomen. "If you're not bringing girls home then you have to be taking care of things yourself. No celibate could make love the way you do. That kind of control comes from taking matters into your own hand from time to time. Am I right or am I right?"

"Jesus!"

"Just tell me what you like and where it's at. I want to try something I've never done before." His eyes widened. She could tell his mind was racing.

"What do you have in mind?" he asked, shock replaced by something that made his eyes gleam. He stacked his hands under his head in such a purely masculine fashion she had to smile.

"Uh-uh-uh," she said, wagging her finger at him. "Tell me where it is. If I tell you what I'm thinking you might not be interested."

"Trust me, sugar. I'm interested. In anything. Everything," he said, giving her a sexy grin that almost had her forgetting her plans, and instead, climbing on top and riding him senseless.

"Where's the stash, big boy?"

"In the bathroom," he said, shifting his leg to brush against her hip.

She ignored the impulse to run her fingers straight to his cock.

"Top shelf of the medicine cabinet."

"Be back in a flash," she said, hopping off the bed and running to the bathroom. She closed the door and took care of a few personal issues before trying to straighten her mussed hair. She retrieved the big, square jar and opened the door.

"Petroleum jelly? I was thinking maybe some spicy-scented massage oil."

"Nah. Things would be over too quick." His eyes caressed her from head to toe and she hoped she could pull this off.

"Heaven forbid. It's pretty unfair I didn't get to taste you," Vicky said when she crawled back onto the bed. "And I only barely touched you before you made me stop."

"Never let it be said I was unfair," he said, spreading his arms wide. "I'm yours, sugar."

Vicky pushed that last statement aside and ran her finger over the crest of his cock before stroking him firmly. "Oooh. Like velvet stretched over steel."

She looked at his face. He wasn't smiling anymore. In fact, he actually looked like he was in pain.

"Did I do something you didn't like?"

"No," he ground out, nostrils flaring as he breathed in and out through his nose. He wrapped his hand around her wrist and gently disengaged her fingers. "This is borderline pathetic. One touch of your hand and I'm ready to fuckin' blow."

"Well then. It's a good thing I'm not planning on touching you with my hand anymore. Get up on your knees and turn around. Face the headboard."

His gaze narrowed and she thought he might refuse but then he rolled onto his knees and did as she asked.

"Thank you for obeying. I thought for I minute there I might have to go in search of that riding crop," she teased.

She watched his ass cheeks tightened and couldn't help but run a nail over the defined muscle, grinning at his small shiver.

"Remember this when it's my turn, Vicky. I know exactly where that crop is."

His voice had dropped to a seductive whisper and she shook her head to clear the graphic images his words induced. She sat down in front of him, propping all the pillows behind her back before sliding her legs between his spread knees. She twisted the lid off the jar and held it out to him.

"Make yourself nice and slippery."

He held her gaze, dipped two fingers into the jar. "You know this stuff is not latex's friend."

"I know. But I don't think I'm up to having you inside again so soon anyway." She offered him a tiny smile then whispered, "Newsflash, studly. You're pretty well hung."

"You should have told me you were sore."

"And what would you have done?" she asked, watching as he brought his fingers to his shaft.

"Kissed it. Licked it. Made it all better," he said in a husky voice, spreading the lube along his length with just his fingertips.

"Maybe you can do that later," she suggested, shifting her legs against the predicable rush of warmth his tone caused. "Rub it all around, Andy."

"Why don't you do it, sugar?"

"I don't want to get it on my hands."

"So that's how it is. I get to do the dirty work," he said, wrapping his fist around his erection, letting the warmth of his hand soften the jelly before he worked it around in long strokes.

"That's not dirty," she said, swallowing hard as she studied his light motion. His shaft shone when he pulled his hand away, the dark tip weeping a solitary drop of pre-cum. "It's beautiful. Scoot up here."

She placed her hands on his thighs as he moved up her body. She loved the fine golden hair that covered his legs, remembering how it teased her bottom when she sat on his lap. She smoothed her hand over it and then moved to the crease of skin between his torso and his thighs. He stopped moving.

"A little bit more," she said, wrapping her hands around the back of his legs and urging him closer until his knees were pressed under her arms. She ran her hands over his ass, brushing between his cheeks lightly.

"What are we doing, Victoria?" She didn't miss the tinge of wonder in his voice or the way his muscles contracted and she smiled up at him.

"Well, Andrew," she said, pulling her hands from him to run her fingertips along the outside of her breasts. "You got to feel every dripping ounce of desire you wrung from me. I want to feel your desire too. Every drop of it."

He tried to think of a response but the mere sight of her cupping her breasts robbed him of speech. Her hands pushed the globes of warm flesh together to cradle the sides of his cock and he groaned loudly.

"Jesus, that feels good," he admitted, unable to stay still. The sensation of his cock sliding against the hardness of her breast bone while being surrounded by her soft breasts was unbelievably sensual. He thought about asking if she was truly certain she wanted to do this but she chose that moment to press tighter around him and he gave up all rational thought. He pumped slowly against her, watching the way her index and middle fingers cradled her hard nipples. He was certain if she gave those tiny nubs a little squeeze he'd explode.

"Mmmm. I like this warm resistance when your cock rubs against me. So different than when you're inside me. And I can see how your cock head's swelling, getting darker. Do you like this or should I not hold you so tight?" She relaxed her grip and let her breasts fall a fraction away from him.

"Oh baby, I like it. Shit. Don't let up, sugar," he pleaded, leaning forward to grab the headboard with his un-lubed hand for support.

"Slow down and I'll make it tight again."

"Oh, yeah. Tighter would be perfect," he gasped.

"Andy? Have you done this before?"

"Never." His response was hoarse. He gritted his teeth and lessened his speed and she immediately applied the promised pressure. And then she shifted her grip so every time he thrust through her ample flesh one thumb brushed over his hyper-sensitized tip while the other one stroked down his shaft.

"You're so hard."

"Vicky. Dear god." He couldn't take any more and picked up speed. "This is so fuckin' good.

"Better than being inside me?"

"Sugar. No. Not even close. You gotta... Vicky. Please." He threw his head back, groaning as his balls rose higher, perspiration broke out on his chest, his back, his forehead.

"What do you want me to do?" she asked, her voice a mixture of awe and pure seduction. She pulled her thumb away and he almost cried.

"Tighter, baby. Tighter."

"God, Andy. I can feel everything. Your cock's so red it looks like it's ready to burst into flame."

"It might," he ground out. "Don't stop."

He felt her chest rise beneath him. A rush of cool air caressed his steaming cock on the next forward thrust as she blew against to swollen tip and his legs began to shake.

"Oh, *fuck*."

"Are you going to come for me, Andy?

"Christ, sugar," he panted, sweat dripping down his back. "I'm almost there. If you're not sure, let me back up now..." He looked down at his cock' plunging between her breasts, before meeting her hot gaze.

"I'm more than sure. Let me feel it, Andy. All of it."

He watched, gasping like a dying man, as he came. Watched her blue eyes close, and then she tilted her head back, moaning as each pearly path of warmth shot over her upper chest. Watched her never let her grip slacken until she had milked ever drop from him. Watched as she blinked her eyes open and gave him a satisfied grin as she let the weight of her breasts fall away from him.

His legs felt like rubber but he managed to hold his weight off her chest, and get his heart rate under control by taking slow, deep breaths.

"Let me get you a tissue," he said when he could finally speak.

"Not yet," she said, staring so intently at the end of his cock he looked down to see if something was wrong. She leaned forward and the tip of her tongue darted out, licking away a lone drop of cum that clung to the cleft. "Mmmm. Yummy."

"That's it," he said, heaving himself off her and flopping down onto the mattress. "You've officially blown my mind. I surrender. I give."

"You sure do," she teased. "A lot."

"You asked for it," he shot back lightly, stretching over her to pull some tissues from the box on the nightstand. "I hope you liked that because my cock's probably gonna be useless for the next few hours."

"I *did* like it," she replied, reaching for the tissues.

He moved his hand out of her reach and then gently wiped her clean.

"What did you think?" she asked softly, threading her fingers through his hair.

"I think you're insane for even asking that question." He covered her lips in a gentle caress and on impulse kissed his way down her neck to the still-damp hollow of her throat. He nipped the skin and then quickly licked the bite, the remains of his salty taste a far cry from her musky sweetness and he grimaced.

"Not so yummy to you?" she asked.

"Not at all, sugar," he said, pulling her leg over his hip until she was half opened to him. He sat up and placed a wet kiss on the inside of her knee before kissing his way toward the apex of her thighs. "There has to be something around here that can get that taste out of my mouth."

She dropped her head back, a long sigh reverberating through the bedroom. It was the sweetest sound he'd ever heard and it brought a smile to his lips.

# Chapter Four

## ❧

Andy hummed as he whipped up a batch of pancake batter. He wished he had more to choose from but Vicky's options for breakfast in bed were sorely limited. Actually, if she didn't hurry up with her bath, it would be pancakes in the tub, which would work out fine since he was currently brainstorming inventive uses for leftover maple syrup.

He had showered quickly then run a hot bath while he moved around the living room and kitchen retrieving their discarded clothing. He'd tossed everything on a chair in the bedroom and slowly kissed her awake before pulling her from the bed and personally lowering her into the tub. He was pleased he'd surprised her and had sat on the closed lid of the toilet and watched as she sank into the bubbles. Her oohs and aahs sounded so orgasmic he'd been poised to join her when his stomach had rumbled loud enough to get both their attentions. That was how he'd found out she loved pancakes.

He searched the lower cabinets until he found the griddle pan and put it on the front burner and turned the element on. She said chocolate chip was her favorite but he knew he didn't have chocolate morsels lying around. He rummaged and found a packet of dried cranberries, ripped them open and tossed them into the batter. He liked them in oatmeal, why not pancakes? He carefully poured four dollops of batter on the hot pan. When he turned toward the sink a movement from the couch startled him.

"You're singing," Tom said, with a lopsided grin.

"What the fuck are you two doing here?" Andy looked from his oldest brother to his youngest brother. He'd never even heard them come in, let alone make themselves at home.

M.A. Ellis

"You never sing," Sam said, puzzled.

"I'm not singing," he glanced at the bedroom door, happy he had closed it on his way out.

"Z.Z. Top, right?" Tom asked, leaning back and propping his ankle across his knee.

"It was humming, not singing."

"*Pearl Necklace*, if I'm not mistaken."

"That's a song? For real?" Sam looked at Tom then slowly turned his head and stared at Andy, eyes widening. "Dude! Did you get *laid*?"

"Can you please get the hell out of here? I've got a ton of shit to do today."

"Why are you making breakfast if you've got so much to do?" Sam asked, ever reasoning.

Andy didn't miss the way Sam leaned back and mirrored Tom's action but with the opposite leg. The kid adored his eldest brother. Tom was the only one who didn't think Sam's attraction to the computer was totally unhealthy.

"Most important meal of the day, asshole," Andy replied. "Please leave."

"We were supposed to meet you a half hour ago upstairs to go over the new purchase order software that Geekazoid here installed," Tom said, hitching a thumb in Sam's direction. "I guess that slipped your mind, Aunt Jemima."

Andy met his bemused look and frowned. With any luck Vicky was still in the bath. He'd give Tom some lame excuse, which he wouldn't believe but he'd pretend to and Sam would be none the wiser. They'd leave. There wouldn't be some awkward scene to totally fuck up whatever was going on with him and Vicky. He was ready to give it his best shot when he heard the creak of the bedroom door.

"Andy? I couldn't find my panties so I borrowed a pair of—"

108

She stopped on the threshold, finally realizing they weren't alone. His worn Minnesota baseball shirt came to her thighs. She'd picked his favorite pair of boxers, the ones that had three stick men surrounding a campfire on the front with the accompanying message *It's all fun and games until someone loses a wiener.* Her chestnut hair was tousled and her lips were still puffy from his kisses and if his brothers weren't present, he'd walk over and make love to her in the middle of the floor. He heard someone clear his throat and tried to focus.

"Your pancakes are burning, Auntie," Tom said and Andy rushed to the stove and flipped the charred circles into the trash.

"I'm so sorry," Vicky said, placing a hand against her chest. "I didn't know you had company."

Andy walked around the counter and was pleased, for purely selfish reasons, she hadn't gone screaming back into the bedroom. Once she was near, he didn't want her to leave. His brothers stood and he walked to her side, ran his hand up her spine and gave the back of her neck a little squeeze.

"Vicky, these are my brothers. Tom…"

"Hello Tom. It's very nice to meet you."

He watched Tom wrap his fingers around her outstretched hand, meet her eyes longer than seemed necessary, then give her an easy smile. Andy was encouraged. Tom wasn't easily swayed by the fairer sex. His brother loved women, he just didn't trust them.

"Likewise," Tom said, sliding a sidelong glance at Andy, which he was forced to ignore when his younger brother came closer.

"Hi. I'm Sam. But you can call me Sammy and if it sounds as hot as when you say that 'ee' sound like you did when you called Andy's name, I'll be in heaven."

Andy stared in disbelief. The kid would barely speak to girls his own age. *What the hell's he doing hitting on my girlfriend right in front of me?* Girlfriend? Okay. That sounded pretty damn good.

Vicky laughed and wrapped an arm around Andy's waist as she smiled at his sibling.

"Nice to meet you too, *Sammeeee*," she purred. "How was that?"

"Perfect," Sam sighed, placing a hand over his heart.

Tom punched Sam lightly in the arm and shook his head. "I'll give you a call later, man. Maybe we can look at that software tomorrow?"

"Tom," Vicky interrupted. "May I talk to you for a sec?"

Andy watched her lead his brother to the wall of windows and motioned Sam to follow him to the stove.

"Dude." Sam tapped him on the shoulder as he poured more batter on the pan. "She's smokin'."

"I know," he agreed, watching her arms move emphatically as she talked. Maybe he and his dick were the only ones noticing how enticingly her breasts jiggled.

"Minnesota didn't make the playoffs this year but holy shit. The twins are lookin' prit-ty good right now."

Andy whacked him on the arm with the spatula. "Keep your eyes above the strike zone, turdhead."

"That *hurt*. Geez. First Jason, now you. It's freakin' scary, dude."

"Relax," Andy said, flipping the circles before they burned again. "You've got years before you're afflicted."

"Not if I fall for some seriously fine Level Eight wood elf and run off to Vegas."

"You gotta' quit playing those computer games and meet some flesh and blood females, Sammy."

Tom walked to the elevator and Sam vaulted over an easy chair to join him. Vicky was nearly to his side when the elevator doors closed shut.

"I like them," she said wrapping her arms around him.

"Yeah. So do I," he said, looking backward and giving her a wink. "When they're not driving me crazy."

"Smells good enough to eat," she said, rubbing her nose against the back of his shoulder.

He shut the burner off, moved the pan and tossed the spatula aside. He pulled her into his arms and nuzzled her neck until she was squirming against him. "It sure does, sugar."

# Epilogue
*One month later*

ॐ

"You're pretty fast," Vicky said, gazing into Andy's half closed eyes.

"That's really not what a guy wants to hear when he's in a beautiful woman's bed, you know."

They were lying face-to-face, legs entwined, his hand resting protectively on her hip. She was so content she could barely stand it.

"Not that way," she smiled, leaning forward to teasingly nip his jaw. "Sometimes, you make love to me so slow I think I'm going to lose my mind. I was talking about the magic you've worked in a month's time."

"I didn't do anything. It was all you."

He brushed her hair behind her ear and Vicky turned and kissed the palm of his hand.

"You're so full of it, Andrew Henderson. You introduced me to Tom—"

"You took the initiative, in a pair of underwear and a threadbare T-shirt, to talk to him on your own. I keep trying to convince myself those fantastic breasts of yours didn't sway him into renting you this place at half price."

"Jealous?"

"Hell yes. Of every guy who looks your way."

"That's weird," she said. "I never notice anyone looking at me because the only man I see is you. And don't try to change the subject. You found me the office space."

"That was Marissa, not me. It made perfect sense to offer you the remainder of her lease since she's moved to a bigger place."

"She's a sweetie. But you definitely talked to your mom about me."

"That, I did do."

"See," she said, tracing the top of his stony pecs with one finger.

"But we didn't talk about your mad designer skills. Your past work did the convincing there. We talked about other stuff."

She looked into his eyes and furrowed her brow. "What kind of stuff?"

"Stuff I'm not sure you really want to hear right now."

Her heart started hammering in her chest and she stilled.

"Try me," she whispered.

"I asked if she thought it was wrong for someone to eat cranberry pancakes while their lover was going down on them in the middle of the kitchen."

"You did not," she said slapping his chest playfully. "And, if memory serves, I offered to share them with you."

"I had my mouth full at the time," he said, the corner of his lips rising as he hefted himself onto one elbow and looked down at her.

"Be serious." She moved her hand, resting her fingers over his heart.

"I asked her what she thought about wanting someone so badly you couldn't stand the hours you had to be apart."

*Oh, goodness.* Maybe she shouldn't have pressed him.

"I asked if she thought pure out-of-control physical attraction was enough to keep what seems like a good thing going."

"What did she say?" Vicky asked, not sure she wanted to hear that answer.

He chuckled and shook his head.

"She told me there was nothing like a good fuck. She said it. Just like that. She's picked up some great language from an all-male household over the years."

"I can't believe she said the f-word."

"She said if there wasn't some heart-to-heart involvement though, it was just sex."

"Just sex," Vicky whispered, looking at the ceiling, the design an exact copy of the one in Andy's bedroom. *You asked for this, Victoria.*

"Yeah. And then I asked her how she knew my dad was the right one. She told me she fell in love with him the day they met and when he finally talked her into his bed she knew for sure because the passion wasn't like anything else they'd ever experienced."

"Wow, that's unbelievable," Vicky said, eyes welling.

"It's disturbing to find out your parents went at it like jackrabbits."

She couldn't help but laugh and turned her head, trying to let the pillow catch the tear rolling from her eye. He caught her chin between his fingers and forced her to look at him.

"Vicky. My heart actually hurts when you're not with me."

He bent down and licked the other tear rolling down her cheek. "I love you."

Her heart was full, so saturated with emotion she thought it might actually implode.

"Andy," she whispered. To her horror it came out a sob.

"Don't cry, sugar. I understand if you're not at the same place. I just needed to tell you." She heard the hurt in his voice.

She couldn't see through her blurred vision but felt something drop onto her cheek. She blinked the tears away and rubbed her thumbs over his cheekbones, shocked when they came away damp.

"Oh, Andy," she rose and kissed him soundly. "You're such an ass."

"A good ass or a bad ass?" he asked raining kisses over her face.

"The best ass. The only ass I'll ever want. As long as your preternatural cock comes with it," she said with a watery laugh.

"So...everything comes back to those vampire fantasies, huh?" His lips curved into a mock frown.

"Hey. If it wasn't for my hidden lust for Dracula I would have never found you. My Hallow's Eve hunk."

"I guess I should be happy you weren't having wet dreams about circus clowns. Those big ass shoes and red rubber noses might have put a crimp in our lovemaking," he teased, wrapping a strand of her hair around his finger as his lips lowered for a leisurely kiss. "I'm glad you like Vlad. He's willing to rise anytime you want."

His wicked smile warmed every inch of her.

"Oh. I like Vlad a lot." She took his face in her hands and looked deeply into his golden brown eyes. "But I love you more."

# LOVE'S ALLY

80

# Dedication

## ❧

*P. Andrew Miller – creative writing guru – this one's for you. Your encouragement means more than you'll ever know. And when you coined that particular piece of my writing – the sex poem – we should have all realized it would one day lead to this!*

# Acknowledgements

## ❧

*My thanks to whatever powers saw fit to grant my wish for an amazing editor.*
*Pamela Campbell – listen close and you'll hear Tina singin'. Thank you for being simply the best.*

# Trademarks Acknowledgement

## ❧

The author acknowledges the trademarked status and trademark owners of the following wordmarks mentioned in this work of fiction:

American Chopper: Discovery Communications, Inc.

Energizer Bunny: Energizer: Eveready Battery Company, Inc.

Mountain Dew: Pepsico, Inc.

The Prisoner of Azkaban: Warner Bros. Entertainment Inc.

## Page of Cups

The Page of Cups prompts us to partake of all the Cups suit offers—romance, feelings and the inner life. The Page is recognized as Cupid and as such, the card brings the opportunity for love. In readings, the Page represents a possible event that could touch us emotionally or bring us great joy. He prompts us act quickly when such an opening presents itself. He urges honesty and sincerity. If the Page of Cups is standing sentinel over a relationship, it will be blessed.

# Chapter One

❧

Tom Henderson pulled up to The Rusty Angler and killed the engine. The streets were practically barren. The locals had a few more months before the seasonal elite descended on Grand Harbor and while they loved the surge in income the summer flux provided, most of them relished every minute of peace and solitude the off-season brought. In his opinion, the only downside was the lack of female companions whose favorite pastime, right after paying homage to the martini gods, was partaking in a little tongue-to-tonsil foreplay on the dance floor, which, he noted, was completely empty as he pulled the heavy door open and walked into the bar.

"Tommy boy. Where've you been, bro?"

He looked at his brother Luke and grimaced. "How long have you been here and how much have you had to drink?"

"Well, hello to you too, asshole. We left work at four-thirty. Blue Lagoon," he said shaking his glass. "Drink of the day. I've had three."

"Keys," Tom demanded, sticking out his hand. "Who all's here?"

"The twins have come and gone," Luke said, relinquishing his keys. "Matt has a date. One he didn't want to bring around—and I quote—'us crazy fuckers'. Sammy was late for a raid."

"A raid?"

"Yeah, some computer thing. Andy and Vicky are at the bar upstairs."

"Where're Jason and Marissa?"

"Up by the boards. Wait 'til you see Jay."

Tom headed upstairs toward the dart boards, anxious to see what Luke meant. One never knew what to expect from Jason and his girl these days. Jason's relationship with her had struck like lightning and roared out of control ever since. At first, Tom assumed it was all about whatever was going on between the sheets but Jason swore he'd fallen for Marissa the moment he saw her. And that's what really baffled Tom. That kind of shit didn't happen in the real world.

"That crazy chick's here too," Luke said, following close behind.

"Which crazy chick?"

"The one with the bad dye job who dresses like she's on the prowl one day and queen of the earth muffins the next."

He knew exactly who Luke was talking about. He had noticed her on more than one occasion. Her long hair was a mass of wild curls—a dark shade of red that couldn't possibly be natural. The color accentuated the paleness of her skin. He thought that might be pure calculation on her part. When she entered a room everyone, men and women alike, turned and stared. He'd been no exception but he liked to think he had covered his ogling fairly well.

"And how's she dressed tonight?" Tom asked, more than a little curious.

"Somewhere in between."

"Great," Tom said under his breath.

"I'd screw her, though," Luke said wistfully.

"You're drunk." Tom laughed, looking over the crowd.

"No, man, listen. She looks at you with those eyes... Have you ever seen her eyes? They're this weird-ass shade of brown and green."

"It's called hazel, moron."

"No, it's different. Anyway, she gives you this look like all she wants to do is fuck you into oblivion."

"We're definitely not talking about the same person." But he knew they were, even though her come-and-get-me looks had never been directed his way.

"But then she opens her mouth and fuck, dude. She can cut a guy to ribbons with that tongue."

"She can be sarcastic," Tom admitted. He'd overheard her talking more than a few times when Jay and Marissa had their little get-togethers. She wasn't some simpering spoiled socialite. She was self-assured to the nth degree and let a man know it.

"Tom. Over here." He looked up and saw Jason and Marissa. His brother had his arms wrapped around her, his chin resting on top of her head, a look of utter contentment on his face. She waved at him and he raised his hand in response.

"What are we celebrating?" Tom asked when he reached them.

"Nothin'," Jason said offhandedly.

"Yeah," Marissa agreed with a dazzling smile. "Nothin' but *this*!"

She held her left hand up to his face and wiggled her fingers. Tom took a step back to focus on the glittering diamond.

"We're engaged, Tommy!" She squealed, grabbed his face between her hands and kissed him full on the mouth. "I'll run and get you a piece of cake," she said and hurried away.

"Con-congratulations," Tom stammered, offering his brother his hand.

Jason laughed and pulled him in for a hug. "Thanks, man. And don't read anything into that kiss. She is on a champagne high—says we all look alike after a couple of drinks."

"Wow, that's flattering," Tom said. "Does that mean all six of us could have been doin' her for the past year?"

"Real funny, dickhead," Jason said playfully. Tom didn't miss the way his brother followed Marissa's path through the other partiers. "Although, if the truth is told, I think Matt and Sam may have tried."

Tom laughed at the thought. "Like those two brats could ever breach your cake queen's defenses."

"Cake babe," Jason corrected. "And you're right. She's a force to be reckoned with." Jason lowered his voice, "I know you don't believe it but she's not a rare breed. There are others out there."

"Don't start. Not interested," he admitted as Marissa and her friend approached.

"Hey, Danny Zuko Junior," Jason said, lowering his voice. "You can't live that summer-lovin'-had-me-a-blast lifestyle forever, man."

"Watch me," Tom countered.

He was saved further interaction with his love-struck sibling when Marissa walked up.

"Tom. You remember Tessa," Marissa interrupted, handing him a piece of engagement cake.

"Sure do. How's it going?"

"Great," came the sardonic reply. "Business is dead, your brother's stealing my best friend away from me and I haven't been properly laid in over two months."

"That long?" he remarked dryly, forking a bite of cake into his mouth. He'd first seen her at Jason's Labor Day barbeque. He'd never been close enough before to see the smattering of freckles across her cheeks and nose. She was attractive, had a cute little nose and nice full lips but certainly was not the type of woman he generally made a play for. But she looked damn good in a silky blue blouse and a paisley skirt made out of some crinkly fabric. She put her hands on her hips and the fabric pulled taut against her curves and he was barely able to swallow. She looked him square in the eye and opened her mouth.

"Why, Miss Ward," Luke interjected with a mock southern drawl. "Allow me to perambulate you toward the corner booth and see if my presence might alleviate that latter problem."

Marissa laughed, Jason groaned and Tom shook his head in disgust. That was just the sort of corny-ass line Luke pulled that usually had women hopping into his lap fifteen minutes before they followed him straight to bed. It was totally ridiculous. And he doubted it was going to work on her.

"I've got a better idea," Tessa said, shocking them all by taking Luke's arm. "How about you buy me a drink, Rhett, and we'll see what the cards have to say about the future?"

Tessa stared at the man who had been sitting across from her for the past half hour trading sexually charged banter like cheap baseball cards. The Henderson clan were all smooth as silk and sexy as could be. Their parents could have made millions bottling that gorgeous guy gene. And women would have paid. Hell, she would have been first in line.

Luke's smile fell into a seductive grin that, on any other guy, would have had her grabbing his hand and running for the door. She glanced, for about the twentieth time, toward the other side of the room where his eldest brother was throwing darts. Now *there* was something to stare at. Tom Henderson was tall and broad and sculpted in all the right places. She couldn't tell that tonight by the loose country club polo shirt he wore but memories were a beautiful thing. She'd seen him in those skin-hugging T-shirts on more than one occasion and dutifully filed each image away for future reference.

"Are you ready to go, darlin'?"

"Oh for cripssake, stop it," she said, pulling the deck of cards from her purse. She found that simply shuffling the vividly colored deck over and over relaxed her nerves. And said nerves were stretched to the max. She wasn't sure why she had encouraged Luke. "We are not going to have sex."

"You say that now." He leaned back in the booth, stretching his arms along the back. She could relent and be home and wrapped in those strong arms in no time flat.

"And I say it with great conviction," she replied, shuffling the cards then spreading them facedown across the table in an arc.

"Why are you such a tease?" he asked softly, leaning his head back and closing his eyes.

"I am not a tease."

"Are too..." he whispered, his voice trailing away to nothing.

Perfect she thought, looking at his adorable features. *Just perfect.* Did they all look that hot, even when they passed out? She imagined that blond hair darkening a few shades, the smooth jaw taking on a stronger angle. And when those eyelids opened, eyes, not brown like Luke's, but a beautiful shade of deep green would stare back at her. Just as they had earlier when they had drifted over her chest. Thank god Luke had come to the rescue. She didn't need Tom Henderson knowing the effect one quick glance had on her nipples.

"Down for the count?"

She jumped and stared upward into the eyes she had just been daydreaming about. Her heart thumped in her chest and Tessa stopped herself before she splayed her palm over the rapid beating. *Aloof is your middle name, girl. Yeah. Right. Tell that to my libido, the one that's been waiting nearly a year for him to get close enough for a little one-on-one.*

"What's the future hold?" he asked, spinning a nearby chair around and straddling it, looking down at the cards. His muscular thighs drew her attention and she curled her fingers to keep from running a hand up his leg.

"For your brother?" she asked, finally finding her voice. "A raging hangover."

He laughed, his lips parting in a small grin. His smile was perfect except for a tiny chip off the bottom of his top left tooth. Tessa wondered what it would feel like to run her tongue over the tiny indentation if he leaned forward and gave her a hot, open-mouthed kiss.

"And what about you?" he asked, crossing his long fingers on the back of the chair. *Don't look, Tessa. Do not look at those hands.* She remembered all the delicious things those fingers had done in her dreams and she squeezed her legs together against a surge of warmth. She forced her gaze over his shoulder and saw Marissa grab Jason and pull him down the stairs without a backward glance.

"Since my ride just left, too preoccupied with your brother to leave her keys, I'm going out on a limb and predicting a cab ride home, a hot bath and hopefully a nice, long…" she paused and met his eyes. *Fuck,* she wanted to suggest. "Sleep," she finally said.

"You can tell all that without even looking?" he asked, placing his finger on the corner of one card. He slid it out of the deck to the edge of the table.

"What can I say? I'm good," she said, pushing the other cards together to re-shuffle.

"I'll bet you are," he said softly, his gaze stopping her breath before he looked down at the card.

Her stomach clenched and she gripped the cards tightly. She shot a glance at him. He was still staring at the card, his eyes moving as he studied it. He hadn't meant a damn thing by those words but when he looked up and met her eyes, she really, really wished he had.

"I'll give you a ride home. You live over your store, right?"

"Yes."

"You'll have to ride along to my parents so I can deposit him," he said, motioning to Luke, "then I'll take you home."

"He lives with your folks?" she asked in disbelief. *Ignore all thoughts of him taking you* at *home, Tessa.*

"No," he said, tossing the card on the table and rising. "But whenever one of us has to carry another one out of a bar, the first thing we get to deal with the next morning is my mom. It's a penance we've all experienced at one time or another. I'm going to close the tab. Be right back."

She watched him walk away, his khaki-covered ass putting the denim ones lined up at the bar to shame. She picked up the card, turned it over slowly. The Page of Cups. Uh-oh. She would generally read it as Cupid offering romance, not of the one-night stand variety but something formed from a deeper emotion. That thought was a little hard to believe since rumor had it Tom Henderson was the master of the twelve hour fling.

She looked up to find him staring at her intently. He turned and she hurriedly put the card on top of the deck and stuffed it in her purse and tried to ignore the way her heart picked up its already accelerated pace. A cab would be prudent if little images of his tight buns, dazzling smile and sexy eyes were going to continue their seductive slide show in the back of her mind. The whirring sound was clearly her common sense spinning out of control like a broken movie reel.

"Ready to go?" he asked, bending to pull Luke to his feet. He reached into his front pocket and handed her a set of keys. "My truck's out front. Go on, I'll be right behind you."

She rushed down the steps and held the door open as he effortlessly hauled his brother along. She double-clicked the remote and the lights on a large white pickup went on. She rushed forward and opened the door.

"Hop in."

"Will he be okay next to the door? He won't fall out?"

"He'll be fine. Get your butt up there, he's getting heavy."

Tessa grabbed a handle and pulled herself into the cab. *When did trucks get so plush? The leather upholstery was finer than the couch in her living room.* Tom folded Luke over his shoulder and placed him in the truck as carefully as if he were a baby. He pulled the seat belt out and handed it to her. "Can you strap him in?"

She clicked the buckle into place and sat back as Tom got behind the wheel and put the key in the ignition.

"Safety first," he said softly, reaching around her body to dig the belt out from the back of the seat. His face came within inches of hers and the distinct scent of sandalwood floated by. He fumbled for the strap, his warm hand brushing her hip, setting her nerve endings into a delightful tingle that worked its way directly to the valley between her thighs.

"There you go," he said, clearing his throat. He handed her the buckle then slowly moved aside.

His big body was too close for her to see him clearly through a sideways glance and she was not about to turn and stare at him like some cow-eyed teenager. *God, it's not like he grabbed your boob, Tess.* She could only imagine what would be happening right now at the party in her panties if he had. She clicked her buckle into place, somehow avoiding touching him in the process.

They drove in utter silence. She had no idea what he was thinking but whatever it was, every so often his strong fingers would flex around the steering wheel, which in turn had her nipples aching. She couldn't help but think how those hands had reputedly teased a large percentage of the female tourists out of their clam diggers and halter tops. *Out of sight, out of mind, Tess ol' girl.* She let her eyes drift shut. *Let him think I'm asleep.* They bumped along one of the old streets and the truck slowed.

Tessa had never been a squealer but she did just that when a big hand unexpectedly palmed her breast. The truck lurched to a stop and a huge weight pushed into her side. She opened her eyes to find Luke sound asleep, head against her shoulder, his fingers plumping her breast. His heaviness pressed her back between the steering wheel and rock-hard biceps of Tom's right arm. She looked up into his face, a contrast of shadows and light in the glow of the dashboard. Was that spark in his eyes real or just wishful thinking? His eyes were staring at her chest and Tessa's breasts swelled beneath Luke's slender fingers.

"Well…" she said on an intake of breath, waiting for someone to move. "When I dreamed of being in the middle of a Henderson hoagie, this wasn't quite what I had in mind."

Tom watched Luke's hand knead Tessa's breast, his thumb brush back and forth, before it fell limply to the seat. He couldn't drag his gaze from the tight little peak straining against the fabric of her top. He'd done pretty well ignoring those breasts before tonight. Oh, he'd noticed them at the Labor Day bash for sure. She'd had on a hot little baseball tee that advertised the fact tequila had been helping women lower their standards for years. It had hugged her ample bosom like a second skin. He'd tried not to stare like some of the other guys had but he'd thought about them later that evening when he'd hit the shower. And a few other nights to boot.

Tonight his peripheral vision caught all the little bounces and wiggles every time the truck hit a bump. When he had turned onto Market and its historic brick streets, he'd had to grip the wheel with both hands to keep from touching her as his brother, lucky bastard that he was, even in sleep, just had. He looked on as Luke's head nuzzled against her chest.

"You thinking about pushing him off you anytime soon?" he asked harshly, turning off the engine. "Or should I just leave you two alone?" He was suddenly having a hard time ignoring that threesome comment and he shifted uncomfortably.

"In case you haven't noticed…" *shithead*, her hesitation implied, "my arm's stuck underneath him."

There it was. That warning tone she was renowned for. He ought to throw it right back into her pretty little face. She seemed to be taking his brother's groping pretty well. "Lean up," he said instead.

He pulled his arm out from under her, grabbed Luke's shoulder and pushed him unceremoniously toward the door. Luke slid to one side, his head dropping backward. She hadn't moved, just stayed in that half-reclined position. If he were naked, all her springy little curls would be teasing his cock, which was pressing painfully against his zipper. *Where had that thought come from?*

Tom studied her. She didn't look angry now. She was staring at his mouth as if it held the secrets of the universe. When her full lips parted, he couldn't pass up the silent invitation. He reached down and unhooked her seat belt with one hand, tilted the wheel up with the other, then effortlessly pulled her up and onto his lap. Pure masculine pleasure shot through him at her shocked expression. He imagined few people were able to elicit that response from her.

They were on eye level but the darkness was obscuring. He couldn't see her eyes clearly but the sound of her rapid breathing was encouraging. She definitely wasn't as detached as she might like to pretend, which was good, because neither was he. He ought to take the time to work her up slowly. He was an infinitely patient man but he couldn't wait to touch her. He cupped her breast, the peak poking into his palm.

"Hard as a marble," he said, brushing his thumb lightly over the center and moving his head to her neck. "Remind me to thank Luke for his assistance."

He felt her stiffen and gently nipped her neck as he tweaked the hard bud. Whatever she was about to say died on a quiet moan.

Her fingers threaded through his hair and she tugged, the light pressure of her nails against his scalp sending a bolt of lust directly to his cock. He could feel her pulse against his lips and ran the tip of his tongue up and down.

"Come back up here. I want to kiss you," she demanded.

"Is that part of your fantasy?" he asked, ignoring her request. He dipped into the hollow of her throat and licked lazy circles on the sensitive skin. His teeth grazed her collarbone and he was rewarded with her shiver.

"I don't fantasize about you," she said, tipping her head back, turning, offering the other side to his trailing lips. He worked open-mouthed kisses up to her ear.

"Not me, huh? So which of my brothers get to be the lucky members of your little three-way, sweetheart?" He shifted his fingers to the buttons of her shirt. "Are you lusting after your best friend's man, Tessa?" He felt her bristle in his arms and wondered if he'd hit a nerve. This time, when she tightened her fingers, he let her pull his head away.

She narrowed her eyes and studied him for longer than he liked. He waited for her legendary tongue-lashing but instead she offered him a sexy smile.

"Maybe I'm just hot for my best friend. The fact she'd bring along your hunk of a brother would be the big fat maraschino cherry on the sundae of lust."

She wasn't serious. Was she? He could easily block out any images of his brother and Marissa together but throw the woman wiggling on his lap into the equation and a tableau of tangled limbs, full pink lips and sultry hazel eyes blurred his vision and had blood rushing to every pulse point in his body.

"I just felt your cock leap at the thought," she said, a controlling edge in her voice that he was quickly learning to discern. She was good at the art of deflection, he'd give her that.

"You're lying," he challenged, quickly working the buttons of her blouse free.

"About you getting hard?" she said, rotating her hips.

"About who you want buried in your pussy." He slid the shirt down to her elbows roughly. "And who you want pressing someplace a little...tighter." His heart kicked up when he saw her reach for the front closure of her bra but he covered her hands with his, running his fingertips across the lace trim that rested against the swell of her breasts. Both were smooth as silk.

"Which two of us do you dream about, Tessa?" She craftily pulled her hands away and he was left holding two handfuls of soft, warm flesh. She pressed herself against his palms and he lessened the pressure teasingly. He wrapped an arm around her back and cradled her neck, urging her backward.

"Who gets to do this," he asked, opening wide and taking one soft globe into his mouth. He swirled his tongue around the turgid peak and she dropped her head back farther and groaned. "Answer me," he ordered, moving to the other breast and repeating his actions.

"Yesss," she moaned but refused to answer. He had all the time in the world, despite the fact his brother was passed out beside them. At the moment, he couldn't have cared less if they were standing in the middle of Main Street during the Fourth of July parade. He switched back and forth between her hard nipples, ignoring her pleas, intent on nothing but driving her to the point where she would tell him the truth.

"Do you want Luke? Most women do," he reasoned, alternating between flat-tongue licks and grazing nips until he felt her legs quiver. He skimmed his hand up her leg, resisting the urge to burrow under her skirt.

"I know as well as you Marissa isn't sharing Jason. Andy's just as devoted to Vicky, so you're out of luck there," he said, pulling her foot up to rest flat on the seat, her knee falling open. He walked his fingers down her leg to the juncture of her thighs, pressed lightly and was rewarded with a whimper.

"The twins have that youthful endurance," he said, rotating the heel of his hand. Her hips started to move and he backed off. "Think we should give them a call?"

"You need to perfect your technique," she said breathily, pulling his hand back to her crotch. "You're walking that fine line between cockiness and being a total prick."

He laughed, fighting against the rapid movement she was trying to force his hand into. He rubbed slowly and smiled when she cursed loudly.

"Your choice of fantasy, Ms. Ward. I can make it happen. Very quickly, if I have to call for reinforcements. *Right now*, if you want me and Luke."

"Ha," she snorted and then caught her breath as he increased the tempo. "A third of our possible trio is dead to the world, so you really can't promise a damn thing."

"Oh, sweetheart, I can promise two things. Every man and his cock come to attention at the sound of a woman crying out in ecstasy, so don't discount Luke."

"And what's that second promise," she asked, her breathing labored.

"I can promise you're going to come," he said, staring deep into her glazed eyes. "So if you're not all talk, throw that beautiful head back and scream to the heavens."

Tessa stared him down, refusing to close her eyes as her desire coiled tighter. The man definitely spoke the truth. She *was* going to come. Her pussy was already convulsing. She had to assume his other offer was just as truthful. She had lied about dreaming of two of the handsome brothers taking her. That fantasy was strictly reserved for Olivier Martinez and her eleventh grade science teacher, Mr. Comby.

But she had dreamed of Tom. The reality of how he had sucked her breasts. The way he was teasing her now through the fabric of her skirt eclipsed anything she might have imagined. The sleep gnomes had sorely misrepresented his talents. He rotated his thumb against the corded area above her clit and she gave up thinking. He had made her so wet. A few practiced caresses and her pussy was clenching so hard she couldn't help rocking against him and closed her eyes against the incoming storm.

"Decision time, Tessa," he whispered huskily, moving his lips close to hers until his breath warmed her. He moved his hand, shifted the tempo again until his fingers were bringing her toward the peak.

"Oh, shit," she gasped, abandoning all traces of glibness. "What if," she forced her eyes open, "I only want…one of you," she panted. "Just you."

He brushed her lips and offered a groan of his own. "Then come and kiss me, sweetheart," he ordered.

And she almost obeyed. She kissed him, then she came.

# Chapter Two

**ഇ**

Tessa had curled up on his lap, her head against his shoulder, that wild hair tickling his nose. She hadn't made a sound since he'd swallowed the cry of her orgasm.

"You sleeping?" Tom asked, shifting against a hard-on that hadn't lessened one degree.

"No," she said softly. "Just thinking. I've never done anything like that in a vehicle before."

He found that hard to believe. "No teenage groping and grinding for the queen of the teases?"

"Why does everyone say that?" she asked in a petulant voice, then quickly changed the subject. "Did I scream when I came?"

"You did. Straight down my throat. Why?"

"Your brother has a pretty prominent boner."

Tom looked to his right and shook his head. The unmistakable bulge was clearly visible in the moonlight streaming through the passenger window.

"I thought for a second maybe you weren't exaggerating about guys hearing screams of delight in their sleep. And I was very delighted," she said, resting her hand on his chest.

He blamed the sudden jumping of his heart on her light caress, nothing more. Women had told him how good he was before. Tessa would too. Later. When they were somewhere a little more conducive to the mind-blowing sex his dick was impatiently waiting for.

"I refuse to talk about Captain Pervert's nocturnal erections when—"

"When we could be talking about yours," she said, tilting her head back and planting a hot kiss on his jaw, one that made his already aching balls tighten a notch.

"Jesus. You're something else." He laughed and reached down to quickly unbuckle Luke's seat belt with one hand and gently ease her away with the other.

"Do you need help?"

"No, I've got him." Tom threw his door open, hurried around the front of the truck and opened the passenger side. He eased Luke out of the vehicle. "Keys?"

She pulled them from the ignition and handed them over. His eyes snapped to hers when their fingers touched as a jolt of electricity coursed through their flesh. "Hurry back," she purred and his dick all but led him to the front door.

He fumbled for his parent's house key while holding Luke up with one arm then stopped dead when he heard the whispered voice next to his ear.

"With a little more finesse on your part she'd have gone for the a little three-way action, dickwad."

Tom stopped himself from flinging his brother away from his side and hurried to get the key in the door. He doubted Tessa, for all her worldly bravado, would appreciate knowing they'd had an audience. When the heavy wood shut behind them he pushed Luke through the living room archway. "You little fuck."

"Yeah. That's me," Luke said. "And not so little, as someone who secretly wants group sex noticed."

"You weren't passed out? At all?" Tom felt the shock wearing off. It was quickly being replaced by an alien form of anger.

"Hell, no, dude. It was pretty clear two minutes into my conversation with her that she was more interested in you. I couldn't even keep eye contact, for shit's sake. I thought you'd pass me off on Andy but my hopes were raised there for a while. Until you ruined everything."

"Andy was already gone, dickhead. I can't fuckin' believe you sat there and let us think you were asleep. You are a sick fuck," Tom said, getting into his brother's face.

"Hey! She's the one who mentioned the three-way," Luke defended, hands in the air.

"After you grabbed her tit!" Tom yelled and then quickly lowered his voice for fear of waking his parents. "What the hell was that all about?"

"I *had* fallen asleep by then, asshole. It was an automatic reaction when I slid against her."

"Bullshit," Tom said, moving his brother into the darkened room with a flat-handed push.

"What the fuck's your problem? Leave me alone and get out there and get a little somthin', bro. Has it been so long you can't recognize a golden opportunity when it's squirming in your lap asking 'did I scream when I came?'" he said in falsetto.

"Shut up," Tom warned.

"I'd take another run at her myself just to see those nipples again. Sorry, dude, I had to peek. You know I'm a tit man."

Tom clenched his fist and seriously considered driving it into his brother's solar plexus.

"What were you doing, reliving some teenage over-the-clothes memory?" Luke went on, as if steam weren't all but coming out of Tom's ears. "You couldn't have pulled that skirt up and fingered her, could you? God, I would have loved to have seen that. You think she dyes her bush the same color as that hair?"

Tom pushed him against the wall, a forearm across his throat. "Shut. Up," he growled.

"Or what," Luke taunted, "You're gonna choke me to death?"

138

Gazes locked, they studied each other. Tom couldn't begin to understand why he wanted to apply a little more pressure. The urge multiplied when the corners of his brother's mouth turned upward.

"Christ, Tommy. Not you too? You haven't even fucked her."

Tom didn't move, just narrowed his eyes in question.

"Let up, shit for brains," Luke whispered disgustedly.

Tom lessened the pressure but didn't back away.

"Tell me something. If she had wanted us both, would you have gone for it?" Luke asked.

Tom stared into his brother's eyes. "Not a chance," he said finally and the truth of the statement had him dropping his arm and turning away from Luke's disturbing stare. *It's going to be one night with her. That's it. End of story.* He suddenly felt the need to reassure himself of the fact.

"Is that because you wouldn't want our balls accidentally slapping into each other or the fact you want her all to yourself?"

Tom turned slowly, looked at Luke propped against the wall, arms and ankles crossed. *Fuck!* He could deny it. He might be able to pass it off as some contagious vibe from Jason and Marissa. Or Andy and Vicky. Either way, Luke wouldn't buy it.

"Shit," he said and turned toward the door, not wanting to give an iota of credence to what Luke insinuated.

"Yeah," Luke called from behind, as if he'd read his thoughts completely. "It's a fuckin' epidemic."

Tom rushed back to the truck and climbed inside. Tessa had scooted into the passenger seat and was holding one of the brightly colored tarot cards in her hand.

"Look, I know what you're thinking," she said matter-of-factly.

"No," Tom said, sliding a little closer to her. "You don't." Somewhere between the front door and the seventeen steps it had taken to reach his truck he had decided to ignore the voices in his head and press his luck.

"I want to explain why whatever you're about to do isn't a good idea."

He stared into her eyes. His brother was right—they did look like they belonged on an animal. Some sort of exotic cat. The trepidation he saw surprised him and he softened his tone. "I'm going to kiss you, Tessa."

"No! See, that's not a good idea. You don't understand how vulnerable you are right now," she cried, waving the card in front of his face.

"Vulnerable?" He looked down at the man in medieval garb holding a large goblet. A fish was poking his head over the rim. It might have been smiling but before he could look closer the dome light went out, carpeting the cab in darkness.

"Yes," she said. "Let me explain what this means and you'll understand."

"I don't care," Tom said, covering her hand with his, leaning close to her ear. She wore a scent that smelled like vanilla and fresh lemon. He breathed in deeply then exhaled slowly along her neck.

"This can't end well—oh, god." She shivered and then straightened her shoulders. "Look. I'll concede that you're great at manual stimulation and I have no doubt you totally rock in the sack but I can't justify allowing anything to happen with this," she jiggled her hand, flapping the card back and forth, "between us."

"That's your only objection?" he asked, pushing her heavy veil of curls aside to cup her neck. Her skin was warm and soft. He felt her nod and jerked the card out of her hand. "There," he said, tossing it onto the dash. "Now there's nothing between us, Tessa." She looked at the card then back into his eyes. It was too dark for him to see what she was thinking.

"Nothing between us?" He thought he heard relief in her tone.

Tessa had a few more comments she wanted to share but he slanted his mouth and kissed her silent. She'd expected hot, urgent kisses, not the gentle onslaught she received. She threaded her fingers through his hair and he deepened the kiss then backed off when she tried to be the aggressor. He took her face between his hands and ran his thumbs over her cheekbones. She knew he was tracing those dreaded freckles, though she doubted he could see them in the darkness.

She tried to bring their lips back together but he held firm.

"Why are you always in such a hurry, Tessa?" One hand slid downward, his thumb burning her lips as he traced their contours.

"Because I've been sitting in a puddle since we left the bar," she said, parting her mouth as he pulled her bottom lip down and ran the pad of his thumb back and forth lightly. It was rough, calloused. *His cock won't be rough, it will be smooth as satin when it's rubbing there.*

"Poor baby," he whispered, gripping her chin. He ran the tip of his tongue along the inside of her throbbing lip. "You taste like licorice."

"I'm addicted to those little gray after dinner mints," she admitted softly, wishing he'd never stop.

He kissed her again, slow and steady, before stroking her tongue with his own. She sucked him into her mouth and was rewarded with his small moan. Good. Now she had his attention.

"You're not planning on screwing me in your parents' driveway, are you?" she asked, hoping he just might.

"Screw you?" he asked after a moment's hesitation then turned sideways on the seat. "No, that's not what I have in mind."

She watched him press a button on the door and recline his seat back a little farther. He pulled one long leg onto the seat and extended it toward her, the scuffed toe of his boot tapping her hip to get her to move. His pants were tented, hiding what she knew could only be an impressive erection, and any remaining shred of resistance crumbled. *The card could actually mean nothing, Tess. It wasn't even in a spread. One card on its own meant jack shit.* Rationale. It was a wonderful thing.

"Come here, Tessa," he commanded, extending his hand. "Let me feel how wet you are."

"Oh, god," Her pussy was wringing desire from deep within. He might as well have hooked her in the jaw and reeled her in. She gave him her hand and let him urge her across the seat. When she moved to swing her leg over the one he rested on the floor and straddle him, he spun her around and, with one steely forearm against her lower belly, pulled her into the vee of his thighs.

His other hand moved around to grab her hair and pull it across and over her shoulder.

"It won't stay," she said, taking an ever-present hair tie off her wrist. She raised her arms and pulled the mass of curls onto the top of her head and secured them in a loose, floppy topknot.

"Keep your arms there." His voice was rough, urgent. "Don't lower them."

Tessa halted. His breath tickled the back of her neck and the hand on her abdomen squeezed, then disappeared. She waited, hands resting on top her head like a petty criminal. *You have the right to remain silent. You have the right to an attorney.* If he ordered her to "spread 'em" there was a high probability she might come right there on the spot. Strong hands gripped her ribcage and his thumbs brushed the outer curve of her breasts. She arched her back and a tiny moan escaped.

"So much for keeping quiet," she said under her breath.

"No need," he responded, rubbing his nose against her tender skin at the base of her neck. "The cab's all but soundproof. Nobody will hear you when you scream."

"Well that sounds pretty serial killer-esque," she said, tipping her head to the side.

"Hell. It does," he chuckled, placing featherlight kisses randomly about her neck. "No one's every pointed that out before."

His fingers hadn't moved, just those big thumbs making lazy patterns along her sensitive skin over the silky material of her shirt. What in the name of all that was holy had prompted her to put it back on when he went into the house? Call her horny or call her preemptive. At least she'd pulled the bra off while he was in there and stuffed it in her purse.

"How often do you do this?" she asked, trying to gain a little control. Her heart was beating double time to the movement of his fingers.

"This? You mean wanting to play with someone so badly I couldn't wait to do it somewhere a little roomier than my ride?"

She'd had enough. She lowered her arms and covered his hands, forcing them to her breasts. "Yessss."

"Not often. Twice in fact. In this exact spot," he admitted, opening his hands flat to brush her nipples lightly. If they became any harder she thought they might just snap off.

"You're joking," she said, arching into his hands, only to have him pull away.

"I'm not. And the other girl wasn't anywhere near as anxious as you are."

Clearly his nether regions weren't pounding to beat the band or he would be moving quicker than a snail's pace.

"Maybe she just got tired of all your talk and lack of action," she goaded.

"You could always ask her. She lives next door."

"Still?"

"Still," he rested his chin on her shoulder. "Unbutton your blouse for me, Tessa. Thanks for ditching the bra."

"My pleasure," she said, glancing at the cute cookie-cutter house. At least she hoped it was going to be her pleasure, and soon. If he'd just move it along.

"Do you know her husband? Does he talk her to death during foreplay?" Tessa asked, popping the buttons free as quickly as possible.

"She never married."

"A testament to your mad lovemaking skills?" She pulled the fabric aside but it caught on her distended nipples and she squirmed against his lap.

"It was over twenty years ago. Long before the days of insertion," he said, taking her earlobe between his teeth and tugging gently. His breath against her ear caused goose bumps to rise. "Nothing more than some shared rubbing between friends. Let me see you."

"Is that what you have in mind for us?" she asked, slowly pulling the fabric out and away from her breasts. "A little mutual masturbation?"

"Is that all you want, Tessa?" He voice took on a deep timbre, reverberated against her shoulder, and she felt him swallow.

"At this point," she snaked a hand around his neck and pulled his lips closer, "I'd take anything. In fact, if you don't touch me soon, I'm going over there, ring her doorbell and ask to borrow a vibrator."

"How do you know she has one?" He laughed, nipping at her upper lip.

"It's a must have, trust me. Every girl needs one."

He leaned back far enough to look into her eyes. "Not tonight," his husky voice promised.

He kissed her long and hard, his tongue stroking and thrusting in a precursor to the main event. He threaded his hand into the hair at the back of her head and tugged their lips apart.

"How do you want to play this, Tessa?" he asked, applying a little more pressure with a twist of his wrist. "You talk a good game, sweetheart, enough of one that I know you like the power. We can do this fast and hot..." He lowered his head to the hollow of her throat and licked a smooth path back to the soft skin under her chin and bit playfully, a direct contrast to his words. "Or, we can stretch this out 'til you're ready to burst."

Her juices dribbled at the thought and she studied him through lowered eyelids. He was right, she preferred taking control. She hadn't flopped back and let someone have their way with her in a very long time. Maybe, just this once, it wouldn't be so bad.

A cloud shifted and the interior of the cab was washed in moonlight. He was staring intently at her, waiting. That really told her all she needed to know but she couldn't give in without a parting shot. She closed her eyes and smiled seductively. "Show me what ya' got, slow hand."

Tom liked a little sexual repartee as much as the next guy but, oh baby. The woman had a mouth on her like no other and he wasn't just talking about the stuff that came out of it. No, her lips were soft and sweet and he could have been content just sitting in his parent's driveway kissing her over and over and over again until she begged him to take her to bed.

She was so hot and ready. When she'd off-handedly asked if he was going to fuck her, his cock had grabbed that thought like a last minute shovel pass and concentrated on running toward the goal line. There wouldn't be any penetration. Not here. Not now. But later? He hoped to be mentally dancing in the end zone.

He wisely hid a smug smile and slid his hand out of her hair to lightly caress her back. His dipped his thumb into the curve of her spine and felt her tremble. He worked his hand between his thigh and her hip and reached down to squeeze her ass.

"Where should I start, Tessa?"

"Wherever you want," she said, wiggling against his palm. "You're in charge."

"We both know that's not true," he said, sliding his hand free. He caught her wrists and moved her hands to his knees. "Your arousal's driving us both. I can feel it, smell it. And you know, eventually, I'm going to taste it. Keep your hands there and don't move."

He trailed a single finger up each silk-encased arm before skimming over her chest. He bunched the edges of her shirt together and pulled them away, down to her elbows, until her torso was bare. He switched his head to her other shoulder and hummed appreciatively.

"You have freckles on your breasts. I can't wait to kiss each cute little spot."

"Elaborate, please." Her voice hitched. "Are you talking about the freckles or my breasts?"

"Your breasts are perfect," he said, honestly. He'd seen enough giant tits to last a lifetime. Touched them, tasted them, fucked them. He gently cupped her, his long fingers spread over the firm globes. "In ten years they'll still be high, just begging for someone to tease them." He brought his fingers together and pinched the extended tips until she arched against him. "Did you feel that all the way to your pussy, sweetheart?"

"Oh, god yes!" Her hands tightened above his knees.

He rolled the darkened peaks between thumb and forefinger and her raspy reply turned into a long moan. "More."

"Oh, yeah," he said, kissing his way down the side of her neck. "There'll be more. Lots more," he placed an open-mouthed kiss at the base and bit down gently. Her ass ground into his crotch and he broke contact.

"If you're doing that to tease me into hurrying, it's not going to work," he whispered against her ear, stroking the lobe with the tip of his tongue when she cursed. "All it does is make me back off and count to ten slowly so I don't spurt in my pants before I have you screaming in my arms. Did I tell you how convenient it is you're wearing a skirt?"

"No," she said, starting to rock backward when his hands touched the top of her thighs and then, remembering his warning, stopping. "But you could shut up and show me."

He couldn't help but laugh as he inched the material up her smooth legs.

"Oooh, more freckles," he teased, working the fabric over her knees.

"Yes, yes, yes," she hissed. "I'm flecked from head to toe. They're everywhere."

"Everywhere?" he questioned, moving the skirt all the way up until the tiny scrap of fabric covering her pussy was fully exposed.

"Just about," she said and he felt her heartbeat vibrating against his chest.

"I can't wait to get you in the light, see if you're telling the truth," he rested his palms on her inner thighs and stroked his thumbs up and down.

"If I'm lying, will you punish me?" she purred and a wave of heat shot through him.

"Definitely." *Crack the window before you combust, idiot.* "What would be appropriate, do you think?"

"A sound spanking?"

His fingers stopped teasing and he actually had to count to ten. Twice. *Could she be any hotter, really?* She had teased his cock to a point of physical discomfort he'd never experienced before with nothing more than some sexy words, breasts custom fit for his hands and a flash of pale thigh. He hadn't even breached the sanctity of the silky black fabric he was dying to touch. *Shit, man, take control.*

"Spread your thighs." The command was stern. Tessa felt the muscles of his chest jump against her back and the fingers at her thighs increased their pressure. She'd used that tone herself. Many times. Now, as unusual as it was, she had no trouble obeying.

"Like this," she asked innocently, opening a fraction.

"Wider," he said, straightening his left leg to pull her thigh over his so she was stretched wide, the cheek of her ass off the seat until she was half on his lap. He put her other leg on top of the one he rested along the back of the seat and raised both their knees as one. Tessa gasped.

The motion forced the material of her thong tight against her swollen pussy. His voice stopped her before she had a chance to move the bothersome scrap of silk to a more comfortable position.

"Don't move. I want you aching as badly as I am," his breathing was short and shallow.

Tessa held still. "I am." Her heart, temples and pussy were beating in tandem.

"I don't think you are," he finally replied, his voice a little more even.

She was about to contradict when his hand covered her mound, his middle finger so long it pressed far beyond her slit and she sucked in a breath. She clutched his thighs, unable to concentrate on anything but the exquisite sensation of him finally touching her. The heat from his hand all but sizzling her wetness.

"So hot, sweetheart," he said, dragging his finger slowly upward, rubbing a slow, winding path over her swollen labia. "Guess you should have worn your waterproof panties. Exhale, Tessa."

She did, not realizing she'd been holding her breath and then gasped again when he touched the uppermost part of her clit, barely brushing against the damp fabric that covered the throbbing ache.

"Hope these aren't your favorite pair," he said, ripping one side of the thong off her hip. His fingers moved to trace a path through her curls. His surprise was evident when he suddenly stopped. He spread his fingers wide, moved his hand first one way and then the other.

She turned her head and whispered against his mouth, enjoying his shock. "Smooth as a baby's bottom, huh?"

Their groans mingled as he plunged a finger deep inside her.

"Oh, baby," he cradled her jaw and ran his tongue over her bottom lip.

"Please don't tell me you're going to keep talking." He pulled his finger out, then slid it and another slowly back in. It felt so good, having something alive and warm buried inside her. "We can talk later."

"Right. Later," he said, rubbing his thumb across her smooth pubis. "What will we talk about?"

"I don't knoooow," she moaned as he gave her nub a quick flick.

"Can we talk about how freakin' tight you are?" He pulled his finger free and she grabbed his wrist.

"I'm just small, it's not that tight. Put those back. Right now."

He ignored her.

"How about the fact you're completely shaved?"

"Actually, it's waxed. Aaaaaah."

He stuck just the tips of two fingers in and rotated slowly. She wanted to push against him but knew better than to try. He'd just pull away, tormentor that he was. She hoped he was enjoying the way her juices were drenching his fingers. Hoped it was driving him at least a little wild. She reached behind and rubbed his rigid length through the fabric of his pants.

His fingers began twisting harder, driving her skyward in tiny increments until she was panting, barely able to get the button of his pants undone before giving up and falling back against him. He thrust his fingers upward once, stopped long enough for her to catch her breath and then began rotating again. With pinpoint accuracy, each little bump to her hidden spot stoked the building fire within her.

She moaned, afraid to move, not wanting to throw off the pace. His hand slid from her jaw, down between her breasts. He circled her navel and her thighs began to tremble. The pressure had built to the point of no return. With two spread fingers he teased along each side her clit — once, twice — never actually touching it until the moment the hand between her legs plunged deep and in a rush of hot, throbbing wetness she exploded.

It was a long time before the tremors eased slowly to a halt. He waited, dick ready to burst, then lazily pulled his fingers from her and rested them against her thigh. She sighed contentedly and turned in his embrace.

"That was worth the wait," she said, tugging his shirt free so her hands could roam over his hard abs before creeping teasingly upward to his pecs. He rubbed her wetness across the curve of her ass and she crawled up his chest and kissed his jaw. She pushed herself up to her knees and smiled.

"What?" he asked. "You look like the cat that ate the canary."

"Oh, I'm thinking it might be bigger than a songbird," Tessa said, smiling at his crotch. "Can you spring the little guy free for me?"

She watched his brow furrow and rolled her eyes. "You can't honestly believe I think you're anything less than hung like a god? After all the stories I've heard from Marissa about your brother's miracle dong?"

"You two talk about Jason's *cock*?" He sounded truly shocked.

"Well, we did. At first. Then she clammed up." She saw his hand poised over his zipper but he wasn't moving. "Women are no different then men. Guys talk about great boobs and hot asses all the time. Don't pretend you don't."

He lowered the zipper carefully. "Jay's never said anything about Marissa. You don't share details about someone who's special."

"Forget I said anything. Please." She waggled her fingers in a "gimme, gimme" manner.

"All right," he said, reaching inside his pants. "But no comparing apples to oranges." He pulled his cock free and leaned back, one hand cradling his head, the other stretched over the steering wheel.

Tessa stared at his hard length and dropped her hands to her lap. She let her gaze drift over him, sprawled against the soft leather before her like an X-rated poster boy for heavy duty pickup trucks. She had a good idea where that *Like A Rock* marketing campaign came from.

"What if I compare big cocks with bigger cocks?" She watched the tip twitch and wet her lips.

"That would probably be okay, depending on which category I fall into."

"Fishing for compliments?" She laughed, reaching out to run the pad of her thumb up the underside of his erection. It gave a little come-and-get-it leap and she smiled. "I wouldn't have thought you that vain."

151

She lay down on her stomach and stretched out along the bench seat, bending her legs at the knees and resting her feet against the cool window.

"Do you know any guy who doesn't like to hear how well endowed he is?"

"Even if it's not true?" she asked, rubbing the tip of her nose across his burgeoning cock head.

"That's just cruel," he said on an exhalation of breath.

She wasn't sure if he was talking about her comment or her action but the musky smell of him turned her on more than she could remember. She couldn't wait to taste him.

"Upon closer review, I don't think I've had anyone fall into your specific category." She stuck her tongue out and touched him lightly. His cock head was sticky, salty. Apparently she hadn't been the only one leaking.

"Are we through talking?" he asked in a tight voice.

"You feel free to carry on," Tessa said, looking up his body to meet his hooded eyes. "But I know my manners." She wrapped her hand around his iron heat and smiled. "I never, ever, talk with my mouth full."

# Chapter Three

## ✖

Tom knew her mouth was going to be hot, he just wasn't prepared for the force with which she drew him in. There was no insertion by degrees, just one long, tortuous decent of her lips teasing him on the outside while she sucked him deep and then released him just as slowly. His balls contracted and he wished he were naked, not sticking through a pair of snug underwear. It could only be better if she were naked too.

Again the tight suction drew him deep and he fought the urge to move. She'd done so well when he'd taken the lead, it was only fair to let her set the speed. Her orgasm had been strong but he doubted the pressure that had built in her tight little cunt could compare to the maelstrom brewing in his balls.

He watched her head move up and down, her eyes closed. God, she looked like an angel. *Angels don't suck dick. Well this one does.*

"Jesus, Tess. That's unbelievable." She picked up the pace and he pushed his pants as low as they would go. His eyes started to drift shut but he forced them open. He needed to see her, wanted to watch until she pulled those hot lips away and pumped the final strokes. She wrapped her fingers tightly around his base and he gripped the steering wheel.

"So good, sweetheart." He moved his other hand to her head, delving into the curls until he felt her scalp, not needing to guide her but wanting to touch her.

The hand on his shaft began to move, coming up to meet her lips in an age-old rhythm that had his mind starting to spin. She consumed him, hand and mouth working together until he gripped her head and begged her to stop.

"Tessa, I can't hold back," he warned, tried to pull away and felt her grip his hip firmly. She opened her eyes, looked at him and told him without a single word she knew exactly what she was doing. He closed his eyes, desire roaring through his loins as his semen shot deep into her throat.

Tessa rose to her knees and watched him catch his breath, head tilted back against the window, eyes shut. God, she so wanted to get him in bed, fuck him into a dreamy sleep and sit quietly and stare at him. It really should be a sin to be that gorgeous.

"Was that as good for you as it was for me?" she teased, leaning forward and kissing his jaw. His mouth was slightly parted and she wanted to plant a big wet one on him but wasn't sure if he would enjoy tasting himself on her lips.

"Better," he said, cracking his eyelids open, giving her a lopsided grin.

"So I surmised from the decibel level of that scream," she joked.

"Don't worry, you'll give me a run for my money soon enough," he cradled her face with both hands and kissed each eyelid.

Tessa smiled at the gesture. "Tonight?"

"Hell yes, tonight," he said in a surprised tone. "You didn't really think it was going to be the ole' magic fingers, an equally impressive blowjob and then I drop you at the curb?"

She stared into his eyes and didn't speak. What had she thought? Her body was still humming from the orgasm and she couldn't recall anything but her long-hidden desire to simply touch him. Taste him. He had let her do both.

He moved his hands to her shoulders and said, "Unless you want me to take you home and drop you off."

"No," she answered quickly. To hell with remaining impersonal. She had perfected that sort of relationship. Even if this was only one night, she didn't want impersonal. Not with him. She hadn't been lying earlier when she'd told him she didn't think it was going to end well but right now she truly didn't care. "Take me home."

She saw his triumphant male smile and couldn't let it slide.

"If you think you're up to it." She grinned, looking down at his crotch. His cock lay soft against his clad thigh. She reached for it but he beat her there and tucked it away.

"I'm up to it, sweetheart."

He started the truck and repositioned the wheel and seat while Tessa quickly slid out of her ruined thong. As it joined her discarded bra she glanced at the dash. That damn Page of Cups was lying there, face up in the moonlight, taunting her.

"It's been a long time since I've had a beautiful woman riding next to me. Scoot back over here and buckle up."

Tessa slid next to him, clicked her seat belt and snuggled against his warmth. He dropped the truck into drive and draped his arm across her shoulder. He rubbed slow, lazy figure eights against her upper arm and she sighed heavily. Did he really think she was beautiful, even with the plague of freckles and unruly hair? With a mouth that tended to say exactly what was on her mind before all the internal filters did their jobs? *Here's where your bullshit meter should be ding, ding, dinging, Tess.* But it wasn't. And that scared her to death.

\* \* \* \* \*

Tessa unlocked the side door to the bookstore and turned on the light. Her heartbeat had increased with every mile they drove closer to her home. Now, as she weaved her way through boxes of unpacked books with Tom right behind her, her mind raced. She couldn't remember if the apartment was even remotely tidy. She knew for a fact there weren't any banks of candles to set the mood, maybe one beer in the fridge and a half bottle of red wine if she was lucky. At least the bed was made.

"Don't hold the state of the place against me," she said over her shoulder when they reached the small landing. His arms circled her waist before she could open the door.

"All I'm planning on holding against you is me, sweetheart," he said huskily and dipped his head to nuzzle her. The pressure of his lips and the swiftness in which he pulled her into his embrace robbed her of breath. He was harder than stone and pressed against her ass in one sexy little rotation.

Worrying about refreshments, ambiance and whether her domestic skills would be considered "a good thing" proved to be moot the second she opened the door and turned on the kitchen light.

He spun her around, kicked the door closed and pushed her back against it with a force that might have been scary if his emerald eyes weren't sparkling. She would have preferred that raw look that usually promised hot sex and a swift departure sometime before dawn. That pattern was the norm. But if she were honest with herself, she'd known the minute he smiled at her in the bar that nothing was truly going to be ordinary again.

He nudged himself between her thighs, dipped his knees and pressed his length against her pussy, bare and throbbing beneath her skirt. The contact sent a gush of desire onto the silky fabric.

"You know I'd love to bury myself in you right here but I'd like to prove I'm a little more skilled than the sophomoric behavior displayed thus far."

He brushed his lips against hers, took her face in his hands and slanted his mouth over hers, alternating between bruising pressure and soft force until her head was spinning.

"But sophomore year was my favorite," she gasped when he finally let her up for air. He laughed against her mouth and she tightened her arms around his neck.

"Is that when you learned to suck the chrome off a trailer hitch?"

It was her turn to laugh as she raised her leg high around his waist and leaned back to meet his eyes. "What a compliment. I didn't learn that 'til college, thank you very much." No one had ever parried with her like that and certainly not in the midst of foreplay. She loved it and grinned wickedly.

"Point me toward the bedroom and let me show you what higher education taught me." He reached under the back of her skirt, his hand hot as fire against her skin. He caressed her ass in firm circles that brought his fingers closer to her wetness with each stroke.

She leaned into his chest and arched her hips to allow him better access. Her clit instantly swelled in anticipation. He ran the tips of each index finger up and down her outer folds and she moaned, thinking how hot his tongue would be there.

"I hope..." She gasped when one finger circled her. "I hope you learned something Italian."

"Oh yeah," he chuckled. "But what you're thinking is actually Latin, sweetheart. I learned a little French too."

"French," she repeated a second before his lips descended and his tongue slid across her teeth and demanded she open for him. As if her mouth were some delicious confection, he licked and stroked and sucked, all the while his fingers mimicked the process against her dripping pussy. She would not let herself come again without him, though he was more than willing to accommodate her, she was sure.

She gripped his shoulders and gave a little push. He loosened his grip and let her slide down his body. His fingers caught the material of her skirt on the way down, the cool air on her exposed ass making her shudder as his hands rested on her hips.

"Did you study any of the fine arts?" she asked, pulling his belt free and tossing it aside before running a hand up and down the bulge at his crotch.

"Such as?" She saw him swallow when she eased the zipper down.

"Oh, I don't know," she said in a voice that was certainly very knowing. She squatted down, her knees between his legs and undid the laces of first one boot then the other before moving seductively up his body. She gave herself credit for not staring greedily at what was peeking out of his loosened pants.

"Drawing," she suggested, pushing his shirt slowly up his body until he pulled the fabric out of her hands and over his head in one motion. Lord, he was chiseled. Abs tight and pronounced. He could have been carved in marble.

"Sculpture," she added, running her fingers lightly over his chest, brushing his tiny nipples, before laying her palms flat against them. She could feel his strong heartbeat against the fingers of her right hand.

He covered her hands with his long fingers, his thumbs brushing back and forth across her knuckles as he toed his boots off. They fell with soft thuds, echoing the sound of her heart beating in her ears. She wanted him. Fiercely. More than she could remember wanting anyone in a long, long time. *Or maybe ever.*

"No drawing. No sculpture." He shrugged then smirked.

"How about painting?" she asked, walking backward. He followed her step for step, never allowing the distance to separate their bodies. His eyes darkened and he tilted his head to one side but his sexy smile never wavered.

"What kind?"

"The face kind," she said with a grin of her own.

She was either trying to shock him or kill him. He didn't know which. And he truly didn't care as long as she ended up screaming his name sometime in the not-too-distant future. He'd been teased before. A little innuendo here and there. A wink. Maybe a little pantiless flash. Not the full frontal assault that had every nerve ending in his body humming.

"I'll get the light," she said, then hesitated. "You don't mind the light, do you?"

"Hell no. Is there anyone who doesn't want the light on?"

"You'd be surprised," she said.

He heard the tiny *click* and the bedroom was suddenly filled with a soft, golden glow.

"Who wouldn't want to be able to see every fuckin' inch of what you have to offer?" he asked, backing her toward the low platform bed covered with fuzzy purple fur. He pulled his wallet from his back pocket and tossed it on the night stand.

"Someone who doesn't want me to see every fuckin' inch of what they *don't* have to offer," she laughed, looking into his eyes. "But we're not going to have that problem tonight, are we?"

Tom stood stock still as she hooked her thumbs in each side of his khakis and pushed them down his legs. Her gaze never left his until his pants were on the floor.

She cast her eyes downward to where he strained against the material of his boxer briefs. "I don't even need a tape measure."

She looked back up and he nearly lost his breath. Her eyes gleamed with a mix of desire and mischief. She rose onto her toes and whispered against his lips.

"That's a legal muskie."

Standing there with a raging hard-on, he threw his head back and howled. She was unbelievable. "Your opinion as a professional angler?"

"Absolutely. I'm a catch and release kind of girl," she said, snaking a hand under his waistband. His balls rose to meet her single, downward stroke and he pushed his fingers into her curls.

"Well you caught him, Tessa. Let's see about that release part," he whispered sexily and covered her mouth with his own.

Good *god* the man could kiss. His lips were firm and hot and they teased her in minuscule increments until her thoughts swirled and she forgot where she was. But not whom she was with. His mouth, the one she had watched time and time again from afar as he conversed with his brothers, was crushing her lips with kisses that had her breasts swelling.

His tongue, the same one that nearly had her creaming her cut offs last September when he'd methodically and thoroughly licked his lips clean after the wing eating contest, was teasing its way along the crease of her lips. This time, the tell-tale wetness slid unrestrained down her thighs.

When he broke the kiss, Tessa noticed he was breathing just as heavily as she was. She also realized she was still holding his cock in her hand. She made a move to pump him and he shook his head.

"Not right now. I want to see you." He stepped back and she was forced to let go. He shucked out of his underwear, his erection tall and pale against his tanned skin. "Take off your clothes," he ordered in a deep voice as he moved to the bed, sat on the edge and took his cock in hand.

"You know I don't do well with orders," she said, pushing the buttons of her blouse free. To hell with the tantalizing striptease. She wanted to be naked. Now.

"Humor me."

"Why should I?" she asked, tossing the blouse aside and undoing the side zipper of her skirt.

"Slower," he barked and then softened his tone. "This first time, please, just shimmy out of that nice and slow." He let go of his cock and placed his hands on the bed.

She tried not to think about that "first time" comment. It inferred she'd be taking her clothes off for him again and that was too much to absorb at the moment.

"Again—why should I?" she challenged but inched the skirt down to just above where her pubic hair should be.

"Because I asked nicely," he said, voice strained.

"Damn," she said, lowering it a bit more. "I'm a sucker for niceties."

He swore and she pressed her legs together tightly and let the material pool at her feet.

She watched him stare at her smooth mound, shocked when she saw his cock swell farther. He raised his eyes and she gasped at the raw desire.

"You are beautiful," he said reverently, then looked her over, head to toe. "All of you. Come here, Tessa."

Her mind raced for some retort as she slowly padded toward him over her forgotten clothing. She'd never had anyone look at her that way. Never had anyone who rendered her speechless. His dark eyes captured hers as she made her way toward him and halted an arm's length away.

He grabbed her hips in his huge hands and pulled her closer. His fingers moved to the fullness of her bottom, taking her firmly in each hand. He squeezed and kneaded, slowly working his fingers toward each other until they were pressed teasingly against the small area of skin between her pussy and her asshole. He stopped, alternately applying little compressions until she was forced to grab his shoulders for balance.

It felt so good she couldn't make up her mind what she wanted to do. If she rocked her hips backward he'd be poised at her dripping slit. She knew exactly what those fingers could do when deftly employed to that area. But if she shifted her hips...

Just as she thought she couldn't get any wetter, he tightened his legs, his thighs forcing her knees together. The motion made his hands seem bigger, the pressure more pronounced and she closed her eyes as the throbbing in her pussy seemed to radiate throughout her lower body. And then his tongue touched her.

The single action seemed to last for minutes as he ran one hot, wet caress from the base of her exposed pussy lips upward, over her clit and pubic area, ending with a tiny swirl around her navel. And then he did it again. Then once more, varying the degree of pressure each time. Tessa thought she had the pattern figured out, waiting for the firmness of his tongue, only to be strung tighter when he barely touched her.

She tried to open her legs but he would have none of it, just continued the unrelenting torture with his tongue and fingers as she bit her lip and whimpered.

"Mmmm…" He hummed against her clit and she dug her fingers into his shoulders. "Still in a hurry."

Her breathing became erratic as he showered attention on the tiny nub until her legs were shaking. When he sucked her button between his lips she sobbed. When he clamped down, she screamed his name and burst against his mouth.


Tessa had slumped forward, her chest resting against his forehead. Her breasts were at eye level, her hard, rosy nipples begging for his taste. He slid his hands to the back of her thighs, amazed at the amount of moisture coving his fingers as he supported her wobbly legs. When the woman came, she *came*!

"I'm sorry I neglected these," he said, nuzzling into her cleavage. "But your pussy's an attraction all its own." He moved a hand to her back and toppled her onto the bed. She had a lazy grin on her face but still remained silent. He wasn't sure he liked that. He much preferred to hear her telling him exactly what she thought. Because, unlike the women he usually took to bed, he'd be surprised if there was an ounce of sexual subterfuge in her entire body.

He rolled onto his side and stared down at her. She was flushed, her freckles not as pronounced with the heightened color beneath her skin. Strands of her curly hair scattered around her head and stuck to the side of her face. He brushed them back and then carefully pulled the hair tie from the bright red mass and she opened her eyes a crack. Gently, trying to hide his smile, he spread her curls over the comforter until they surrounded her head.

"What's so funny?" she asked.

"It's like a devil's halo," he said, rubbing a few strands between his fingers.

"Clearly you would know. You take temptation to a new high." She reached down and cupped her hand around his balls.

"And you don't?" he asked, shifting until his cock nudged her outer thigh.

"It's apparent I'm slipping. Either that or you have more control than twenty men."

"Mind over matter, sweetheart," he stated, moving her hand to his shaft, inhaling sharply when she stroked him.

"Well, would you mind moving your matter out of my hand and into my pussy?"

Tom growled as he pulled her hand free and covered her body with his. If truth be told, his control was quickly reaching the end of its tether. She was a tease, whether she believed it or not. He pulled her hands above her head, anchoring both wrists with one of his hands. All that talk about spankings and face painting had his cock harder than he could remember. The taste of her cum against his tongue had almost made him go off like a rocket right there on the edge of her bed.

He pushed a leg between her thighs and raised his knee to open her. Her musky essence wafted upward. He wanted nothing more than to bury himself in her slickness. He let his gaze roam over her. Tiny freckles covered her chest but the tight peaks of her breasts diverted his attention. He nipped one and then laved it soothingly. He moved his free hand to the other one and rolled it firmly. She bucked beneath him and he moved his other leg between her thighs, felt her open for him.

"This is gonna be good, Tessa," he promised, reaching toward the nightstand. He had a condom out of his wallet and covering his dick in record time. "Better than good, sweetheart."

She was drenched and he rubbed his cock up and down her slit and then eased in slowly. *Fuck.* He should have loosened her up with a finger or two. *Lord, almighty!* She was way too snug. He felt her wince and started to pull back.

"Don't you dare," she warned, hooking her ankles around his thighs, pressing upward.

She opened her eyes and he read her desire, as raw and wild as his own.

"If you don't make love to me this instant, Tom, I'll never forgive you."

He felt the corners of his mouth rise. *Make love. Now doesn't that sound interesting for a change?*

"I wouldn't want to disappoint," he said, pushing steadily into her until he was sheathed deep within her warmth.

"You haven't yet," she said, tugging against his hands. "Let me touch you."

"I don't think so, sweetheart," he said, slowly pulling halfway out before thrusting in with a little roll of his hips. "I'm hanging on by a fuckin' thread and you're still talking."

"Aaaaah," she moaned, struggling harder against his hands, as he picked up the pace. "I've come more in the past hour than I have —"

"I know," he said, jaw clenching. "Two months of going without." It hadn't been that long for him but it suddenly felt like he'd never fucked a single soul. Her cunt had stretched to accommodate him but gripped him tighter than his own fist.

He bent his head, took her nipple into his mouth, and sucked. Hard.

She moaned again and he knew he had to be deeper, so deep he'd touch a part of her no one else had. He let go of her wrists and she immediately grabbed his face and urged him toward her mouth. He slanted his lips over hers, opened them and ran his tongue around her sweetness. Her tongue touched his for a brief second then roamed back and forth across his upper teeth and it was his turn to groan.

"Don't wait for me," she whispered against his mouth. "I'm not going to come again."

"Like hell," he swore. He grabbed her waist and rolled onto his back. He held her suspended and then let her sink slowly down onto his shaft. *Don't think about her cunt closing in on you, pal.* Distraction. Something. Anything.

"Oh, god. I don't know," she sounded concerned. "You're so big and it's so deep."

"Set your speed, sweetheart," he said, cradling the globes of her ass in his hands, resisting the urge to grab tightly and work her up and down his throbbing length.

She started to rock, a gentle little rhythm that had her breasts swaying just out of reach. He closed his eyes against the tempting sight and listened to the soft noises she made every so often. She placed her palms on his chest, resting her weight as she leaned forward. Little grunts turned into quiet groans and she moved quicker. He pulled her cheeks apart and flexed his hips as she pounded down until he heard her sob.

He opened his eyes and met her gaze. Her lids were hooded, her lips parted, hair flying about her shoulders. He felt the contractions begin. "Sit up," he ordered.

"I can't," she said, riding him harder.

"Up," he punctuated his demand with an opened-hand slap to her ass. Her cunt clenched around him and she jolted upright. He looked down to where their bodies were joined, watched her swollen folds move up and down, her little nub gleaming, begging for attention. He moved his thumb until it was less than a centimeter away. He could feel the heat rolling off her. Feel the quickening around his cock.

"Please," she begged and their eyes met. "Please. Touch me."

Five little strokes and she went over the edge.

He followed in her wake, yelling her name.

# Chapter Four

෨

Tessa only half listened as one of the members of the Saturday morning book club explained her take on Lord Byron's *Don Juan*. Her thoughts were on a different legendary lover. The one she had left sleeping upstairs in her bed. The one who had kept her up most of the night, who had said he'd have fucked her again if he had more protection and then had laughed when she'd opened the drawer and pulled out a box of multi-colored condoms that had barely fit. God, he was huge. She shifted against the slight soreness and tried to focus, to no avail, on what the octogenarian was saying.

Flashbacks of entwined limbs and cries to the deity drifted into her thoughts. They were the same images that woke her at five that morning and found her wrapped in his arms. She had been hesitant to move but eventually had disengaged without waking him and gone to the bathroom. She'd taken a quick shower and still he'd slept. She'd stood by the side of the bed and watched him sleep. As she'd thought, he was just as gorgeous in repose. She had made herself a cup of tea and dug through a stack of books on the coffee table until she'd found the one she needed.

She had curled up in her chair and read the section on the Page of Cups, focusing on the section of the combination of elements. Water and Earth in complete harmony. *Right.* The Page demanded honesty and sincerity in matters of the heart. She'd quit reading when she reached the part that stated he was a strong ally to lovers. It would be so easy to grab that idea and run with it, embrace the general thought that the card represented the start of a new relationship. *Oh, how I'm so ready for one.*

But not with a man like Tom Henderson. He was drop-dead gorgeous, had the stamina of the Energizer Bunny and a raunchy sense of humor that rivaled her own. But he was going to wake up and realize they had made a big mistake. Everyone knew he wasn't looking for more than recreational sex. She thought that was exactly what she had wanted as well…until he'd pulled out of her that last time, gathered her into his arms and kissed her tenderly. She hadn't been prepared for that.

She also didn't want any awkward feelings because of their relationships with Marissa and Jason. He had given her some great memories, ones she'd never forget. In appreciation, she had done the mature thing and offered him an easy escape.

Tom had nodded off, anticipating the feel of Tessa in his arms when he awoke. He was disappointed when he reached around and didn't find her and became a little concerned when he called her name and she didn't answer. He relaxed when he found his clothes in a neat pile on the corner of the tub with a fresh towel, toothbrush and short note.

Now, rinsing the vanilla-scented soap off his body, he was pissed. How dare she imply that he should take a flying leap right out of her life. He climbed out of her shower and wrapped the towel around his hips. As if he were going to walk away without a backward glance after last night.

Her note said she was in her store hosting a book club. That was fine. He'd wait for her. He didn't have any plans except watching the game with his dad and brothers. That wasn't for hours. He walked to the kitchen, rummaged around until he found the coffee and filters. He started a pot and roamed around her living room, looking at photos and knick knacks as he went. He picked up a picture of her and Marissa and smiled. They were wearing large sombreros and each had a bottle of Corona nestled in their cleavage. He had no doubt there were a few good stories to accompany that photo.

He sat down in the oversized armchair and shook his head. He rested his elbows on his knees and considered all the times he'd walked out on sleeping women he'd made love to. *You never made love to them, buddy. You fucked 'em and left 'em.* But Tessa? He'd made love to her. Numerous times. Thoroughly. And the way his cock was pushing against the terry cloth covering his crotch, he wanted to do it again. Numerous times. Even more thoroughly. She wasn't going to be a one-shot wonder. She might not realize it yet but they were going to be lovers.

*Lovers.* Tom stared at the book lying open on the ottoman. The word jumped out at him. He picked up the book and began reading. Within minutes, her morning departure and "have a nice life" note became perfectly clear. She was scared. Tom didn't blame her. If he actually believed that cards and runes and crystals were a guiding force in life he'd have dropped the text and run through the streets of Grand Harbor screaming like a girl. He might not subscribe to her beliefs but he wasn't about to mock them.

He grabbed a cup of coffee and returned to the book, looking over it with renewed interest. The guy in the short tunic apparently elicited active emotions like being moved or touched by a specific person or event.

"Check and double check," Tom said aloud, smiling over the rim of his cup as he replayed the highlights of the evening in his head. If he were able to edit, he certainly wouldn't have flaunted her easily stoked passion in front of his brother but what could he do? Other than hope the asshole kept his mouth shut.

Tom finished his coffee, enlightened to the fact the Cups suit offered the wonder of romance. That was an alien thought but one that was becoming more palatable with each passing second. He continued on, reading that an opening might appear that could bring happiness. He read the final sentence once and then twice more.

*When a chance at great joy presents itself, act on it.* He nodded his head slowly and slammed the book shut.

Tessa was ready to comment on Mrs. Grady's observations on Canto six when the door that separated the bookstore from the back room flew back on its hinges.

"Excuse me, ladies," Tom said, beating a path directly to her side. "I need just a minute of Tessa's time."

He grabbed her hand and pulled her behind one of the tall racks and spun her around until she was backed against the R's. If she wasn't mistaken, her ass was resting against *The Prisoner of Azkaban.*

He trapped her between his arms and moved closer. His hair was still damp and her fingers tingled with the urge to touch him. His shirt was untucked and barely buttoned, a nice little vee of tan skin peeking out the top. If she was succumbing to the attraction, she'd be placing her lips there right now.

"You've got some major *cojones*, Tessa," he whispered. "You think it's going to be that easy to get rid of me?"

She didn't answer but her eyes opened wide when he pressed his hips against hers and rubbed back and forth.

"I wish you could see your eyes right now. Did you know they get greener when you're excited? And I do excite you, don't I, sweetheart?" He molded his body against hers and cradled her jaw with both his hands.

"We make each other so fuckin' hot it's scary. You might be too frightened to admit there's something more than a screw-me-any-which-way-you-can dynamic here but I'm not so blind."

He brought his mouth down in a scorching kiss, one that branded her his and his alone.

"This is far from over, Tessa." He pulled back and his eyes were filled with hunger...and something else. Determination? "Far from over."

He walked briskly away and she heard the back door open and slam shut. She clutched Lord Byron to her chest, suddenly realizing she was shaking like a leaf.

"That's what you think," she said under her breath, turning to find the entire book group standing on the other side of the rack. The audience of ladies, young and old, were staring at her with dreamy looks on their faces.

"'And whispering, I will ne'er consent, consented'," Mrs. Grady said with a broad wink. "*Don Juan*, Tessa dear. Canto one."

\* \* \* \* \*

"Anybody need a drink?" Tom asked, rolling himself off the couch. He couldn't concentrate on the damn basketball game and Luke kept giving him sideways glances that had his teeth on edge.

"Grab me another beer, Tommy," his dad said.

"Make it two."

"Three."

"Four."

"I'll have a dirty martini," Sam said and they all stopped and stared.

"Just kidding," he added. "Can you grab me a Mountain Dew?"

"I'll give you a hand," Andy offered and followed him into the kitchen.

Tom opened the refrigerator door and handed the beverages to his brother.

"What's up?" Andy asked.

"Nothing," Tom replied.

"Let me rephrase. What's up between you and Luke?"

"Not a thing."

"Whatever," Andy said, grabbing a handful of beer and turning toward the family room.

"Wait," Tom said. This might be a giant mistake but he certainly wasn't going to say anything to Jason. If Tessa wanted Marissa to know anything, she'd tell her.

Andy unscrewed the top of his beer and met Tom's gaze as he brought the bottle to his lips.

"I slept with Marissa's best friend," he blurted out.

"The redhead?" Andy choked in disbelief.

Tom nodded and Andy took another quick swallow.

"Man. She is hot," Andy said and Tom grimaced. "You know, in an 'I'm going to rip your balls off and toss you to the curb' kind of way," he added with a grin. "How was she?"

Tom crossed his arms over his chest and narrowed his eyes. "I really don't think that's anyone's concern." He watched his brother's eyes widen and he looked away.

"Are you planning on seeing her again?" Andy asked incredulously.

"She made it clear she wanted it to be a one night thing."

"Oh-ho! That's rich," he laughed. "A little bit of your own coming back to bite you in the ass, huh?"

"Screw you," Tom said. Why the hell had he even brought it up? "Not all of us walk around waiting for our dream girl to throw herself at our feet in adoration."

"You've had women throwing themselves at you for years, Tommy."

"Yeah. Well this is different," he said, running his fingers through his hair. "I don't know what to do. I really like her. *Her*, Andy. Not her boobs, not her pussy, not her tight little ass. They're just added perks this time. I can't fuckin' understand it."

"Can't you?" Andy asked in that all-knowing voice that was generally annoying.

"Shit."

"You'll figure it out, bro," Andy said and patted him on the shoulder. "C'mon. Let's go watch those Wildcats kick some ass."

The only wildcat he wanted to see was the one with crazy red hair and soft, inviting lips. *Shit*. Life was officially hopeless.

\* \* \* \* \*

"I slept with Tom." There, she'd said it. Maybe admitting that fact should be approached like a twelve-step program. She would have preferred to tell Marissa in private but Vicky had invited them both over for margaritas and the American Chopper marathon. How could she refuse when she sorely needed a diversion?

"Tom who?" Marissa asked absently, salting the rim of a glass.

"Tom your soon-to-be husband's brother," Tessa said testily.

"Oooooo," Vicky squealed.

"You slept with *Tom*?" Marissa yelled.

"Shit," Tessa swore. "You want to holler a little louder? I think there's someone on the fourth floor who might not have heard you."

"Oh my god. Sorry. I'm sorry, Tess. It's just," she paused and shook her head. "I'm shocked. Wow. That's...shocking."

"You're getting a thesaurus for your birthday," Tessa muttered, holding her glass out for Vicky to fill it.

The kitchen became uncomfortably quiet.

"See," Tessa said. "This is exactly what I was afraid of. The eggshell effect."

"Well I'd usually grill you on all the details but that doesn't seem right since he's like a brother to me," Marissa said.

"It won't stop me," Vicky chimed in. "Tell all, Tessa. Tell all."

"Wait," Marissa said. "There's no reason to be crass. Here. How about this? Let's just watch the show and every time Junior says something's "awesome" we'll ask a question."

"Brilliant. And if the answer shocks us beyond belief we do a shot," Vicky added, grabbing the tequila and heading toward the couch.

"Great," Tessa said, embracing the idea. "And if Mikey's in the episode we drink twice."

"Deal."

"Deal."

* * * * *

The Cats lost. He'd neglected to get Tessa's phone number. And she wasn't home when he drove to her house intent on nothing less than making her accept the reality of what lay between them. Returning home, he rode the elevator up to the top floor of his building and knew something wasn't right the moment he stepped inside his condo. He could hear the television in his bedroom. He hadn't left it on. Normally, he would assume one of his brothers had let himself in and taken control of his domain. It happened more often than he liked. The perils of living around the corner from their favorite bar.

He walked through the spacious rooms of the converted warehouse and halted at the foot of his bed. There she was, in all her semi-naked glory. His cock leaped for joy until he quickly realized she was undeniably drunk. The smell of tequila permeated the room and he saw a half-empty margarita on the nightstand. There had to be a logical explanation. But right now all he wanted to do was strip off his clothes, crawl in next to her and close his eyes. He pulled his shirt over his head and heard her mutter something about a camel.

"Tessa?" he asked, sitting down on the corner of the bed.

"Thirsty," she said, trying to open her eyes.

He went to the kitchen, filled a glass with ice and water and grabbed two aspirin.

"Sit up, sweetheart. Take these," he said, putting the pills in one hand and the water in the other. "Drink up."

She drank the entire glass and plopped back on the pillows. With great effort, her eyes blinked open.

"Tom," she said in a surprised tone. "Howyoudoin'?"

"Great," he said. Even totally fucked up she was gorgeous. "How about you?"

"Good. I've been dreamin' 'bout you. You and Paul Senior," she slurred. She wrapped both hands around one of his biceps and grinned. "You know what? You two have great arms."

"Really?" he asked, mildly amused. "Me and Paul senior?"

"Mm-hmmm. Don't tell Jason but Marissa likes Nubs better than any of the other guys and Vicky has the hots for Rick because he's so quiet, just like Andy." She put her arms over her head and stretched to each side and sighed deeply. "I'm saving myself for Mikey."

"C'mon, baby. Under the covers," Tom said, his mouth suddenly dry. She was doing little catlike moves on his bed in nothing but a pair of white panties and all he could think about was the fact that Mikey, whoever the hell he was, had a leg up on him and there was a cast of characters his brothers might want to know about. He had her all but tucked in when Andy called his name and stepped into the bedroom.

"Hey. Just wanted to check and see if you needed anything," Andy said. "She's wrecked, huh?"

"Pretty much. I'm not sure what the hell happened?"

"Drinking game from what I've pieced together from Vic's mumbling. Marissa's trashed too."

"Damn," Tom snorted. "Is this what we're like?"

"Probably," Andy laughed. "You're not pissed that Vicky used the spare key and let her in, are you?"

Tom looked down at Tessa and felt his heart clench. "Hell no, I'm not pissed. Remind me to give your girlfriend a big wet one the next time I see her." Tom brushed his knuckles against Tessa's flushed cheek and smiled.

"Not fuckin' likely," Andy said. A small moan escaped Tessa's lips and he chuckled. "You prepared to hold her hair when she pukes?"

"I never puke," Tessa replied sleepily, then bolted upright in the bed, clutching the sheet to her chest. She looked back and forth between Tom and Andy and scooted back against the headboard. "Tom?"

Her sharp whisper brought him to her side and she grabbed his hand in a viselike grip. "He's not here for the— you know."

Her eyes widened and she pulled him closer. "Marissa told me you gave all your brothers keys to the place. Oh my god. How many more are coming? I wasn't serious about that whole sandwich thing. I've never been with more than one guy at a time. I've never done anal...it's all I can do to fit you inside me...I can't imagine having enough room for another Henderson. I think you all are probably hung like Clydesdales." She rambled on and he heard Andy chuckle. "No wonder your mom had so many kids. You guys probably get it from your dad. I can't imagine anyone being as good as you were but maybe he is. Maybe his penis is just as huge."

He did not want to think about anybody's cock but his own. At the moment, it was making less than subtle suggestions on various methods to get her to quit talking. But at this point in her alcohol-induced ranting, there was only one way to get her to stop.

"Get lost, Andy," he said and silenced her with a long, deep kiss.

# Chapter Five

## ဆ

Tessa awoke just as the sun was illuminating the eastern half of the huge bedroom. She blinked her eyes open, her confusion lifting a second later. She was in Tom's bed and he was breathing, slowly and steadily, next to her. She barely remembered how she'd got here. Girl Night had turned into margarita madness with a little tequila truth or dare thrown in for good measure. She had spilled the beans on her attraction to the man sleeping by her side. She'd thought she had presented a fairly sound case for why getting involved might be a humongous mistake. Her opinions had been soundly overturned by the other women, who had effortlessly employed a spare key as part of their solution to her predicament by letting her into Tom's apartment.

The plan had been to wait for him, spread out seductively on his comforter and tell him she was sorry. But she'd made the dreaded mistake of drinking that one-for-the-road margarita. *Crap!* She recalled bits and pieces of the remainder of the night. Tom semi-clad. Cold water that had tasted like manna. A kiss that had spun her right back into la-la land.

She eased out of the bed, grabbed her purse and headed to the bathroom. She dug around until she found her travel toothbrush and eased the medicine chest open in search of toothpaste. Everything was neatly lined up on the shelves and she picked up a frosted bottle of cologne and sniffed. She loved sandalwood. His scent. On a whim she pulled the cap off and misted her chest, her belly, the front of her panties and then inhaled deeply. It was almost like the real thing. She brushed her teeth and padded softly back to the bed.

She crawled back under the covers but didn't scoot over. She didn't want to wake him and he looked so peaceful in the early morning light. She lay on her side and simply watched him sleep, the laugh lines around his eyes and the deeper crevasses across his forehead totally relaxed. She closed her eyes against the sudden welling. She had been a giant ass to think she didn't want him around. Wouldn't it just serve her right if he'd changed his mind?

Tessa slowly rolled onto her back, only to have his big arm snake around her waist and pull her back against him. He nestled his erection between her butt cheeks and she held her breath, waiting for him to speak but his warm breath tickled the back of her neck in a steady rhythm. She snuggled against him and fell promptly back to sleep, a grin on her face.


I am definitely going to have to change my panties, Tessa thought. Lick, lick, lick, *liiick.* "Aaaah," she said, rubbing her face against the soft sheet as a jolt of wet heat shot through her pussy and dribbled out.

She pressed against the pillow stuck beneath her abdomen and realized her panties were gone. Lick, lick, lick, *suuuck.* "Oooooh," she groaned, opening her eyes and finding Tom's side of the bed empty.

She had a pretty good idea where he had gone. Lick, lick, lick, *nip.* "Tom," she gasped, about to roll over when he spread his hand over her lower back to keep her in place.

"I'll get you some breakfast," he said, flicking the tip of his tongue rapidly against her clit. "Right after I finish mine. And then we'll talk."

"Talk?" she asked, shifting her ass higher.

"Talk. You remember talk don't you, Tess?" He blazed a solitary path from her aching clit, delving between her heavy pussy lips before opening wide and sucking on the pouting flesh. "It's that thing you like to do when you're standing before me with your nipples begging me to kiss them."

His tongue entered her and she clutched the sheets. Moisture was rolling from her slit, its wet path teasing her throbbing nub.

"It's what you do when my fingers are here." He slid his middle finger into her pussy, rotating until it was deeply seated and his other fingers rested against her ass cheeks.

"Oh, lord," she whispered, then called out louder when the finger inside her started tapping against her inner flesh.

"Let's talk, Tessa," he said, his free hand rubbing her clit a fraction off pace of the finger inside her.

"I can't," she cried, amazed at how quickly he was bringing her along. She was coiling harder with each pass of his hand. "I can't concentrate."

"Join the fuckin' club, woman."

He pulled his hand and finger from her, tossed the pillow aside and flipped her to her back. He was hard and sheathed and the fierceness in his green eyes made her catch her breath. He grabbed her thighs roughly, spread her wide and filled her with one long, hard thrust.

"You're a distraction I didn't want to admit," he said, lowering himself to his elbows as he started to move. "You were the termagant, the temptress, the tarot-reading tease who could emasculate a guy with a single glance."

She wrapped her hands around his bulging biceps, shocked by the honesty reflected in his gaze.

"Who do you think I am now?" She sucked in her breath, nearing the peak. He hooked her legs over his shoulders, buried himself deeper and pounded harder.

"You're a challenge. Still a damn tease," he swore, a fine sheen of sweat breaking out across his brow. "The woman who, if you walk out that door and don't come back, will make me cry like a fuckin' four-year-old who's lost his best friend."

"Oh. Tom." She wrapped a hand around his neck and tried to pull him down for a kiss.

He pulled away and met her eyes. "If you want to believe this is all about your Page of Cups, go right ahead. But that fish boy has nothing to do with this, Tessa. You snagged me months ago. We just didn't realize it."

She tried to answer. Her throat was closing with emotion, intensified by the release rolling through her.

He came, telling her how much she was adored. For once, words failed her.

"Well, that was amazing," Tom said a short time later when they had each caught their breath.

"You're a sex machine," Tessa admitted with a smile, tracing his six pack, then the fine line of dark hair that disappeared under the sheet he'd covered them with.

"Not the sex," he teased, grabbing her hand and bringing her fingers to his lips. "I'm talking about the fact that I finally got the last word."

She tried to pull away but he held her hand tighter and nipped her thumb. "I bought you a present yesterday. Wait here."

Tessa watched him roll out of the bed and sighed contentedly. *Mmm, mmm, mmm.* So tasty. And all hers! She rolled onto her stomach, buried her mouth in the pillow and screamed in delight.

"Don't peek," he yelled and she closed her eyes. She loved surprises. She felt him get back into bed, heard the rustle of plastic as he set something down between them. "Go ahead."

Tessa looked at the produce bag filled with dark gray after dinner mints and pushed herself up. "You remembered," she said, genuinely touched. She undid the tie and grabbed a handful of sweetness.

"How could I not? It's my second favorite flavor," he said, wiggling his eyebrows and opening his mouth.

She smiled and tossed a mint in.

"When did you buy these?"

"Yesterday. I stopped by your place while you were here pining over a bunch of biker dudes. I thought bribing you with a pound and a half of pure sugar might help you to see reason."

"I'm sorry I wasn't at there."

"I'm not," he admitted, reaching into the bag and popping a few more mints into his mouth. "You were exactly where you belong. Even in your altered state."

"Really?" she saw the amusement in his eyes.

"Oh, yeah. You in a Cuervo haze is enlightening. I found out more than a few things about the real Tessa Ward."

"Like what?" she asked cautiously.

"You're not as brazen as you let on, sweetheart." He brought a mint to her lips and she accepted it and then sucked on his finger in an attempt to disprove his point.

"I'm the queen of brazen," she said, sticking her tongue out, offering him the dissolving mint on the tip. He leaned forward and was a little brazen himself.

"You thought Andy showed up to form that sexual trio."

"I did not."

"You admitted you weren't a group sex kind of gal."

"Oh god." Apparently she hadn't been impaired enough to mention that long-running fantasy of a chemistry lab ménage. After last night, she could probably delete that from her erotic memory bank.

"It was nice to learn I'm the only one you want," he said, leaning forward to kiss her softly.

She smiled against his mouth.

"The fact you questioned if my brothers and my dad might be hung like horses was another matter."

"Oh my *god,*" she groaned, hanging her head. "I couldn't have said that."

He set the mints aside and rolled her under him. "Andy found it humorous."

She felt her heart clench as he looked into her eyes. She adored him. Big time. "And what about you," she said teasingly. "You didn't feel threatened?"

"Don't worry about me, Tessa. I've got big shoulders," he said with a devilish smile as he ground his cock against her. "I come from sturdy stock, sweetheart."

"Do you now?" she asked, more content than she'd ever thought possible.

He bent his head and nipped her shoulder. She dissolved into laughter when he whinnied next to her ear.

# TWISTED STEEL AND SEX APPEAL

ॐ

# Dedication

∞

*For Katelin — loyal fan and lover of all things Henderson. Your support truly touches me. Not as deeply as imagining #87 skating across the blue line wearing nothing but a male thong, but it's a close second. And it's sincerely appreciated.*

# Trademarks Acknowledgement

∞

The author acknowledges the trademarked status and trademark owners of the following wordmarks mentioned in this work of fiction:

007: Danjaq S.S. Corporation

Bacardi: Bacardi & Company Limited

Chippendale: Chippendales USA, LLC

Flintstones: Hanna-Barbera Productions, Inc.

Frappucinno: Starbucks U.S. Brands, LLC

Geek Squad: Best Buy Enterprise Services, Inc.

Home Depot: Homer TLC, Inc.

Labatt Blue: Labatt Brewing Company Limited

Precor: Amer Sports International

Sesame Street: Children's Television Workshop

Trojan Man: Church & Dwight Co., Inc.

# Chapter One

**ଛ**

Luke Henderson watched his brother wrap an arm around his girlfriend of the past eight months and pull her in for a long kiss. There was a time in the not-too-distant past when Luke would have made some smartass comment but seeing one of his brothers fondling his significant other was becoming so commonplace he barely noticed.

"Odds on how long we have before Vicky says she forgot something in the bedroom and asks Andy to help her find it?" his brother Jason asked.

"No way in hell," Luke said. "I've been burned too many times putting money down on you and your cake babe…or Tom and the tarot queen."

Luke leaned his head against the back of the leather couch and tried to divert his attention. He knew from experience if his brother's girl didn't get her ass moving he and Jason would have to concoct some reason for a hasty retreat.

"Enjoy the movie," Andy said, running his hands up and down Vicky's arms. "And tell the girls we all said hello."

"I will," Vicky replied. "And I'm supposed to point out that if you guys plan Tom's bachelor party around anything that remotely resembles a strip club, Tessa already has formaldehyde-filled jars with your names on them, waiting for three pairs of testicles. She's certain she can sell them online to one of the many women you guys have left pining after you over the years."

Her voice dropped but not low enough that Luke couldn't hear.

"And I like your balls right where they are, Andrew," she crooned softly as her hand disappeared between their bodies.

"All right." Jason slapped his knees and rose from the couch. Apparently he'd heard Vicky as well. "That garlic bread's gotta be all but done. C'mon Luke. I'll grab it while you call the dynamic duo and find out where the hell they are."

Luke hauled his tall form vertical and fished his cell phone out of his pants pocket as the elevator door to Andy's apartment opened and the sound of his twin brothers' raucous laughter filled the room.

"Hey, Vicky," they said in unison and Luke noticed the perturbed look that passed over Andy's face when they totally ignored everyone else and made a beeline for her.

"We're glad you're still here, Vic. We need to ask you something," Matt said.

"What would you pay to be sitting on Matt's lap, back plastered against his naked not-as-ripped-as-mine chest, while I straddled your thighs, ran my hands through your hair and sang 'Happy Birthday'?" Sam asked.

Luke watched her give the question some thought, wondering what the hell his youngest siblings were up to.

"Well I don't know. Andy, honey, what's the going rate for a twenty-something twofer?" she asked with sincerity.

"Not a whole lot when the male participants have their faces bashed in and their dicks in slings." Andy walked up behind Matt and pushed him out of the way and over the back of the couch.

"Take it easy, dude," Matt said, rolling straight to the floor and onto his feet. "This is important."

"Yeah," Sam agreed. "We got a call from Mrs. Wakeford that she's looking for a couple of guys to dance at her friend's birthday party next month and she remembered us from that charity auction Mom signed us up for last spring."

"Well, shit. Why didn't she call our brother, the centerfold?" Jason asked from behind Luke. "He can wrap a sock around his cock and bump and grind with the best of them."

The sharp 'snap' of a dishtowel made stinging contact with Luke's shoulder.

"You're still pissed about that, aren't you," Luke joked, snatching the towel from Jason's hand and spinning it into a tight little cylinder. "It's not my fault the size of your hammer couldn't compete with the length of my flamin' hot metal. And no padding needed, shitface."

"Flamin' is right," Jason said, twisting away just as Luke whipped the edge of the towel. The crack of sound echoed through the room, barely missing his brother's arm. "I might have been relegated to Mr. August but at least I don't have every ass pirate in the tri-state area squealing my name when they roll into town for the weekend and see me on the street."

The twins chuckled and Luke laughed right along with them. "Hey, man. It's all about community pride," he said, tossing the towel at Jason's face.

"Yeah," Andy chimed in. "And who better to appreciate the efforts of the Grand Harbor Garden Club than the anal cartographers of the world?"

"Technically, dude, that term has nothing to do with gayness," Sam interjected.

"Well you would know, turd burglar," Andy teased, wrapping Sam in a bear hug and making kissing noises by his ear.

"You guys are soooo bad," Vicky said.

Luke watched her walk around the other side of the couch to give Jason a consoling hug. "You looked just as sexy in your tool belt as Luke did twisting his steel."

"Is that what they're calling it now?" Matt joked.

"Twisted Steel and Sex Appeal," Sam said, breaking free of Andy's grip, elbow to ribs. "That's what the *Packet* called him."

Luke wasn't likely to forget that moniker…or the headline that started it. The personal attention had been a little embarrassing at the time but he'd gotten used to women bringing it up. He'd met more than a few ladies who had used it as a conversation starter before happily finding out later in the evening it wasn't over-inflated journalism. Not only had the press helped his mother's club sell enough calendars to reclaim and beautify one of the town's parks, it had caused a major increase in the sale of his wrought iron creations.

"Sex appeal—that goes without saying," Vicky added, stepping in front of Luke and giving him a quick hug as well before walking back to the elevator. "You all have that in spades. Marissa and Tessa and I always say we'd be gazillionairs if we could find a way to bottle it. Have fun and remember—no bare nipples and G-strings," she said, raising her hand as the doors closed.

Luke noticed they were all standing there returning her wave and dropped his hand first. It was easy to see why Andy had fallen for her. She was smart and funny and had the heart of an angel. If he thought about it, all his brothers' women were pretty much cut from the same cloth. Maybe that was the secret trio of qualities that led to Henderson happiness?

*Get a grip, moron. Now isn't the time to become philosophical.* Planning Tom's final bout of debauchery was the order of the evening. There'd be broads and booze and, despite Vicky's warning, there'd definitely be boobs.

Now *that* was a trinity of qualities that always brought Luke bliss.

\* \* \* \* \*

Luke was too full from dinner to partake in his usual bedtime treat of a glass of whole milk and one of Marissa's homemade cookies. Jason's wife was a master baker and Luke was pleased for all their sakes that his brother had found her and her kick-ass oatmeal raisin delights.

He climbed the back staircase of the historic duplex he lived in, thinking how, in theory, he should be the next one in line to have the woman of his dreams appear before him to fill that little gap his older brothers swore he wouldn't even realize was there until the minute he found her.

One by one it had happened to them. Like lemmings they had followed each other away from free and easy lifestyles to being so utterly committed it was beyond frightening. As close as he was to Sam and Matt, Luke missed the camaraderie he'd shared with his older siblings when they'd gone out howling. He would never believe that rush of excitement could be replaced by one woman.

He wasn't looking for love. Lately, he hadn't even been looking for lust. Every summer the new wave of hot seasonal pussy was getting bolder in their advances and demands, which he had absolutely no issues with. He'd be first in line to welcome them to town in another few weeks. He loved ladies who knew what they wanted. He just wished their mental acumen would match their implant size. And he was completely fed up with women reaching for their cells and texting their friends before they had the common courtesy to climb off his dick.

He hit the top step and padded across his bedroom to the French doors that led to the covered balcony overlooking his half of the small backyard and the river beyond. Tom continually offered him prime living space in the warehouse he'd converted but Luke always refused. He loved this place. It was peaceful and he got some of his best ideas sitting in the old rocking chair on the balcony. Or he could jump in his boat, follow the river and quickly hit the inner coastal for some backwater fishing or keep on going and ride the waves of the Atlantic.

Luke opened the door and stepped outside, reaching behind his head to peel off his T-shirt, letting the late spring breeze swirl around his body. He tossed the shirt aside and leaned over the railing, watching the watery reflection of the lights from the houses on the other side of the river contemplating how well the evening had gone. Until the movie ended and the women descended.

He rubbed his chest, remembering the little stab of something that felt a lot like jealousy when his older brothers had been gifted with looks from their women that had ranged from adoration to pure lust. *Not jealousy, moron.* Jealousy wouldn't have had him scrolling through his cell phone the minute he'd said goodnight, looking for someone who might offer a diversion. He had pulled up number after number, nearly dialing a few and actually hanging up on one woman as her phone clicked on when he realized she wasn't what he really wanted. *What the fuck do you want?*

With a heavy sigh he grabbed one of the beams that ran across the low ceiling, stretching his tired muscles as the truth hit him. He—the man who had never met a pussy he hadn't liked—had become vaginally jaded. He moved his other hand downward, sucking in his abs to make room for his palm to slide into his jeans. It looked like he and his right hand would be renewing their on-again, off-again long-standing relationship.

"Well, doesn't that just suck?" he said with a little snort as he gripped his semi-hard dick.

"Not from where I'm sitting."

Shelly Latimer raised the wine glass to her lips as her hulk of a neighbor whipped his head around and met her amused grin.

"Holy shit!" He lowered his thickly muscled arm and turned, affording Shelly a great view of the rippled flesh of his torso as he yanked his hand out of his pants. "I didn't know anyone was out here."

"I'm a closet stalker," she said, taking a healthy swallow of wine, wondering if it was the *vino* or the expanse of firm, profiled flesh that had a burst of moisture breaking out above her brow. She refused to believe it was another hot flash. *Probably option number two.* She'd seen him shirtless before and it was a sight that guaranteed a rise in heart rate. Throw in the fact that he'd been playing with himself—she could have easily sold attraction tickets. *Yeah, Shelly. You have to be this tall and have the body of a goddess to ride.*

His semi-nakedness wasn't all that rare. *So why is it making your private parts tingle?* He was always a welcome addition to the backyard scenery, whether working in the raised beds of his garden, cutting the grass or sweating all over his siblings during one of their shirts versus skins football games. That was Shelly's favorite. On those occasions, she'd grab a cool drink, a magazine she'd pretend to read, sit down at her patio table and take in the delightful site, her ogling safely hidden behind the protective lenses of her polarized sunglasses.

But it wasn't daytime and the darkness hid a good portion of his yumminess. Which made him appealing in a whole new way. The moon highlighted the ridges of his hard abs and his set jaw, causing him to look somewhat fierce. Or maybe it was the thirteen percent alcohol level of her beverage of choice that was making him appear all Roman-Greco warrioresque.

"C'mon over, Spartacus," she said, the security found in the deep, dark night affording her a bit boldness. "Want some wine?"

She watched him reach for his shirt and in her best imitation of a two-pack-a-day voice said, "Don't spoil the party by putting that back on."

He laughed, his full lips parting to show very straight, very white teeth and Shelly's stomach tightened. Lord, but the man was gorgeous.

"Are you drunk, Professor Latimer?"

He swung first one and then the other denim-clad leg over the low partition that separated their balconies and walked slowly toward her, his worn jeans resting low on his hips.

"Not entirely," she truthfully replied, shifting in her seat and crossing her legs against a little zing of unexpected desire. She hadn't felt that in forever. Well, not really forever, more like the four months her ex-husband Howard had been gone and maybe another six months prior to that during their trial separation. Tack on another five from when he had pretended he was too busy or too tired or too whatever to show her any interest and…yeah, that *was* pretty much forever.

The thought was sobering and she pushed it aside, refusing to ruin the perfectly good wine buzz that was working its way through her bloodstream, along with the little sparks that glimpses of his pure buffness tended to ignite.

"I've got red," she said, rocking her glass from side to side, picking up the nearly full bottle of Meritage with her other hand. "Or I've got red."

"Tough choice," Luke said, easing into the other wicker chair. "I think I'll go with the red."

Shelly filled the glass two-thirds of the way full and handed it to him.

"Where's yours?" he asked.

She clinked the lip of the wine bottle against the rim of his glass and raised the bottle to her lips. She watched his throat work as he took a sip of the bold blend. He had a nice neck. Thick…solid. Just like the rest of him.

"What are we celebrating?" he asked, his voice blanketing her in its sexiness.

She took a little swig of the wine and reached for the tiny, coffin-shaped box sitting on the table to her side and offered it to him, a little blue spark of static jumping between their fingers as they touched.

"Shocking," he joked, setting his glass down. He opened the lid and looked, for a long time, at the silk lining that cushioned her wedding ring. "Is it polite to say happy divorce?" he asked.

"It's extremely apropos." Shelly turned her head and he saluted her with his glass.

"I hope my friends and I didn't make too much noise," she said, setting the bottle down. She knew from years of living in the duplex that the walls were fairly thin.

"No way. I wasn't even home."

"Hot date?" *Now why the hell did you ask that?*

"Nope. Brainstorming for my brother Tom's bachelor party."

"Uh-oh. Should the banks be expecting a shortage of ones?" she asked.

His low chuckle echoed through the still night. She liked the sound of his amusement.

"There are other venues for celebration other than exotic dancers."

"His fiancée threatened to kick your butts, didn't she?"

"Our butts we could have defended. Threat of castration is an entirely different story," he said, shifting in his seat.

"Ouch."

"We were feeling pretty bold at first but we caved."

"Smart men." She laughed.

They sat staring into the night, the sound of chirping crickets a backdrop to their silence. She had no idea what he was thinking. Her thoughts were centered around the fact that it had been so terribly long since she had simply carried on a conversation with a man that had nothing to do with seventeenth century poets or the division of twenty years worth of assets.

They each sighed heavily and reached for the bottle at the same time, laughing when their fingers fought for control. He won the struggle and refilled the glass, then offered it to her, waiting for her to drink before bringing the bottle to his mouth. *Gorgeous and polite.* There was a combo she hadn't seen in a while.

He tilted his head back and the reflection from the light inside her bedroom door made his eyes sparkle as he gave her an extremely relaxed, very hot look.

"Did I have you?" she asked suddenly.

He coughed, covering his mouth with the back of his hand as he fought for air. "Oh, Professor...you'd have definitely...remembered...if you had me."

*Is he flirting?* Probably not. She was so out of practice. Flirtation today meant something altogether different than it had when discussing the latest Ted Nugent song had been a precursor to backseat sex. Now everything was sly innuendo and rules that Shelly needed explained in detail.

"I meant in class," she said, reaching over and patting his back. She knew she had erred the minute she touched him.

His skin was as warm as embers compared to the coolness of her hand and the heat rolling off his body radiated straight up her arm and took a magical journey through her extremities before landing at her core. The rock-hard muscle beneath her fingers jumped and she couldn't stop herself from running her hand over the taut flesh covering his shoulder blade.

"Did you go to GHU?" she asked, reluctantly pulling her hand away.

"No. Tech school in Baltimore and then two years on a practical apprenticeship in Germany. Thanks," he said, clearing his throat. "I'm fine now."

*Oh yes. So very, very fine.* She needed neutral ground before she reached forward and did something totally embarrassing. Like see if the little dark spot above his left pec was a mole or—if it truly was the luckiest evening of her life—a drop of forgotten chocolate that, if she crawled into his lap, he'd beg her to lick away.

"Are your mom and dad still running the business?" It was the first thing that popped into her head. Probably because she was thinking how wrong it was for a woman of her age to be mentally lusting after her much younger, hotter-than-Hades neighbor. He represented the current fantasy of newly single forty-somethings and while Shelly didn't usually follow trends, her mind was telling her, in this instance, being a sheep might not be a bad thing.

"I wasn't aware you knew my folks."

"I doubt they'd remember me. It's been a long time. Your mom helped us—my ex and me—decide on a model. Your dad and his crew built our first house. A four-bedroom split entry on West Jefferson. I remember a few of his sons working with him but I don't think you were one of them."

"That would have been my older brothers. Dad never took us on site until we were at least sixteen."

Shelly looked out over the river and tried not to think of how it had hurt to sell that house. How with each passing year she didn't get pregnant Howard had fought harder to downsize, urged her to be practical. *We don't need this much room if it's just going to be the two of us.* What a joke.

"So, you sold and moved over here, farther away from the university. What prompted that?"

Luke's chair creaked as he leaned forward and Shelly resisted the urge to look his way, keeping her eyes firmly focused on the water instead. She was done going down memory lane. Actually, she was pretty much done. The wine had been a bad idea. It wasn't mellowing her out. It was making her tense. Tense enough to realize Luke was staring at her and waiting for an answer.

"What's so desirable about Oak Street?" he asked, his voice dropping to a low tone she'd heard many times before, though he was never aware she'd been listening. Was there anything sexier than a man with a deep voice? Goose bumps broke out along her arms as her mind answered that question with a resounding *no*.

Little wonder the door to his bedroom all but revolved! With an arsenal consisting of breathtakingly good looks and a voice that could melt every bone in a woman's body? Preoccupied with her professorship, Shelly had always been somewhat insulated when it came to local news but the tales surrounding the libidinous Henderson brothers didn't stop at the university's stone walls. Of course, Shelly really had no use for second-hand rumors.

Her gaze strayed sideways to the way his elbows rested on his knees, how he held the wine bottle in one large hand and traced the foil-raised image on the label with his thumb, following the edge with slow precision. Her breathing increased as she imagined how thorough he'd be at other things, how he'd take his time, how he could focus on one thing and rub it over and over. She hurried to set her glass aside before he noticed how badly her hand was shaking.

"Killer view," she finally replied, shocked to hear the huskiness in her voice.

He moved his arm and she heard the soft thud of him setting the bottle on the planked porch floor.

"The view is pretty damn stupendous," he said softly.

The calloused pads of his fingertips brushing her cheek startled her. He tucked a strand of hair behind her ear, flicking her lobe with his thumb and a slow shiver ran from the tip of her head down to her toes. She turned her head sharply and met his gaze.

"What are you doing?" she asked, heart pounding in her chest, its accelerating rhythm reverberating in her ears.

He studied her features and she felt the tiny flutter in her belly quicken when he leaned forward and brushed her cheek with his bristly jaw.

"What do you want me to do, babe?" he finally said.

If it hadn't been for that overused endearment, one she knew for a fact was his favorite, she would have walked over to the porch swing, thrown herself down and told him to rock her usually sedate world until she had slat marks embedded on her butt and a kink in her neck.

"Classic. Smooth as ever," she said, drawing away from him and narrowing her eyes. She definitely needed practice on reading signals. "Well, thanks but no thanks, Scooter. I'm not so desperate that I'm willing to use pity as a prelude to…whatever."

His deep, sexy chuckle wrapped itself around her body and, traitorous little bitches that they were, her nipples came to life.

"I prefer Luke, but if you want to do some sort of teacher-student fantasy thing or…whatever…I'll roll with it, Professor." His long, slender fingers threaded through the hair at the base of her skull, his power unmistakable as he pulled her head closer and lowered his voice.

"Pity generally doesn't give me a boner," he whispered. "But that hot little once-over you gave me when I climbed over the railing sure as hell has."

Shelly tried to ease her head backward but he held her steady. His wine-scented breath teased her lips in warm little bursts. She so wanted to kiss him. Just throw herself at him and see how he'd react. She already knew what he was capable of. But would he do all those things to her? *Of course he will…he'll do it to anyone.* That thought slapped the reality back into her lust-filled mind.

"Anyone with a pair of decent boobs gives you a chubby, Luke Henderson," she eventually said.

"A *chubby*? I haven't heard that term in years." He laughed and brought his lips close enough that Shelly knew if she stuck out her tongue she'd be able to taste him. And she knew he'd taste good.

"You can't make slanderous accusations without backing them up." He rose slowly from his chair and pulled her to her feet, sliding his other hand around her hip and over the curve of her ass as he stepped his lower body into hers. "Prove it, Professor?"

It wasn't like the movies or the historical romances she been secretly addicted to since she was seventeen. He didn't grab the pale globes of her rounded flesh, forcefully pull her against his erection and grind against her, showing her without words how much he wanted her. What he did was much more subtle…and way more erotic.

It was as if he knew the exact dimension of her hips and legs and thighs. His body warmed her, yet only the material of his fly touched her — barely — just enough that she got a hint of the hardness behind his zipper and her knees began to shake. She was out of her element and she didn't care for the feeling. Oh, she loved the way her body came to life — she'd really thought she was past the point of feeling the long-forgotten rush of want. But as totally revved as she was, she was too old for the current fuck buddy trend.

Shelly grabbed the hand behind her head. At first, it didn't budge and then he let her yank it away, his smile widening when she wrapped her palm around two of his fingers and tugged.

"Come here," she said, leading him between the chairs and into her room. He followed her to the bed and she knew if he hadn't wanted to be propelled backward onto the matelassé coverlet it would have never happened. He was the consummate V of manliness — broad shoulders, beefy arms, tapered waist. He was built like a small mountain, one she continued to convince herself it would be disastrous to climb, her reserve slipping a little at the sudden image of the huge bulge in his jeans becoming the perfect hand hold.

She looked up and he gave her a lopsided grin, one that said he knew exactly where she'd been looking as well as possibly having a damn good idea of the track her thoughts were following. One thing was certain, she had to act quickly and prove how she knew he was just as predictable as any other male who embraced the penis-driven life.

"Stay there," she said, pointing her finger at him. "Listen and learn."


Luke propped himself up on his elbows and gave her his most charming smile. His body had surged with energy when she'd grabbed his fingers and urged him toward her room and onto her bed. Her cheeks were flushed. Maybe from the wine, hopefully from the fact that she wanted what she'd been staring at. God knew he wanted her with an intensity he wouldn't have imagined. And he hoped the theory she wanted to prove would at some point involve her ditching the oversized T-shirt because, when it came down to it, the Professor was absolutely correct. He did love a nice rack.

It was blindingly clear he'd wasted his time speed dialing. This was going to be exactly what he needed. He'd had rebound sex before. Never with someone who was determined to prove a point before the frantic divestment of clothing began but either way the heat level would be blazing. Shelly Latimer was clearly an omen that he'd been over-thinking the loneliness shit. He didn't need a now-and-forever woman like his brothers. He just needed the "now" part and the curvy woman with silky brown hair and full, lush lips was to be his.

"I'm all ears, honey," Luke said, stacking his hands under his head. Shelly stared down at him and he realized he'd never been close enough before to see the color of her eyes. They were a light bluish gray — the color of finely cast pewter.

She turned on her heel and walked toward the balcony.

"What are you doing?" he asked, enjoying the way her hips rocked as she stalked out of the bedroom. She wasn't Barbie doll extreme but that hour-glass shape was still there and his dick gave an approving twitch.

"Proving my point," she called out, her voice distant.

He could tell she'd climbed onto his half of the balcony, not at all concerned she was in his room when he heard her voice, muffled but still discernable, on the opposite side of the bedroom wall.

"Ready?" she asked.

"Go ahead," he replied, glancing around the room. Their bedrooms were flip flopped. Where his flat screen hung on the wall, she had a row of built-in book shelves, filled to the max, with cupboards underneath. He had a collage of family vacation pictures hanging over his fireplace, she had a wall of diplomas with gaping spaces where her ex's similar degrees must have been hanging at one time.

"Oooooh, Luuuuke," she moaned, her voice so clear Luke bolted upright and looked at the wall between their rooms.

"Holy shit," he muttered. He knew the interior walls were thin but—

"C'mon, *babe*," she said in a lower voice and Luke grimaced.

"That doesn't sound anything like me, Professor. It needs to be deeper," he teased.

"Right," she called. "'*Deeper*' doesn't usually get screamed until a lot later. Quit interrupting."

Luke laughed aloud and listened, shifting his erection to try to garner a little bit of comfort. He honestly couldn't remember a single time when humor and a hard on had gone hand in hand, so to speak.

"C'mon, *babe*. Let me see 'em."

"They're not as big as Dana's, Lukie."

He dropped his head into his hands and groaned. She was mimicking one of the Anderson triplets. Donna...no, Danni. *Shit.* He'd hooked up with her a few months back, after years of adhering to his personal promise that he'd never touch any one of the crazy siblings again. It had been a moment of desperation he wasn't overly proud to admit.

"Oh, *babe*. They're perfect," Shelly's voice got louder and deeper and Luke shook his head. *So she'd heard a little bit of sex talk. Big fuckin' deal.*

"Let me lube them up and pump off between them."

Luke shot to his feet, only to stay rooted to the spot when he heard the rhythmic pounding echo through her bedroom.

"Mmmmmm."

"Jesus, *babe*. That feels awesome."

Luke gritted his jaw, caught between embarrassment and the fact that he actually liked what he was hearing. *FYI, pal. She's got issues with the whole 'babe' thing.*

"Oh, Lukie. I can't wait to feel you," she moaned.

The thumping against the wall increased and Luke found the wherewithal to move, missing whatever she said between the time he rushed from her bedroom, scissored over the partition and hit the doorway to his bedroom. He came to an abrupt halt.

She was kneeling in the middle of his bed, her body in something similar to the one yoga pose women loved—the one that afforded the male mind a clear image of rear entry sex and absolutely nothing else. Her hips shifted to and fro in little rocking motions that slammed the mattress against the wall and his balls against the base of his dick.

"Christ, *babe*, I love your tits," she said in her faux male voice. "Hold me tighter. Mmmm. And I love your cock."

Luke's vision actually blurred and he clenched his fists against the sudden urge to turn her—his brainiac neighbor who had been polite but had shown no signs of finding him remotely attractive—onto her back and lick every inch of her body until he heard those words again. Directed at him. Spoken in her distinct voice and not a take-off of someone else's.

"That's perfect *babe*, don't let up," she said, body gyrating quicker. He eased up to the side of the bed and looked his fill. The fabric of her lounge pants was stretched taut over the globes of her full ass and he was ninety-nine percent certain nothing stood between the knit fabric and her bare skin. She was all but covered from head to toe but he couldn't have wanted her more if she was stripped bare.

"Will you come all over me?" she asked, adding a tiny giggle that was so air-heady and dead on that Luke cringed

"Oh yeah."

"And still be able to fuck me?"

*Shit.* Luke reached for the Professor's ass and then quickly curled his fingers into fists.

"Oh yeah."

"Long and slow?"

"Oh yeah."

*Help me, jesus.* Luke's erection surged uncomfortably behind the zipper of his jeans. She was driving him wild. He knew she wasn't doing it on purpose. She was clearly in the zone. But that grabbable fanny, the unmistakable thumping...her pleading voice.

"Promise you'll bury every inch of that big cock inside me."

"Oh—"

*Fuck it.*

"Yeah," Luke interrupted, putting an end to her thespian skills as he buried one knee on the bed and flipped her to her back, looking down into her startled face.

"Every inch and then some, Professor."

# Chapter Two

🔊

Shelly felt a rush of adrenaline storm through her body and stifled a shocked squeal as he threw his leg over the top of her thighs and leaned his naked chest over her. Blood rushed to her temples and the little haze of inebriation evaporated in a flash, leaving her stone-cold sober and staring up into his questioning chocolate-colored eyes.

"Would you like that?" he asked, wrapping his hand around her forearm, her body tightening in conjunction with the circular pattern he was teasingly rubbing over the smooth skin at the crook of her arm.

Her gaze moved to his lips. She knew he had just asked her something but between the drumming in her ears and the way the small bedside lamp illuminated his features she couldn't begin to determine what it was.

Everything about him was perfect. His long, straight nose, those gorgeous eyes. A single lock of dark blond hair fell against his cheek and if her arms didn't feel like lead she would brush it away from his handsome face. His jawline was smattered with just enough stubble that a woman could easily fantasize that he hadn't shaved due to a session of sheet-twisting sex that had gone on far into the night and made him late for work.

The leg that was pinning her hips to the bed shifted and she felt him press his erection against the outside of her hip. *Oh shit, Shelly. It's been too long.* The simple feel of a rigid cock was enough to turn her nipples hard and send a rush of moisture to her core.

Every time that she and her ex had been unable to fall asleep, or had been awakened from the depths of slumber, due to the sounds of Luke's marathon love sessions, flitted through her mind. She knew he was masterful in the sack—all the moans and screams and pleas couldn't possibly have been fake. She knew well the sounds of contrived orgasms. She'd felt compelled to fabricate more than a few over the years.

She yearned for the real deal. The sheet clutching, the toe curling, the stunning completion that had usually been out of reach unless there was a battery-operated device involved and that had only been since Howard had been out of the house. His ego would have never survived her suggesting their lovemaking could use a little help. She doubted the man hovering over her had self-worth issues. Luke could give her everything she craved, using only his mouth if he so chose.

As if he could read her wayward thoughts, he rubbed his lips together and another dribble of wetness teased her folds. She watched his mouth turn up at one corner. The thought of him finding this whole situation amusing was enough to clear a little of the fog from her head. She was about to raise her arms and push him away when he spoke.

"'No' has always meant 'no', but silence—I'm taking that as an open invitation, Professor."

She watched his head descend, as if in slow motion. It gave her plenty of time to tell him she didn't want to be like the bulk of her divorced friends who went prowling for a little hot sex and if they found it with a younger man, it was ten times better, because according to them, the men were ten times more attentive and spontaneous.

What could be more spur-of-the-moment than the situation she was currently in? It was so foreign she wasn't sure what she should do. But the good Lord and his legion of angels knew exactly what she wanted to do. *Where are you?* she mentally implored. *Get your robed-in-silver butts down here and help me resist.*

She could have stopped Luke, even after the first light brush of his lips against hers, she could have pulled away and retreated to the safety of her own home but the mere fact that he hadn't engulfed her lips in a suction-filled wet kiss was enough to make her wonder what came next and her eyes fluttered shut.

He parted his mouth and lightly caressed her upper lip. Back and forth, over and over, until he finally closed his lips and pulled slowly away, his tongue barely brushing the sensitive skin as he broke free.

"So, so soft," he whispered before lavishing the same attention on her lower lip until it was pleasantly throbbing in perfect unison with her clit. He slid his knee down her leg and between her thighs and rolled over, holding himself a fraction of an inch above her body as he shifted his head to the left. He kissed her firmly, flesh meeting flesh, until she parted her lips and groaned against his mouth. He was taking his time...too much time. It was Shelly who made first tongue contact, pushing against the seam of his lips until he opened and allowed her entrance.

He let her lead, never once plunging ahead, even when she pressed full against his mouth and ran her tongue around the semi-circle of his teeth. He nipped playfully and she pulled back quickly, wondering if she'd done something wrong.

"What'd you have for dessert? You taste like wine and pure sweetness," he said huskily.

*Oh my god.* That voice...all velvety and smooth. It sounded so much better in person than through the layers of plaster and two-by-fours.

"W-we never made it to dessert," she finally said. It was nice to know her vocal cords hadn't melted from the heat pulsing through her body.

"So you always taste this good?" He stared at her mouth as he shifted his lower body, his strong thigh forcing her legs wider. "I missed dessert too, Professor. Want to share something hot and tasty with me now?"

Do or die, Shelly. She could barely breath as the thought assailed her. *Do you, giant dummy? Do. Do. Do!*

He brushed the hair back from her temples, his featherlike touch causing her body to tighten a little more. He met her eyes, waiting patiently for her answer.

"I didn't mean for this to happen." *Forgo the honesty, you idiot.* "I only wanted to prove I knew you really weren't attracted to me, how everyone you've ever brought home is just some babe to you."

"Yeah. I got that."

"You can let me up, now," she said softly.

"I don't think so." His grin turned sexily wicked. He dipped his head, nudging her chin to the side, his hot breath tickling her skin when he spoke. "We need to clear up one thing. I am attracted to you. You're an undeniably hot woman."

"I'm an undeniably old woman."

"That's bullshit." He placed light caresses from the bottom of her ear down the slope of her neck. She waited anxiously for him to touch the supersensitive patch of skin right above her collar bone but his tormenting halted. "I've got a great quote for you on that subject."

She loved quotes, almost as much as she loved the way his tongue had started making hot, wet circles against the pulse point at the base of her throat.

"'You're only as old as you think you are…if you think at all.'"

"Wordsworth?" she asked, trying to concentrate as he nipped around the hollow but the sensations rocketing to her nipples distracted her.

"No," he said. "Let me taste the other side."

Shelly swallowed and turned her head. He started a slow path upward and she found it hard to focus on anything except his lips. "Dickinson, then," she said, making a last-ditch effort.

"Nope. Papa Smurf," he admitted and then moved quickly to where her neck and shoulder met and slowly sucked her flesh into his mouth.

The ridiculousness of his words blended with a jolt of pure desire and the sound that came out of her throat resembled the soulful bleating of a young goat.

"Sorry," he said against her throat, shoulders vibrating with mirth. "I guess words aren't my thing." He pulled back and gave her a matter-of-fact look.

"What is your thing?" Shelly asked in a soft voice, more than aware her words didn't come out in the sultry tone he was more than likely used to but he didn't seem to mind at all.

He rubbed his thumb against the soft skin under her chin and met her gaze dead on. "My thing is living life to the fullest, trying to pack in every moment with all the things I want. And right now," he said in a deep, husky tone, "I want you."

*I want you.* Shelly had never heard those words spoken to her. Not before she married and certainly not during. She and her high-school boyfriends had fumbled their way through sex with very little dialogue. She'd met Howard at her first college party and hadn't been with anyone since. He simply would ask 'do you want to have sex?' There was no prelude before he would utter the statement.

Shelly stared into Luke's eyes, uncertainty gnawing at the pit of her stomach. She'd given a great deal of thought, during the dissolution of her marriage, as to how she would step back out into the dating world. She had imagined the first time would be difficult but she also had imagined it would be in a bar or club, somewhere that would give her plenty of time to think about what she was doing, weigh her options.

She hadn't intended to be flat on her back in bed with a locally known playboy whose words were making it hard for her to keep a firm hold on her insecurities.

"Luke. It's been a long time since, you know. You're gorgeous and funny and I don't know if this is at all the smartest thing to do and I'm babbling like a moron, which isn't like me, so that's a sure sign I'm totally off kilter—"

He brought a finger to her lips, effectively silencing her. "This isn't rocket science, Professor. You either want me or you don't."

Shelly only hesitated a second before responding. "Of course I want you."

"And come tomorrow we're not going to sit around worrying that we shouldn't have indulged?"

She simply stared at him, eyes widening when his thumb replaced his finger and he ran the pad against the crease of her lips until she relaxed the muscles of her jaw.

"No guilty thoughts about giving in to temptation?" he asked, lowering his hips fully between her splayed thighs and rocking into her one time, pinning her against the mattress. The tiny movement brought every nerve ending in her body to full alert and they screamed their displeasure when he eased back a second later.

"I'm really not interested in women who think they have to refrain from all the things they really want, all the treats they definitely deserve. And I'm definitely not a fan of regret. How 'bout you, Professor?"

Shelly stared into his dark eyes and slowly released the breath she didn't even realize she'd been holding. She knew all about regret and she was sick of it. But getting what she wanted, taking what he offered without any sort of strings attached? She'd never done casual sex. *Maybe it's time you give it a try.*

"You willing to partake? Maybe go for a second piece of enticement? I doubt I'll be able to stop after that, Professor, so if you're up to it...we might even have room for thirds?"

He rocked against her again before beginning a slow rotation of his hips that had his erection grinding excruciatingly slowly against her pussy.

"Oh," she gasped, clutching his shoulders as the throbbing between her thighs escalated.

"Oh 'yes' or oh 'no'?" He snaked his tongue between her lips and she gave up on the mental debate, pulling his head down to hers, moaning when the stroking pattern of his tongue began mirroring the movement of his hips.

*When, Shelly?* When would she have another golden opportunity, one tall and tanned and toned to perfection, waiting for an answer? She scraped her nails along his scalp and welcomed his moan into her mouth before she pulled his lips away.

"Yes. I want you."

"Thank god," he whispered, stopping the movement of his hips and closing his eyes. He rested his forehead against hers. "I think my balls would have exploded if you had shut me down."

"That's pretty graphic." She smiled, despite the lust swirling through her body.

"Oh shit," he said, leaning back and giving her an appraising look. "Are you from the quiet, non-potty mouth school of lovemaking?"

A wave of heat surged to her cheeks and he chuckled.

"We'll have to work on that. I'll try my best but there's no way I'm going to be able to tone it down when I get you naked. My fingers are itching right now to pull this shirt up. And it's nice that you know up front, no pun intended, that I'm totally enamored with your tits. I can't help myself. It's kinda like your attraction to my tush."

"What!"

"Come on, Professor. You're an ass aficionado, admit it. I've noticed you watching me when I've been out in the garden, doing the weeding. Or throwing the Frisbee around with my brothers, when we laid the new sidewalk out front and that time—"

"Stop! That's not true," she said, cheeks flaming further.

"It's okay," he said with a big grin, easing back onto his knees. "Just say it. This will be a great place to start. Tell me you love my ass."

"I do not love your ass."

"Really?"

Shelly watched him slide from the bed, unzipping his jeans as he went. A minute later they were pooled at his feet and he was standing in a pair of black briefs that did little to hide his sizeable erection. She wondered how many times a person's heart could race out of control and then stop dead before it simply waved a white flag and surrendered.

He moved to the side of the bed and offered her his hands, pulling her up to sit on the edge before he turned around.

"Go ahead. Look 'til your heart's content."

He crossed his arms over his chest and Shelly saw the way his deltoids strained. She let her gaze roam over his back, from his broad shoulders to this trim waist, hurrying over his covered butt—a lame attempt to convince herself she didn't care how hot his ass looked—to take in the sweep of long, sturdy legs.

"You look great," she said, swallowing against the sudden dryness in her mouth. He looked more than great. He looked like a damn god.

"You know what?" he asked, hooking his thumbs at the sides of the elastic waistband of his briefs. "I've never played tutor before."

Shelly sat and stared as he pulled his underwear down, bending over to pull them off each leg, his tight, muscled ass cheeks less than a foot from her face. She could see the shadow of his balls and her mouth went dry. Without thought, she reached out and ran a fingernail through the cleft, unable to drag her eyes away when his cheeks clenched, first one and then the other.

"That's right...touch me," he ordered, shifting his feet a little wider. "Touch me and tell me what you're thinking."

Her hands were shaking when she reached forward and grabbed his hips. He flinched and she knew it was from the coldness of her fingers.

"Sorry," she said but didn't let go. Now that she had him in her grasp, it seemed perfectly natural to lean forward and rub her cheek against the swell of his ass.

"Now that's a lot warmer," he said softly. "Your face feels as if it's on fire."

"It's not as hot as other parts," she whispered.

His body shook with laughter. "That's perfect. Now tell me what parts of your body are hotter."

"No," she said, thoroughly enjoying the firmness of his flesh.

"Obstinate, huh? That should prove fun. C'mon, Professor. Play along and tell me what's going through your mind. When the time comes, I'm going to tell you everything I see. From how tight your nipples are to the exact shade of pink your pussy is."

Her heart kicked up its beat and she pressed her legs together. Her ex hadn't wanted any sort of talk in the bedroom. Everything had been pretty straightforward. She rolled her head until her other cheek hit his smooth flesh and took a deep breath.

"Your ass...it's...I mean...I'd like to..."

She couldn't get the words out and she buried her forehead against his spine.

"Kiss it?" he suggested.

She shook her head.

"Lick it?"

"No." Her reply was barely audible.

211

"Spank it?"

She shook her head again and he gave a heavy sigh.

"Damn." She heard the smile in his voice. "I was really hoping for that one."

Shelly closed her eyes and pressed her lips to the little swell of his right cheek. She tilted her head and let the tip of her nose brush back and forth and then opened her mouth and gently nipped at his skin. She felt the shudder that rolled through him and waited for him to pull away and tell her she was a total freak.

"Christ," he swore, tilting his hips backward.

She looked up the length of his back...waiting...and then bit him again, this time following the tiny nip with a flat-tongued sweep that brought the salty taste of him into her mouth.

He stepped backward and she spread her knees to accommodate him. "Do it again," he said.

"You like it?"

"No," he said in a lightly sarcastic tone. He grabbed her hand and brought it around his body, urging her fingers around his erection. He worked their hands slowly up and down his length. "I hate it...feel how much."

"Oh my god, you're huge."

"It's sensory illusion. Just do the other side."

Shelly nipped and licked her way to his left cheek and started anew, enjoying the added attraction of his cock in her hand. Each time she bit, the length of smooth steeliness twitched.

"Do you like to have *your* ass nibbled, Professor?"

She pulled her lips away and thought about his question. "I don't know. Howard never did anything like that. He found my ass a little too widespread for his liking."

"What a fuckin' moron," he whispered. Then, in a confident voice said, "We'll answer that riddle in the not-too-distant future. And from now on...let's make it just you and me in the bedroom." He held her hand at the base of his cock and slowly turned to face her.

Shelly stared at the expanse of flesh above her fist and blinked, seeing exactly why her fingers hadn't been able to meet. "Just you and me," she whispered. The broad head of his penis was darkly flushed, a solitary drop of pre-cum glistening like a gem in the soft light, begging her to taste it.

"What about your wingman?" she asked, tracing the rim of his cock with her index finger before leaning forward and taking him into her mouth.

His chuckle died on a small moan and Shelly felt a surge of womanly control.

"Just the three of us then. Your mouth is amazing," he said, cupping her cheek.

Shelly gave a little hum of acknowledgement and his fingers twitched but he surprisingly kept his palm open and relaxed. She sucked his cock a little deeper as a reward for him not grabbing her head and plunging away at his own pace.

She loved giving blowjobs...to a point. She loved the feel of a man's cock pressing against the back of her throat...the tiny grunts and groans that slipped from their lips. It was a true rush. It was something she excelled at. And her reluctance to finish hadn't been a detractor to anyone, including her ex. But as she worked Luke's steel-like length between her lips, she wondered what it would be like to taste a man's pearly release. She grabbed the cheeks of his ass and pulled him closer, relaxing the muscles in her throat to take nearly every inch of him.

"Holy fuck," he said, gripping her chin and urging her lips away. His cock was wet and red and she leaned forward and licked the excess saliva off its crown.

"That's enough of that," he growled. "My turn. Take off your shirt. Nice and slow."

She stared into his eyes and gnawed at the inside of her cheek. He'd had no trouble getting naked, but look at him. He was gorgeous. Not an ounce of fat on his body.

"Can we turn off the light?"

"Absolutely not."

"Luke," she pleaded.

"Michelle," he replied, not giving an inch.

"I didn't think you knew my name," she said, a bit of her uneasiness beginning to melt.

"I've been your neighbor for five years. Of course I know your name."

"But you've never called me anything before. Just waved or said 'hello'."

"You never crawled into my bed before. Which, if you had done before your divorce, I would have found to be a major dilemma. I respect faithfulness above all else. But to have those lips wrapped around me? Had I known, I think I'd have broken a commandment or two. Now quit stalling. Let me see what I've been dying to get a taste of."

"That's such a crock," she said under her breath.

He dropped to his knees before her and took her face between his palms.

"It's the truth," he said solemnly. "Believe me when I tell you I realized a long time ago that the woman next door was prime wet-dream material but completely out of reach."

She stared into his eyes and shook her head. *Do it. Just throw the truth out there.* "I'm turning forty-five next month."

"Great. I'll take you to the Dairy Hut and get you a chocolate man with eyes."

"I'm serious, Luke."

"So am I. Then we'll come back here for your birthday whipping—one lash for each year, my tongue to your pussy. How's that sound?"

"That's ridiculous," she said but the picture he'd painted was forcing drop after drop of dewy wetness from her slit.

"You can't tell me you're not a proponent of oral sex, not the way you give head."

Michelle shifted her gaze and stared at the wall. Honesty was reigning supreme tonight. "I'm really not qualified to offer an opinion. That person I can't mention did it a few times and nothing really happened."

"Your egghead ex was a real piece of work, Professor. But you're in luck." He reached forward and cupped her breast through the thin fabric of her shirt, teasing the undersides of her erect nipples with the tips of his thumbs. "Want to hear my dissertation on the merits of cunnilingus?" he asked.

"Can you spell that?" she asked, the tension she was trying to ease ratcheting tighter when he brushed her beaded nipples lightly until she moaned.

"I can—against your clit with the tip of my tongue."

Shelly had never seen anyone whose eyes could be smoldering one moment and filled with devilment the next.

"And while there's something totally wicked about a man getting his first taste of pussy through a pair of silk panties, I think the effect might be lost if I'm forced to attempt that over these lounge pants."

Shelly looked down at her legs and blinked, suddenly very sorry she wasn't wearing silk panties.

"I really can't wait to see you naked," he said softly, kissing the corner of her mouth, curling his fingers against the sides of her breasts. Inch by inch, side to side, he eased the material of her shirt upward until her stomach was exposed and his fists were full of fabric.

Shelly sat up straighter in an attempt to alleviate the little roll of flesh that would undoubtedly be resting against the waistband of her pants. He took the shift of her upper body as a sign to proceed and gently pulled her T-shirt up her arms, over her head and straight off her body. Heart drumming unmercifully against her ribcage, she watched his wandering gaze study her bosom, inhaling sharply when she felt her breasts swell.

"Aw, fuck," he whispered, brown eyes widening.

Cold uncertainty gripped her stomach and when his hands closed over her knees and he dropped his head to his chest she thought she might actually be ill. Seconds ticked by as her uneasiness increased and she slowly began to cross her arms.

"Don't even fuckin' think about it," he said huskily, chest rising and falling rapidly as he pinned her with his hot stare. "Now that I've curbed the urge to come in my underwear, you've gotta let me see you—right now—every hot, sexy inch. Lie back."

Shelly swallowed hard and eased herself onto the down comforter. It was cool—a stark contrast to her heated skin.

He raised his head and gave her a strained smile as he grabbed the sides of her lounge pants and slid them slowly down her legs and she tried not to worry about the fact that her bush hadn't seen this side of waxing since an ill-fated at-home attempt several years back. Oh, it was trimmed, but not the newborn-butt-smoothness every woman's magazine reported as a trend all females should embrace.

She watched the hem of her pants slide over her toes and drift toward the floor.

"It just gets better and better," Luke said reverently, his gaze traveling from her toes to the top of her head. "You're quite the sight, Professor. Promise you won't blame me if we end up fucking each other to death."

She bit her lip, preparing to over-think his remark when his lips twisted into a slow, wolf-like expression—one that made her catch her breath at the promise reflected in his eyes. A promise that, for tonight at least, she was more than willing to accept as truth.

Luke stared down at the position Michelle had shifted into and knew better than to laugh. Hands clasped over her stomach and legs pressed tightly together—all she needed was a lily. He pushed that thought aside. He wasn't into corpses. Even ones with killer tits and hips that would cushion his thrusts like none before.

He'd make sure she wouldn't stay still for long. Her hunger was there. It was buried but it was there. He felt it in the way she'd kissed him. In the way her nails had dug into his hips as her teeth marked his ass. And sure as fuck, in the way she'd sucked his dick.

"Here." He grabbed an extra pillow and stuck it behind the one already under her head. "I want you to be able to see everything we're going to do."

He watched her eyes darken and this time he did smile. It was going to be pure hell taking things slowly but he'd had years of practice for a moment like this. Making love to someone who hadn't already run the sexual gamut, someone who only wanted to hook up with him to see if there was some hidden kink she'd missed along the way.

"Look at yourself," he said, taking her hands and spreading them wide. Her breasts were full, tipped with large, dusky nipples that had hardened into tight nubs and Luke entwined their fingers to keep from reaching down and tweaking them again.

"I'd rather look at you," she whispered and Luke watched her gaze roam over his body. Instinctively he tightened his muscles and smiled when her eyes studied his dick.

"You're beautiful," she said. "I'd like to—"

He watched her suck her bottom lip between her teeth and stifled a groan. "I think your indoctrination into hot pillow talk might be more of a trial than I thought. Tell me what you want to do?" he asked, pinning her hands to the mattress. She didn't say a word. "You didn't have any trouble talking dirty before."

"That wasn't real. That was recitation."

"Recitation, huh? Well then, Professor, recite in detail, what you'd like to do."

She gnawed at her lip and he stared her down.

"Honey, I have no problem lyin' like this for hours on end. Your tits are a great cushion and I'm happy nestling away in these wet curls," he said.

"Oh lord," she said quickly, closing her eyes. "I don't even know where to start. You're the hottest man I've ever been with."

"Just hearing you say that makes me so fuckin' hard I could burst. Right this minute," he admitted, letting go of her hands to trail his fingers down her arms and over the swell of her breasts. "Listening to someone tell you how turned on they are or what they want you to do is unbelievably sexy but you've never played that game, have you?"

"No," she replied so softly that Luke almost dropped the façade and gathered her into his arms.

He leaned forward to rub his nose against the sensitive skin between her ear and jaw. Her body jumped and he blew a stream of hot air against the column of her throat. "Tell me why you want my cock in your mouth."

She moaned. "This isn't me. I can't talk like that. You should know what I need."

Luke tilted his head enough to see she had closed her eyes tighter and he slid his body over hers, knowing she wasn't going to like what he had to say. But they were putting it out there.

"Men aren't mind readers, Michelle. After your demo on the need for intra-wall soundproofing, I assumed the reason I didn't hear any action coming from your side of the house was because your ex was a total dickwad. But if you were too afraid to give the guy a hint or two over the course of a few decades, it's no wonder your sex life sucked. Sucks—make that present tense, honey. Because it's not about to change anytime soon unless you help it along."

Her eyelids shot open and she brought her hands to his chest and pushed. He dropped a little more weight onto her torso and tried not to think about how warm her palms had become, how that heat was teasing his nipples.

"I gave him plenty of hints, you big oaf. Get the hell off me."

She raised her upper body and he grabbed her shoulders and gently pushed her back down.

"Little moans and 'oh my gods' only go so far, Professor." He ran the pads of this thumbs inward against her collarbone and then up her throat, forcing her head backward as he reached her chin. She glared at him through narrowed lids.

"I know you're pissed. Your cheeks are all pink so you're probably embarrassed to boot and I'm sorry. But I do love how that flush has brought out the freckles splattered over just the very top of your cheekbones. And what—four across your nose?"

She exhaled the breath she'd been holding and the little breeze tickled his lips. He felt her body relax and he shifted his hips, gritting his teeth as he slid his cock against her stomach. "I just want you to realize how smokin' hot the sex between us is going to be. All it takes is a little honesty and openness. I'm more than willing to fulfill any fantasies you have."

"And what if I can't reciprocate when the time comes? I'm not like those other women, Luke. I might beg you to let me deep throat all seven inches—"

"Actually, it's a little bigger than—"

"But I don't swallow. Hell, I don't even spit. And from that piece of imparted knowledge you should logically assume I won't be parting my cheeks and begging you to take your dick, which you're rubbing way too high to be of any use whatsoever, and fuck me in the ass!"

He didn't take his eyes from hers but he felt the rise and fall of her chest beneath him and his smile deepened. He released her shoulders and framed her face with his hands.

"A 'dick'…a 'fuck'…and a hint that your pussy needs my attention — now how hard was that, Professor?"

The silence stretched. He waited for her response.

"Not as hard as your…cock?" It was more of a question than an answer and he gave her a tiny wink.

"I knew it," he said, lowering his lips to the deep valley between her breasts. "You're a natural. And for your info, I'm not looking for an evening that resembles an amateur porno…"

He kissed his way downward, sliding his balls over her wet pussy as he went. God, he'd love to just straddle her face and watch her lick her juice off each tight globe before sucking them into her mouth. *Focus, pal. No porno.*

"I'll be content making love to you however. You want straight missionary…we're nearly there. Throw your legs around my waist. You're drenched enough that I can slide right in." He kissed his way over her left breast and nuzzled the sensitive skin at the outer edge, her heart banged against his cheek.

"Do I want to eat you? Yes! I've wanted to do that since the minute I smelled how excited you were. And the urge to bury my face in your pussy got a hell of a lot stronger when I found out I'd be the first man to make you love it. And yeah, I'm cocky enough to look into your gorgeous eyes and tell you you're definitely going to love it." He turned to find her staring at him wide eyed. "I don't care if I have to go down on you all night and into tomorrow. I'm not stopping until you're screaming."

"Oh lord," she whispered, easing her legs wider.

"I will also accept pleas to the savior as proof you're coming but if my dick's not inside you, feeling those little ripples, then those cries have to be accompanied by you creamin' against my tongue." He felt her hips begin to squirm and he slid his dick all the way down her folds and away from her body. He stacked his hands over her breast bone and propped his chin on top.

"What are you doing?" she asked breathily.

"I'm watching your eyes change colors. Watching the silvery blue get smaller as your pupils dilate. You slicked my dick with every little movement my words were forcing you to make and now it needs to find the safety zone for a few minutes. Your eyes are a beautiful distraction."

Her rapid breathing moved his head up and down and he felt her nipples pressing into the little space between his forearms and his biceps. She really was amazing, in a way that far surpassed the women he usually slept with. She didn't seem to care that her face wasn't made up, that her hair wasn't stiff with some styling product. When he got her out of the bedroom, he felt pretty certain she'd be a woman comfortable in her skin. And that was refreshing.

"Luke?"

"Yes?" His head stopped moving when she held an upward breath and he met her stare.

"My nipples are so tight...they ache."

*Holy fuck.* That little admittance had his balls pulsing. He held his breath the minute she released hers.

"What do you want me to do, Michelle?" He eased himself upward and waited for her answer.

"Make them stop hurting...and call me Professor."

# Chapter Three

༄

Shelly had a moment of sheer and utter embarrassment and then, with his straightforward question, it passed. Honesty and openness, he'd said. If that's really all it took, she'd be insane not to give it a try.

"So you like it when I call you that?" he asked, sliding his hands off her chest, gently caressing her shoulders.

"When we're doing this kind of stuff—yes."

"This kind of stuff? Like you letting me turn fantasy into reality?"

He rolled to his back and she rose up on her elbow, her gaze drawn to his groin as he reached down and leisurely stroked his cock. She watched his hand and nodded. "Only a few people call me Michelle. You can call me Shelly. When we're not…you know." She reached out a finger and ran her nail around his nipple until it rose.

"And do you think we're going to…you know…more than a few times?"

"You're the one who mentioned thirds…Scooter."

"Get on top, Professor," he said with a smile.

Shelly crawled onto her knees and straddled him, looking down to make sure her heart wasn't pounding out of her chest like a cartoon character's, because that's exactly how it felt.

He cradled her hip with his free hand and urged her down, pushing his cock behind her before grabbing her hips with both hands and sliding her exposed pussy lips against his lower abs until his erection bumped her ass cheeks.

"You're soaked," he said, running the palms of his hands over the globes of her ass before manually pressing his hot length between her cheeks. Moisture seeped from her folds at the sensation of his fingertips and the heel of his palm stroking her while he rubbed his cock at the same time.

"I don't think I've been this wet before," she said, pressing hard against his stomach to ease the tickling trail of wetness.

"It's pretty heady, knowing I've warmed you up enough to get that honey flowin' and we haven't even really gotten started. Scoot on up here, bend down and let me taste those tight little nipples."

She couldn't believe the things he was saying. *Don't you love it?*

He ran his hands up and down her back and pulled her breasts to his lips. With slow licks he ran the flat of his tongue against one nipple then shifted his head and laved the other. Shelly sighed and placed her hands on the pillow and held back a groan. The tiny little caresses were only making it hurt worse. She looked down at his face, at his long eyelashes brushing his cheeks, at his tormenting tongue.

"You know what these buds are perfect for?" he asked, suddenly looking at her.

"Sucking instead of teasing?" *God! Did she just say that?*

He nipped at one distended tip and she dug her nails into her palms. "That...and nipple rings."

"Forget it," she whispered, but her cunt clenched at the thought.

"How 'bout clamps?" He pulled his lips away and rolled her nipples gently between his forefingers and thumbs and she tried to tighten her legs against the jolt of pleasure that rocketed to her clit.

"Doubtful," she gasped.

"We'll see." He pinched a little harder and the moan escaped as she ground her wet pussy against him. He didn't seem to mind. In fact, his cock gave a sharp tap against the cleft of her ass. "You stoke my fantasy and I'll stoke yours."

"I'm sure there's a way to do that without my nipples ending up in a vise."

"Sit up and play with yourself."

"*What?*"

He grasped her elbows and pushed her upward. His big hands inched their way down her arms and he directed her hands to her breasts.

"Show me how you stroke them when you're all alone."

"I don't—"

"Honesty, Professor."

*This is too much.* She swallowed hard. Two could play the "I dare you" game.

"Will you show me how you masturbate? On those rare occasions you're alone? Or not driving your horny neighbor to the point she's ready to jump you."

"I'll absolutely whack off for you, any time you like," he said, gracing her with a seductive smile as he reached toward the nightstand and picked up one of three remotes. A few presses of buttons and the muted sounds of Dave Brubeck drifted from the four corners of the room.

"I love jazz," Shelly said, listening to the cry of a lone sax.

"Nothing better to get busy by," he said teasingly.

She couldn't help smiling. "I'm sure that's exactly what - all those early musicians had in mind."

"No doubt about that, Professor. Considering more than a few got their start in Big Easy whorehouses."

Their gazes locked and he gave her a little nod.

"Places where the ladies probably didn't have to be asked twice to show a man what they liked. C'mon Professor. Touch yourself for me."

Shelly let the music wash through her and fought the urge to close her eyes. He was focused on her hands and as she watched him watch her, a little rush of control surged. She ran her thumbs against the outermost fullness and pressed her flesh together to form a deep crevasse of cleavage. She lessened her grip, pushed again, harder this time, and his jaw clenched.

She knew exactly what he was thinking. "Do you think your cock will like my breasts better than Danni's?"

"Yeah." He cleared his throat and added, "Yours are phenomenal. But just you and me. Remember?"

Bolder than she'd ever been, Shelly splayed her fingers across her flesh and gave herself a couple of firm squeezes. In unison, she brushed her thumbs across her nipples, back and forth, and then switched to an alternating pattern that she thought might make him hot, surprised when her touch and his intent gaze soon had her hips rocking against him. He grabbed her waist and forced her tighter against his skin.

"Just you and me," she panted, her inner muscles curling into pre-orgasmic mode. She watched his nostrils flare and the smell of her desire reached her a second later. "That feels so good."

She tugged at her nipples, whimpering each time he forced her clit downward.

"You're scorchin' me, honey." He looked away from her breasts and met her eyes. "So wet and slick. If you keep rockin' you're going to make yourself come."

"Oh god yes," she moaned, working her flesh harder as the first wave begin to roll.

"You look so fuckin' hot doing that but you're not allowed to go that quick." He gripped her hips and lifted her up and away, her clit throbbing as she stared down at him.

"What?" she cried, trying to lower her body but his powerful arms held her at bay.

"I said, as much as I'd love to feel you gush against my stomach, that's not how you're going to come."

"Why?' she asked, the tone of petulance that echoed in her ears a tad embarrassing.

"Because I'm going to make very certain you never forget this night and that means me getting to taste your inaugural orgasm. And then me fucking you," he said, moving his fingers just inside the cleft of her ass and stroking her lightly.

"Oh my god. Not there?" Shelly asked, clenching her glutes at what he suggested.

"Probably not tonight but secretly, you're not averse to the idea, are you?" he asked, his gaze drifting slowly down her body until he was staring at her cunt.

"I'm not interested in anal escapades. At all."

"That dripping pussy's calling you a liar, Professor. Come up here."

Shelly's heart seemed to jump to her throat when his massive biceps bulged and he lifted her forward until her knees were pressed wide and she was straddling his shoulders.

"Damn, Professor. You're perfect."

She looked down, shivering as she watched his gaze flit over her exposed flesh.

"Just a little lower," he said, running his thumbs up and down the crease of her thighs before easing her legs open and bringing her pussy so close to his mouth she could feel the heat of his breath. "Now reach back and put your palms against the top of your ass."

Shelly did as he asked, the position forcing her breasts so far forward she couldn't see his face. She was about to complain when his tongue touched her and she jerked.

"Easy," he said, covering her hands with his and moving her into the previous position. The tip of his tongue delved between one side of her inner and outer lips and traced a path straight to her clit, brushed the soft wrinkles of her hooded clit and slid slowly down the other side. He re-traced his path, two…three…four more times, stopping halfway through on the last pass.

"See how nice that feels," he said, his breath hot against her pulsing flesh.

Shelly couldn't say a word. She clenched her teeth and listened to the little bursts of air rush from her nose in an attempt to keep her mouth closed and hyperventilation at bay. "Nice" didn't begin to describe what she was feeling.

The muscles in her thighs were strung so taut they were beginning to burn but nowhere near as badly as the pressure blossoming in her lower belly.

He tilted his head to the side and pressed his parted lips against the hot, swollen flesh of her labia, kissing her softly and then sucking her skin against his teeth. She dug her nails into her skin and stifled a moan.

"Don't do that," he said, shifting to the other side and showering it with equal attention. "Don't hold in what you're feeling. Let me hear how much you like what I'm doing."

"I'll try," she said, her breath hitching when he let go of her hands and slid his palms over the outside of her hips and snaked his thumbs through her pubic hair until they flanked her swollen nub. He shifted his thumbs back and forth slowly, brushing the root of her clitoris with the edge of his nails, and Shelly let her appreciation for his enticing touch show with a very audible groan.

"That's what I want to hear, honey. Tell me what you want me to do, Professor."

"I don't know what I want you to do," she said in a hoarse voice.

He rotated his tongue against the very bottom of her slit in tight little circles and Shelly closed her eyes. Heat flooded every pore of her body and she gasped when he turned his tongue sideways and slid it up and down between her inner lips, never deep enough to be considered a form of fucking.

"God*damn*, Professor. Your pussy's so hot and sweet—a flavor all its own. I want to lick you 'til you come then do it all over again."

He flattened his tongue and slid it around her entire vulva, his saliva and her juices slicking her hot flesh even more. Light strokes became firm, full-frontal licks that inched closer to her aching clit. He circled her, round and round and round, until Shelly couldn't keep quiet.

"Oh my god. Lick it," she pleaded. "Please…lick the middle."

His tongue bathed her clit with one broad sweep that ended with it swirling through her curls.

"No," she groaned, scooting her legs farther apart, but he stopped her before she could sit fully on his face.

"Too close will ruin it," he said, pulling the top of her outer labia wide and blowing a stream of surprisingly cool air around her nub.

"Shit," she swore, dropping her head backward. The pulsing increased to the point of near pain and she arched her back, ever muscle in her body straining.

"Try to hold back."

"I don't want to," she cried, shifting her hips against his hands, throwing her body forward until she was straight-arming the wall for support. "You don't know how it feels."

"Tell me," he ordered, flicking her clit with the tip of his tongue.

"Oh god," she moaned, low and long, and he stopped.

"Tell me," he said, his gaze far from teasing when he looked up at her. It was intent, seductively demanding. "Tell me and I'll make you come like you never have."

He firmly stroked her clit with the underside of his tongue, the smoother texture driving her straight to the edge. And then he stopped.

"You're making my insides quiver," she gasped, holding his gaze.

"More," he said, teasing her slit with a downward serpentine move that had her sliding her hands to his chest for support.

"*More!*" She had meant to question, not comment. He tensed his tongue, delving into her cunt in a steady rhythm.

"Luke, pleeeease." She moaned as he eased back once more and stroked the entire area of swollen, throbbing flesh with slow swipes of his tongue. "I'm going to burst—the pressure, it's unbearable. Lick me harder."

He did and she nearly rocketed through the roof. "Faster...oh shit...right there," she cried, a sheen of perspiration dotting her back. He was rewarding her, she knew. And in a way that no one ever had. He went back to flicking her clit and she let go of his chest and grabbed his head. "Oh my god!"

The wave hit her and the white dots she'd been looking at behind the lids of her tightly closed eyes exploded into an array of brilliant color and she screamed his name as her pussy contracted over and over and over.

Luke watched her shatter. It was the most glorious sight he'd even seen—her breasts heaving, her licking her dry lips a second before she called his name and crested, creaming his tongue with her cum.

But, fuck me Frances, he'd barely held back again, all but shooting his load straight toward the ceiling when she had run her nails against his scalp and told him exactly what she needed.

He took deep breaths, his goal of getting his dick under control hampered by the smell of her excitement.

"Oh fuck," she said softly and he smiled despite his discomfort. She plopped her ass onto his chest, eyes still closed and slid her hands onto her thighs. "I think I'm still coming," she whispered in an awe-filled voice.

Luke looked at the wet, pink flesh splayed before him. He couldn't wait to feel the aftershocks for himself, bring her back to the point of erupting a second time. And he sure as fuck liked what he was looking at.

"Mount up, Professor."

"I can't move," she said in a voice that was taking on a very satiated edge.

"Don't you bail on me, honey." Luke gave her ass a few flat-handed whacks and watched her eyes shoot open. "Get a leg up so I can fuck you proper."

He watched her eyes darken but she shifted to the side and brought her foot flat onto the bed. Luke grabbed his dick and guided it to her slit, holding his breath as she eased onto the broad tip.

"Oh...damn. That's so...fuckin'...unbelievably...tight." He gritted his teeth and tried to focus.

"It feels even bigger than it looks," she said. He heard the worry in her voice and took a moment to let her words sink in.

He grabbed her hips but didn't pull her away. "You're either too damn tiny or...how long has it been since you've been laid? You're so freakin' hot." *Shit...christ!* "Off! Off, Shelly! I forgot the condom." *What a time for a fuckin' brain freeze.*

"I don't think this is going to work...and you don't need a condom."

"It'll work, just not with you on top." He eased her up and off his shaft and rolled her onto her back. "And I don't go in bare."

"But there's no reason —"

He sealed her argument with a slow, deep kiss. One that went on and on and on until she gasped for breath and he was once again somewhat sane. He palmed her, the heel of his hand resting against her mound as his fingers danced across her vulva.

"How long?" he asked, stroking just his middle finger up her slick folds.

"Ten months, six days," she said, crooking her knee and opening her legs. "But who's really counting?"

*Jesus!*

Luke eased his finger inside her in a slow, steady motion, residual tremors taunting him to hurry up and bury himself deep.

"Relax," he ordered, withdrawing his finger when she arched her back.

As soon as she was flat against the mattress he slid his middle finger back in, this time a little deeper.

"You are tight."

"It feels good."

"It's going to feel a lot better."

"When?"

"Anxious?"

"You're the one who keeps promising to fuck me."

"That's true. But I have willpower, honey." *Liar!* Her pussy was like silk and he let his finger glide nearly the whole way out before adding another digit and stretching her with a little twist of his wrist. He moved his fingers in and out, switching to a scooping motion that quickly had her breath hitching. "Do you have a favorite dildo, Professor? Something nice and slender so your pussy stays snug?"

"No," she replied softly, her eyes watching as he worked her closer to the edge she'd fallen over moments before.

"A vibrator?" He pulled his fingers nearly free and teased her opening with shallow thrusts. She gnawed at her lip and he knew she was well aware he wouldn't stop the torment until she answered.

"Yes," she finally whispered.

"Will you bring it next time you come over to play?" he asked, upping his pace.

"Next time?" she gasped and met his gaze. "I'm not sure I'll survive this time...oh...no."

"Oh yes. Do you have any idea how badly I want you?" Luke asked, watching her eyes scrunch tight when he rubbed the tiny patch of rough skin on the front wall of her vagina. *More than you've ever wanted anyone, pal.*

"Don't wait. Fuck me now." She tossed her head to one side and said in a shocked, throaty voice, "Oh my god. I've never said that to anyone...ever."

Her honesty put him over the edge. He slid his fingers out of her pussy, ignoring her whimper. He yanked the drawer of the nightstand open, got the condom out and quickly sheathed his cock.

He spread her one leg wide and then hooked her other ankle over his shoulder, rubbing his cock head up and down her folds, purposely avoiding her clit. "Let yourself back off a little."

"You already did that once," she whined, opening her eyes and grabbing his sheathed cock, grinding her pussy against it. She'd turned into a damn wanton and he freakin' loved it.

"Let go, Professor."

"Give me what I need, Luke."

"I will, honey. But don't you want to stretch this out a little longer?"

He brushed her hand out of the way and teased her dripping-wet opening with just the broad head of his dick. Pushing in and letting it pop slowly out a half dozen times.

"No," she gasped. "I want you in me. Now. Am I supposed to beg? Tell me," she ordered in a shaky voice, eyes pleading.

"I don't want you to beg," he said, visions of her on her knees being totally submissive reeling through his mind. "At least...not this time."

With carefully measured movements, he buried his cock deep and listened to her welcoming moan. He started an easy rhythm, one that was a bitch to maintain in his advanced state of blinding arousal but one he knew would stoke the embers of her desire into flames.

"Faster," she demanded.

"Soon."

"Now," she cried, reaching under her thigh to graze his balls with the tips of her fingers.

"Oh, christ," he moaned, stopping dead still. *She shouldn't have done that.* His sac curled taut and he felt the pulsing heat begin to burn. Luke dropped his elbows to the bed and began thrusting harder. He could feel her pussy clenching, gripping his dick in tantalizing little spasms that forced him straight to the brink. Her body tensed and he clenched his jaw so hard he thought he heard it crack. *Hold on, pal.*

She dug her nails into his arms and cried his name.

"Shelly," he moaned, dropping his wall of control and pumping his way straight to oblivion.

*Pull out, get the condom off.* Luke lay on top of her, his head buried in her damp hair, his breathing far from normal. *Pull the fuck out.* He felt his erection going down and he attempted to move before another round of voices, which sounded progressively more like those of his brothers, echoed in his head. *Get the fucking condom off, you moron.* Shit. It *was* their voices.

"Mmmm. Don't go," she said in a satiated voice that made Luke want to stay buried in her even longer. She grabbed his ass and urged him closer.

"I'll be right back." He hit the floor and stumbled to the bathroom, trying to get a handle on the fact that he'd just had the most intense orgasm of his entire life. By the time he came back she had propped the pillows behind her back and was sitting upright in the bed with the covers over her lap. He slid in beside her and insinuated his head onto her chest. Was there anything better than looking down at the finest set of breasts on the planet?

"That was amazing," she said, threading her fingers through the hair at his temple.

"Yeah. It was. Thank you for being my horny neighbor."

She laughed and her tits jiggled enticingly. "You're welcome. Thank you for teaching me to talk like a trollop."

"A trollop?" He smiled and ran his fingers up and down her cleavage. "What do you teach, Prof—Shelly?"

She grabbed his hand and brought his fingers to her lips, kissing each one before she answered and Luke felt a stab below his left pectoral muscle. *Must have pulled something at the gym.* Yeah. Right.

"British Literature." She nipped at his thumb and his dick gave a surprising twitch.

"Don't you want to know what I do?" he asked, drawing his hand away and snaking it through her cleavage and down to her stomach. He laid his hand flat, simply loving the feel of her skin under his palm.

"I already do. Number four in the lineup of hot Hendersons. Built like a weightlifter, hung like a god. A mild mannered, extremely talented craftsman by day. By night, a well oiled sex machine. A man who doesn't discriminate by race...and now age. Or multiple births."

"Oh, come on," he moaned, letting the age comment slide as he rolled onto his back. "Can't a kid have one moment of sexual glory without it constantly coming back to bite him in the ass?"

"You're a legend. And you like having your ass bitten."

*Hell yes, I liked that.* "I wish Sammy or Matt would step up to the plate and do something that would make people forget about those triplets. God knows people in this town conveniently forget about all past indiscretions the minute you settle down. Jason fucked half the locals and every rich bitch with a Jag that rolled in each summer but no one remembers that anymore."

"Memories fade when you're in a carrot cake coma," she teased, snuggling against him in a manner Luke found totally comforting. "Your sister-in-law's baking skills could buy off the mob. I used to stop by her shop every Friday. Since the separation, I upped it to Mondays and Fridays. I completely blame her for the extra poundage on my posterior."

"I'll thank her tomorrow. I like your ass. I've got some of her oatmeal cookies downstairs. I'll grab us some later. If they're still here tomorrow Tom's girlfriend Tessa will totally wipe them out."

"Ah, the other older brother. And Tessa? Not Tessa from the book store?"

"One and the same."

"She's quite a character."

"Yeah, my brother seems to love her to pieces. I still can't believe he's getting married. Then Andy'll be the next one at the altar. If it weren't for him not wanting to upset Tom, I know damn well he and Vicky would be married already and on their way to Storkland, which is something I can't even fathom."

"Don't you want kids?"

"Not really. I'll love my nieces and nephews and spoil them rotten but I'm not planning on having kids of my own. My brothers are capable of expanding the family tree without my help."

"I don't have any siblings. You must love them very much."

"We have our moments, that's for sure. But there's nothing we wouldn't do for each other. I don't know if it's a guy thing or a family thing, but yeah, we love each other a lot. Our parents wouldn't have it any other way."

He ran his thumb over the bone at her elbow and tried to focus on the little pattern she was tracing around his navel. Some alien sensation that was blossoming in the middle of his chest shot straight to his brain and he was seeing images of laughing couples who looked way too familiar for comfort. He shook his head and slid his hand down her waist and over the curve of her ass. "How the hell did we get on this topic?"

"It's not your usual post-orgasmic conversation?"

"No. My usual post-orgasmic conversation segues straight into a second round of pre-orgasmic conversation."

She turned her head and placed a kiss on his cheek. He couldn't ignore the fact that his heart stumbled. *Shit.* That couldn't be good.

"Aren't you just full of yourself?" she chuckled, her breath tickling his chest.

"I am," he said, rolling to his side. "Wouldn't you like to be full of me too?"

"Do you have a lot of success with that line?" Her lips quirked in a way that forced Luke to smile back.

"It's worked on most of the other trollops."

Her teeth flashed as she laughed and Luke swooped in and kissed her until her laughter was gone and she'd wiggled herself against his semi-hard dick and wrapped her arm around his back.

"I wouldn't want to be a deviation from the norm, Scooter," she whispered.

"Too late, Professor. You already are."

\* \* \* \* \*

The sound of running water permeated Shelly's dream and she bolted upright in the bed. *His bed.* The bed of the oh-so-sexy man who apparently possessed enough stamina that he hadn't fallen into a doze after he'd made love to her a second time. Or was it three times? Did oral count? *Screw the former president from Arkansas — hell, yes it counts.*

Shelly plopped back onto the pillows and stared at the ceiling. She'd never been fucked that long. Or that slowly. She had thought he'd drawn out their first bout of lovemaking but it paled in comparison. Her pussy clenched at the memory of how he'd had her writhing...sobbing. Dear god. He probably thought she was an emotional wreck.

She rolled to her side and pulled his pillow to her nose and inhaled the scent of pure man. She needed a quick lesson in no-strings sex and a way to pretend his off-key singing wasn't tempting her to join him...and the protocol on post-coital bladder relief. She could easily hop back over into her own house and relieve herself but she didn't want to leave. Not yet. There'd be time for that in the morning, which was another four hours away, according to the bedside clock.

She eased out of the bed, contemplating what a man like Luke could accomplish in that amount of time, wondering if her nether regions could actually take any more. She tiptoed to the bathroom door and peeked in. The shower glass was steamy but she could make out his form. He had his hands above his head, flat against the tile, the spray of water hitting his upper back. He didn't appear to be moving. She glanced to the open door of the toilet area and hurried across the room and shut herself inside.

She sat there long after she'd relieved herself and still the water ran. *His hot water tank must be huge.* That random thought was enough to get her on her feet and turning toward the toilet. Her gaze stopped on the small trash can, the tied-off condom lying on top. She had a sudden vision of a mountain of discarded prophylactics with her body draped over the top of them in a Goreyesque swoon — two little black exes where her eyes had been, to mark the fact that Luke had fucked her to death.

"Possibly better than demise by chocolate," she muttered. She flushed the toilet and opened the door, sneaking toward the sink to quickly wash her hands.

"Mother*fuck*!"

The shower door crashed opened and Luke hopped out, his body dripping wet and looking utterly edible as he stared from her to the threshold of the doorway.

"Sorry," she said, spinning around and turning on the faucet since the damage was already done. She wasn't used to standing naked in anyone's bathroom but her own. She watched his reflection as he moved closer and her throat went dry at the look in his eyes. He shut the water off before she had a chance to wash her hands.

"I thought you were sleeping." His eyes gleamed as he walked up behind her and wrapped his arms around her waist, pulling her away from the sink and into his damp embrace.

"I woke up. I need to wash my hands."

"Running water…right here, honey." He picked her up, spun her around and walked them toward the shower.

"I'm a tub and candles kind of girl," she said, tilting her head to one side when he nuzzled her neck.

"Mmmm. Good to know. But I have something more alluring than a bubble bath."

"God, don't I know that," she admitted, snaking her hand between their bodies to brazenly stroke his soft cock.

"It's going to take a little time to get it back up, Professor."

"Well then, if you're not corralling me into the shower for another bout of mind-boggling sex, I assume this is a subtle hint that I'm harboring the distinct odor of mind-boggling sex."

"Are you kidding? If you hadn't milked every last drop of cum out of me, that musky smell would have your ass plastered against the shower door and my cock buried balls deep all over again."

"Then why am I here?" she asked.

He pulled her into the large stall and the spray from the multiple jets hit her square in the face. He adjusted the taller nozzles so they weren't pummeling her with water and she slicked her wet hair off her face. She felt the sudden prickle of water shooting against her inner thigh and opened her eyes.

"You're here because I'm a man of my word." He licked the water away from her neck as he moved behind her and brought his body flush with hers, guiding her hips to the side until the spray of water was teasing the soft skin above her pubic bone. He bent his knees, wrapped one beefy arm across her abdomen and the other around her waist, slowing raising her until the soft, pulsating jet cut through her curls, its final destination forcing her eyes wide open.

"How 'bout it, Professor? You ready for thirds?"

* * * * *

"Let me walk you home."

She had worried about the awkwardness that morning would bring. She shouldn't have. He was going to make that a non-issue the same way he did everything else that worried her — with his sense of humor and a sexy smile.

"I can manage," she laughed.

"I'm sorry I have to go. I really could cancel. Andy, above all others, would understand."

He'd told her she could stay in his bed. Wait for him to finish with his weekly run with his brother. He'd even tempted her with the promise of returning with a double mocha Frappuccino with extra whipped cream. She'd thought about that while he threw on his underwear and running shorts but she hadn't succumbed.

She should have been up and out of his room before his phone rang and his brother asked where the hell he was. But his X-rated shower massage had been followed by him proving he did indeed know how to spell the Latin word for oral sex. She smiled, the totally inappropriate Sesame Streetesque vision of "G" being the letter of the day drifting through her mind.

He led her onto the balcony and held her hand as she scooted over the partition and then brought her fingers to his lips and met her eyes.

"You're amazing, Shelly. I think somewhere between that first sip of wine and my self-control spinning into the outer realms of the universe, I forgot to tell you that. Last night was beyond memorable."

She'd expected a little 'that was fun' or 'see you around'. She didn't know how to respond. *Tell him the truth.* Right, and watch him dive off the balcony if her words came out sounding needy? *Honesty and openness.*

She pulled her fingers free and looked down, toying with the drawstrings of her pants. "I'm sure I don't have to tell you how special you made me feel."

He hooked two fingers under her chin and forced her to meet his bemused gaze. "I'm a man, honey. Tell me anyway."

"If I admitted you brought me more pleasure in one night then I've ever experienced, would that be enough?" she asked, watching the corner of his eyes crinkle.

"It's a great start."

"You really did make me realize that my love life sucks."

"Sucked...past tense now, Professor." He dug his fingers into her hair and pulled her lips closer.

She assumed they'd part as friends. There was absolutely nothing platonic in the way his gaze bore into hers.

"Anything else you've come to realize?" he asked, brushing her lips softly.

"Yes," she said, taking a step away before she crawled back over the partition and snaked her arms around his waist. "I need an updated shower unit."

He laughed then leaned over and placed four quick kisses over the bridge of her nose, his lips touching each one of her freckles. "I'll stop by Home Depot on my way back and get you an estimate."

\* \* \* \* \*

Shelly read the sentence in her student's thesis, *The Secret Empowerment of Women as It Pertains to the Wife of Bath's Tale*, a fourth time before tossing her red pen aside and walking from her study into her kitchen. The window over the sink was open and the breeze blew the sounds of lighthearted laughter into the room. She hadn't needed Luke to tell her his family rotated Sunday get-togethers. It seemed as if every other month he was entertaining. She moved closer to the window, stopping herself before she partook in a Gladys Kravitz moment. *Good grief!* Eavesdropping was unbecoming and far from healthy.

She doubted Luke would be mentioning her at all, let alone in the middle of a family gathering. Personally, she had no intention of telling anyone about their evening together. *God.* She needed to go online and find out the exact definition of a bobcat—no, that wasn't right—a cougar. She had no intention of becoming a label. No way. She'd let her friend Tilly hold that title.

In the clarity that came with Luke removing his distracting body from her presence, she recognized their liaison for what it truly was. A satiation of his apparent need and enlightenment to all the forms of sexual pleasure she'd been missing. If Howard's little intern rocked his world the way Luke had hers, she could almost understand why he'd ended their pathetic excuse of a marriage and bailed.

She grabbed a diet soda from the fridge and was about to take another run at Chaucer when a sharp knock sounded at the back door. She walked through the sunroom, shocked to find Luke on her doorstep.

"How are you feeling?" he asked loudly, pushing his way into the room. "Thought you might like something for dinner."

Shelly looked at him as if he'd lost his mind.

"Grilled chicken, redskin potatoes and amaretto cheesecake," he said, sliding the foil-covered plastic plates onto her kitchen table before yanking her into his arms and giving her a scorching-hot kiss that had her toes digging into the soles of her sandals. "Did you miss me?" he asked softly.

He nibbled his way to the shell of her ear and she squirmed in his arms.

"You've only been gone for six hours—how could I miss you?"

"That hurts. I couldn't quit thinking about you," he said, trying to tug her shirt downward and then giving up and pushing the fabric up and over her breasts. "Don't you have any shirts with buttons, Professor?"

He cupped her breasts and lightly ran his thumbs over her nipples. They immediately poked against the silky fabric of her bra. He pulled one cup down and wrapped his lips around the distended nub and sucked hard enough that the nerves running from her nipple to her pussy felt as if they constricted.

"Luke! Stop that." She twisted to the side and put herself in order. "You're insane."

"Yeah, I've come to that realization. My dick's been hard most of the day and when I finally got it to behave I saw images of you riding that shower spray and I got hard all over again."

She watched open mouthed as he leaned back and quickly unbuttoned his jeans.

"Even my whacky-ass family can't distract me. I've listened to stories about everything from imported teak nesting tables to the debate over vests versus cummerbunds but nothing's working."

"What are you doing?" For some reason she felt compelled to whisper. "Your folks are right next door."

"Haven't you ever had sex with your parents in close proximity?"

"No!"

"You should try it. It's exhilarating and they're the least of my worries. You're so not deserving of a quick fuck but I thought maybe I could use a little white lie and a home-cooked feast to tempt you into—"

"What? A quick, no-mess blowjob in my kitchen?"

"*Shit!* I was hoping you could just wrap your fingers around me and jack me off in the powder room sink but by no mess do you mean—"

She'd like to believe his words had caused the gush of wetness to dampen her panties but truth be told, every time she'd thought of him throughout the day she'd gotten a little wetter. She grabbed a dishtowel off the sink and thrust it into his hand as she backed him up against the archway.

"We'll try the coming in my mouth thing later. Maybe," she said, crouching before him.

"Oh shit. I might go off just thinking about that."

She looked up at his flushed face and smiled. He made her feel alive...and undeniably naughty. She opened her mouth and stuck out her tongue, then lowered her gaze to the hand he'd stuck in his pants.

"Luke...dude? Is everything—"

Luke had his hands wrapped around her arms and Shelly standing upright before she could think.


"Oooo-kaaay." His brother's voice was dripping with amusement as he stood on the ground and peered through the bottom of the screen door.

"Everything's fine," Luke said in a tone that was anything but fine. "Professor Latimer was just feeling a little lightheaded."

"Probably from that flu you said she had," Matt said.

Luke watched Shelly's eyebrows arch and he shrugged. He'd lied to get away from his family but he hadn't lied to her when he'd said he couldn't get her out of his mind. And it wasn't just his usual after-sex thoughts of how good things had been. He'd found himself wondering strange little things, like what her favorite food was and what her childhood had been like. And how she'd react if he told her he wanted her to spend this night and possibly quite a few others, in his bed.

"Luke?" Matt asked.

"What?" he replied, having lost the thread of the conversation.

"You think it's from the flu?"

"Probably."

"That sucks," Matt offered.

Luke watched Shelly turn her head to the door and look at his sibling.

"Call me crazy," Matt said with a shit-ass grin. "But I've always heard it works a lot better if the person who's feeling faint puts their head between their *own* knees."

*Oh christ.* "She's fine. I'll be home in a minute."

"A minute, huh?" His brother laughed. "There's something to shout from the rooftops."

He gave his brother a lengthy glare, shocked when he heard Shelly giggle.

"Oh my god," she said. "Are you all that funny?"

"Don't forget handsome," Matt said, walking up the stairs and opening the door.

"Get the hell out of here," Luke ordered.

"Relax, dude. It's not even your house. I'm Luke's amazingly suave, not-that-much-younger brother."

"I swear to christ, Matt—"

"I'm Shelly." She offered her hand and his brother shook it. Far too long for Luke's liking.

"I know who you are. My girlfriend swore you were the best teacher on campus."

"That's so kind. Tell her I appreciate that."

"I'd love to, except she's married to some financial planner and we just don't get it on like we used to." He sighed emphatically and gave Shelly a dejected look.

"You poor thing," Shelly crooned and Luke wondered how much it would cost to replace her door when he physically picked his brother up and hurled him through the screen.

"I'll survive," Matt said, placing his hand across his heart. "Somehow…some way—"

"Some other place," Luke added, spinning his brother around and giving him a push to the back.

"Right. Nice meeting you," he called over his shoulder as he walked down the stairs. "Should I tell everyone you're playing Florence Nightingale over here or what?"

"No. Just go."

He waited until he saw Matt's head disappear from view and followed Shelly back into the kitchen. "I'm sorry. This kind of shit happens all the time. Just usually to one of my other brothers. Not me."

"It's fine." She wrapped her arms around his neck and he smiled. From a physical standpoint, it was the first time she'd made the first move and he refrained from pulling her against him. He could tell she was worrying. He was becoming familiar with her little habit of biting her lip.

"Matt's not going to say a word, if that's what you're thinking."

245

"It crossed my mind."

"At some point you're going to have to tell people we're together."

"We're together? After one night?" Oh lord. She so needed a copy of *Post-Divorce Sex for Dummies.* "I'm having a hard time getting my mind around you wanting a relationship with someone my…someone like me."

"Hey," he slid his hands to her shoulders and gave her a gentle squeeze. "Don't backpedal on this age thing. I told you it doesn't mean a damn thing to me. Physically, I find you hotter than any woman I've ever seen. It's no lie that I love your body but there's a part of me that's equally attracted to the fact that you're as smart as you are sexy and another part that's pretty certain you won't feel the need to question my net worth or demand I choose whether your toes look better painted pink or red."

"Oh, please," Shelly said. "I couldn't care less."

"Then do me a favor and don't be concerned with the difference in our ages. Focus on the fact I want to be with you. And I know there's every chance you'll wake up tomorrow and say you want to see what it's like with someone else. That's fine. I've had years to figure out what it is I'm looking for. You haven't. But if you want me, even if it's just for now, let's run with it."

"Luke…I don't know. It's scary, you know?"

"No. I don't know. I've never committed myself to someone for twenty years. I have no idea how painful it is to lose love and security and then end up alone. To have to go out and start again. But I imagine the initial fears are no different than starting any new relationship. It takes time. So let's give this some time, okay?" He saw the indecision in her eyes and pushed her. "One month, Professor. Give it a month and see where we're at. That's all I'm asking."

He'd spoken straight from his heart—the one that was beating out of control while he waited for her reply. It hadn't just been the sex that had drawn him to her. He knew that this morning when he woke and found her curled up against his side as if she'd always belonged there. *Liar. You knew it from the minute she pointed her finger at you and told you to wait.* Deep down, once he peeled away the layers of her hurt, once her confidence shone through, she'd be the woman every man would want. Including him.

"Okay," she finally said and his knees nearly buckled. "One month it is."

# Chapter Four

ᔆᔉ

Shelly smiled as she walked down the poster-lined corridor that led to her small university office. She'd been doing a lot of grinning over the past three weeks. It was utterly amazing how having a hot, virile male in her bed made her existence beyond bearable.

"*Bonjour, Professeur* Latimer."

"Professor Waters," Shelly said, inclining her head to the elderly teacher whose finely etched good looks had a great deal to do with all four levels of his French classes being filled semester after semester.

"*Magnifique*," he said as they squeezed past each other. "Michelle, *ma beauté*. You've done something different. Something with your hair?"

"*Non, monsieur*, I have not."

"Are you certain?" he pressed.

"Absolutely." Shelly smiled and arched a brow. The only thing she'd done was learn to take all of Luke's compliments to heart. Her self-confidence had increased to the point that, for the first time in many years, she actually felt sexy.

"It is amazing. You look, as the students like to say, quite hot."

She laughed and waved at him over her shoulder. He had always been jovial but she had the uncanny suspicion he was checking out her ass. "Thank you, Professor. You're looking rather smokin' yourself."

"*Illusoire!*" She heard his chuckle follow him down the hall.

Delusional? Maybe she was. There were moments when she felt that way…little pockets of time where she actually had to pinch herself to determine if she was dreaming. She was happier than she'd been in forever. Ever-so slowly she was beginning to realize how foolish she had been in thinking a span of ten years was a horrific age gap.

Shelly had been brave enough after the first week of their relationship to ask Luke if he'd told anyone about them and she'd been shocked when he said he had. By the second week, with no gracious way of refusing his mother's offer when they'd run into her at the local butcher's, she had found herself invited to Sunday dinner.

She'd been sweating bullets when she walked through the door of his parents' house. She'd done the calculations. A mere fifteen years separated her from his folks. Either the contagiously happy couple had put up a good front or they truly didn't care. Neither did his siblings, nor their partners.

Their acceptance had been a relief yet, at the same time, totally baffling. She had expected to be grilled, tested perhaps. In contrast, someone made sure she was drawn into every conversation. Family stories about Luke were freely shared until she was doubled over with laughter and he was blushing so adorably she wanted to crawl into his lap and simply kiss him. And she got the vibe that if she'd done that, no one would have batted an eyelash.

That entire day had gone a long way in helping her see that maybe society wasn't as judgmental as she imagined but she'd continued to keep quiet about their relationship to all except her best friend Tilly, whom she had called that first Sunday as she was downing the piece of cheesecake Luke had brought to her door. She'd spilled it all.

Then, two days ago she had, as Luke liked to say, "grown a pair" and shared the news with her two closest colleagues. They'd been horrified, until they found out he wasn't a student and then all stigma dissolved. They had emailed her off and on during the day and when the snippets of info she was willing to share weren't enough, they dragged her out to dinner with them for further interrogation.

By the time she got home, ready to tell Luke about her older woman-younger man breakthrough, he was sprawled naked, facedown on her bed with the sports channel blaring and a biography of Oscar Wilde that she knew came off her bookshelf lying open on the nightstand.

Pulling her key ring from her purse, she shook her head at the memory. Day by day they were finding out all the little things they had in common and all the ways they were different. And that was fine. He wasn't trying to change her. He didn't care that her car had a layer of dust on it while his truck sparkled. Or that she had to re-arrange the top shelf of her dishwasher as fast as he put the glasses where he thought they should go.

She looked at the sign-up sheet taped to her door and unlocked her office. She had fifteen minutes to spare before a student whose handwriting she couldn't read would show up for fifteen minutes of the best advice she could offer. She tossed her book bag next to her desk and pulled out a stack of final papers and started grading them. She'd made it through two before she heard the light tapping at her door.

"Come in. I'll be done in a—Luke?"

"Hey, Professor. I brought you a mocha frap. Thought it might tempt you more than a piece of fruit. That whole apple thing is way overdone."

She stared at him and wondered when she'd ever get over the little flutter of excitement that shot through her every time he looked at her with that innocent expression—the one that turned smoldering hot before she knew what was happening.

"What are you doing here? I've got a student signed up–"

"Yeah. I know." He set the coffee on her desk and leaned back against the door until it clicked closed.

He pushed in the lock and her mouth went dry.

"That would be me."

"You?"

"Mmm-hmm." He walked around her desk and rolled her chair backward, bracing his hands on the arms and leaning forward until his head touched hers. "I've got fifteen minutes, right?"

His fingers moved to the buttons of her silk blouse and he popped them free before she could answer.

"Luke—"

"I never got to have forbidden relations with a teacher," he said innocently, dexterously unsnapping the front of her bra and palming her breasts as they tumbled free.

"And you're not going to now," she said, pushing his hands away.

"Shelly," he said in a tone usually used on children. "You've already wasted a half minute of my collegiate fantasy time."

"My office hours aren't for sex." The moment the words left her mouth she knew that's exactly what she was going to get and her pussy leaked at the very thought. But she still had to show some semblance of reason. "You don't see me storming into your workshop and plopping my fanny on that flat part of your anvil—"

"It's called the face—"

"Begging you to sink your cock into me, do you?" she asked.

"Jesus." He closed his eyes and shook his head. "Bring that wet dream to life! Shit, now there are two faces I can imagine you straddling. I might never be able to work another piece of iron without my dick getting hard. I'll be too preoccupied thinking of something else I enjoy pounding."

"Oh my god. You're incorrigible."

"If by that you mean horny—a minute's already up—then yes, I'm incorrigible. Really, really incorrigible. And you love it."

Shelly threw her arms in the air and then gripped the arms of her chair as it jerked forward. He hauled her ass to the edge of the seat and dropped to his knees.

"I've wanted you, Professor Latimer, since the moment you walked into the auditorium and wrote your name on the board." He ran his hands up the backs of her bare legs and Shelly shifted in her seat. His palms were warm and rough. "Are you wearing panties...or did you take them off when you saw I needed an appointment with you?"

"Of course I'm wearing—"

He grabbed the edges of her lacy underwear and yanked them off her hips and down her legs.

"Pull your skirt up and let me see. Hurry," he ordered.

The urgency in his voice made her body clench. She grabbed two handfuls of gauzy fabric and did as he commanded.

"I knew it," he said, placing his palms against her inner thighs and spreading her wide. "I knew your pussy would be dripping...crying for my touch. Can I taste you, Professor?"

If she had a shred of willpower she would tell him no...think of some sexy little scenario that would turn the tables on him. But with his eyes moving from her pussy to her breasts and down again, that wasn't about to happen.

"Yes," she said in a hoarse whisper. She felt the wetness rolling toward the crack of her ass and she slid a little closer toward him.

"Word on campus is you don't like when guys go down on you." He pressed his thumb against the wetness between her asshole and her opening and stroked firmly upward until he hovered over her clit.

"Talk on campus is wrong." She arched her back and groaned when he touched her. Words she never imagined herself saying whispered through the room. "Make me come, Luke...and I'll up you a letter grade."

"Note to self—"

He removed his hand and blew a fine stream of cool air against her aching nub and she whimpered softly.

"Somebody likes to role-play. If I make you come twice will you use that as extra credit?"

His hot, wet tongue moved against her and she dug her nails into the chair and didn't say another word. He licked her in long strokes that went on forever and then tiny little licks that seemed to come too fast. He nibbled and soothed the tiny bites with the flat of his tongue, working on the pillowy flesh of her labia until her hips started rocking.

"Oh my god. I love when you lick me like that."

"I never imagined you'd talk dirty, Professor Latimer…or be so demanding."

"I had a great teacher," she gasped, feeling the pressure building between her thighs.

He tensed his tongue and thrust in and out of her pussy until she slid her ass completely off the seat, thighs quivering as he held her up with his hands and started the tiny little flicks that they'd both learned would quickly drive her right over the edge.

He wasn't backing off as he usually did. His caresses were insistent, spiraling her straight to the peak.

"Oh god, Luke." She leaned forward, nearly doubling over in the chair as the orgasm started. "I'm going to come…oh god…right now."

"Shhhhh," he whispered against her pussy, placing his hand over her mouth. He closed his lips over her clit and she came, groaning into his palm and rolling her hips as the spasms hit.

She threw her head back, intent on catching her breath but he grabbed her arms above her elbows and pulled her out of the chair.

"My turn," he said, backing her up against the filing cabinet. He pulled her skirt up and pressed her ass against the cold metal, causing gooseflesh to rise.

She looked down, shocked to find his pants unzipped and a condom already in place. "How is god's name—"

"You weren't paying attention, were you Professor?" He hooked his elbow under her knee and raised her leg high. He bent his knees and she felt the tip of his shaft part her pussy lips and ease into her wet heat.

He thrust into her, hard and deep, and her gasp was drowned out by the sound of the filing cabinet hitting the wall.

"You've got my attention now," she said, finding it difficult to catch her breath against the sensation of being unbearably full.

"Do I?" he asked, thrusting again.

She looked up and found him staring at her with such a look of desire she didn't trust herself to speak.

"Answer me, Professor." His cock rocked into her again.

"Yes."

He grabbed the cheeks of her ass and held her up as if she didn't weigh an ounce and started stroking into her in a deep, steady rhythm that had her insides shaking within seconds.

She moaned, burying her face against his neck as his thrusts continued to push her against the metal. "Faster, Luke...oh shit. Harder."

"Faster *and* harder? You sure that's how you want it?"

"Yes...god yes."

He pumped into her with a force that would have been frightening if she hadn't been on the verge of coming again. Her pussy was throbbing and she knew he could feel every little squeeze.

"God, Shelly. I love when you're ready to go. Your pussy huggin' my cock, your little grunts making me so fuckin' hot I can't stand it." He shifted his head and captured a nipple between his lips.

She barely managed not to scream at the coil of pleasure that roiled through her. She pushed her breasts together and held them high for him, no longer able to tell him what she wanted…but he knew.

He growled his appreciation and used his teeth to graze her nipples as he thrust four more times and made her explode, following in her wake with a loud, long moan that couldn't be mistaken for anything but an extremely satisfied male.

"So, Professor," he said a short time later when their breathing had returned to normal. "Did my GPA just hit the roof?"

She smiled against his skin and turned her head and licked a salty little trail of moisture from his neck. "It *and* me. That was incredible," she said, lowering her legs to the floor. "I might never be able to walk again."

"I know I can forgo the upper body workout at the gym later," he teased, sucking her bottom lip into his mouth as he eased out of her. He grabbed a handful of tissues from the box on her desk and masterfully pulled off the condom, rolled it up and tossed it in her trash.

"Is that a veiled attempt at telling me I need to lose weight?" She watched him stalk around her desk and she slumped against the wall.

"Hell no! You know by now I love each and every one of those curves," he said, walking back to her side and crouching at her feet. He tapped the back of her calf and held her panties open as she put one foot and then the other in the leg holes. He stood, pulling her undies up above her knees. "You take it from here, honey. If I go near your pussy again I'm going to want to bend you over the desk and surprise you with the extent of my literary knowledge."

"And what could you show me that I don't already know?" she asked, pulling up her panties and giving him a quick kiss as she did. "From a literary standpoint, that is."

"I could show you a different meaning of the importance of being earnest...as it pertains to my cock getting lubed and sliding, nice and slow, between the cheeks of your fine ass."

He wiggled his eyebrows and she broke into laughter.

"I think the esteemed Mr. Wilde would approve," she said, righting her clothing while watching him tuck his cock away. *Oh, yes. Oscar would most definitely have approved.*

"My fifteen minutes are just about up and I've got a huge knob project I need to finish for Jason's sister-in-law," he said. "I've got a dozen more to forge and then they all need polished."

Her small hands grabbed as much of his massive biceps as possible. "I'd be more than happy to help polish your knobs," she teased.

He looked down into her eyes and took her chin between thumb and forefinger and kissed her softly on the lips as he opened the door. "Don't tempt me, Professor. There's nothing finer than the way you suck my dick."

Shelly watched him leave and would have slid down the wall into a contented heap if she hadn't heard applause and one sharp, high-pitched whistle.

She walked into the corridor in time to see various colleagues from the department standing in their doorways clapping. She watched, stunned, as the Women's Studies advisor stuck her hand out and gave Luke a low five before meeting Shelly's gaze and offering a double thumbs-up.

Her cheeks flamed but she bit her lip to keep from smiling.

"*Bravo, ma petite,*" Professor Waters grinned at her from his office across the hall. "*Bravo.*"

Shelly heard Luke's truck long before he pulled into his driveway. He had a set of dual exhausts that heralded his arrival from a half block away and she walked toward her front door, intent on kissing him before he went inside and took his shower. She loved when he was squeaky clean but she had discovered the unique blend of man and sweat that he carried after a day of work completely turned her on.

She watched him slide out of the truck and nearly clapped her hands when she saw the familiar lime green box that contained his sister-in-law's baked goods. He was always good for dessert. *Now that's an understatement, Professor!* He had taken the first step onto the brick walkway when a car squealed to a halt.

"Hey, Henderson...nice ass." The loud, feminine voice was followed by a round of giggles. A tall, lithe woman jumped over the back door of the ruby red convertible, jogged up to Luke and gave him a hug that lasted longer than Shelly thought appropriate. *Lighten up, Professor. She's a kid.*

She wasn't certain at what point over the past three weeks his voice had started insinuating itself into her head but she was having a hard time buying that last statement. The *kid* was gorgeous and when Luke leaned down, saying something that made her tilt her head back and howl with laughter, Shelly felt her chest tighten. She watched as they talked, Luke's head nodding and the woman's hands and arms moving to and fro.

He walked her slowly back to the car and she could tell introductions were being made then a number being entered in her cell phone. By the time she thought about going back into the kitchen and pretending she hadn't seen a thing the car was driving away and Luke was halfway up the stairs when he noticed her in the doorway.

"Hey, honey." He gave her his usual grin as he stepped onto the porch and handed her the box. "I wish had known you were there. I'd have introduced you to Reggie."

"Old girlfriend?" she asked in an overly light tone. She'd never felt a shred of jealousy where her ex was concerned and he was an attractive man. Not jaw-dropping like Luke but a head turner. She had thought the niggling doubt that Luke might one day look at a piece of firm, hot young ass and simply walk away without a backward glance was in the past. Apparently not.

"No, Double-O-Seven," he said, his smile widening. He clearly knew she'd been covertly watching. "That was Regina Lawrence. Moved in next door to Mom and Dad when the twins were in high school. She was Sam's best friend for years. Nearly lived at our place. She went out west for some higher education and a few career choices that apparently didn't work out. Anyhow, she's back in town for the summer and I was giving her Sammy's number. He's going to shit his pants when he sees her. I'm going to wash up then I'll be right over."

He slid one finger down her breastbone and caught the V of her sweater along with the center of her bra and tugged her forward. "Unless you want to join me...scrub my back." His finger shifted in her cleavage, the simple touch sending jolts of desire through her and pushed any thoughts of jealousy aside.

Over the weeks, Shelly had learned a smidgen of control where he was concerned. At the moment, she could refrain from the temptation of him driving into her until she was moaning his name. Barely...and only because she knew that would be his mission as soon as dinner was over and dishes were done.

"You'll have to go it alone. I've got a rib roast than needs to come out of the oven and rest."

"You're the tempter, Shelly." He gave her a smoldering head-to-toe look. "My dick's already hard and I'm seriously considering just doing you right here on the front stoop."

"Stop that." She laughed, giving him a flat-handed push toward his front door. "There are kids working their way up and down the street selling god knows what. I barely avoided a probationary warning from our last bout of nearly public sex. I don't need the parent-teacher club accusing me of corrupting the moral fiber of our youth."

"I'll go," he said, hanging his head in mock dejection as he shuffled to his door. "As long as you promise to continue to corrupt the moral fiber of this youth…somewhere after dinner and before the white chocolate napoleons."

\* \* \* \* \*

Twenty minutes later the doorbell sounded three times in quick succession. She hadn't locked the door. Or maybe she had accidentally. "Hang on," she called, noticing the lock wasn't thrown.

"Why didn't you use your key?" she asked, jerking the door open.

"Because I don't have one anymore, Michelle."

She stared into her ex-husband's face and gripped the doorknob tightly.

"May I come in?" He started to move and she placed her arm against the door frame and blocked his path.

"No. You cannot come in."

"I see," he said.

She noticed the tiny tic at the inner corner of his left eye, a tell-tale sign that the man who rarely lost his temper was on the verge of doing just that.

"Are you *entertaining*?" the word dripped insinuation.

"Why are you here, Howard?" She heard the soft creak of Luke's front door and when the screen didn't open she knew he was listening.

"To give you some sound advice, Michelle."

"You are the last man on the surface of the earth I need advice from."

"Oh really? You think your Chippendale wannabe is a paragon of guidance? I knew my leaving would affect you but I never imagined you'd become so irresponsible."

He put his hands on his hips in the familiar manner that always reminded her of an impudent child. "You're the talk of the university, Michelle. Word reached me about your office screwfest, probably before he even made it back to the parking lot and climbed into that phallic-enhancing monstrosity sitting in his driveway. How does it make you feel to know that all our colleagues bit-and-pieced together the story behind all the thuds and groans and thumps?"

She watched his neck flush and leaned her shoulder against the doorjamb. "Good news always travels fast," she deadpanned.

"Smugness doesn't become you. It never did."

"Go away, Howard."

"It doesn't bother you that people think this is some sort retribution for my relationship with Amber."

"All that's bothering me at the moment is you."

"Go ahead, Michelle. Be flippant." He dropped his chin and looked over the top of his dark-framed glasses. "Do you realize you're a laughingstock? Are a few minutes of having his cock pounding into you worth your reputation? Do you get some thrill from the fact that he's a common laborer and the only thing you have to talk about is whether you want him to fuck you on your desk or against the white board? You could have told me years ago that you were a closet exhibitionist, that all it took was a layer of grime covering my hands to get you to spread your legs without complaint."

Shelly didn't say a word. She didn't like the way the anger seeping into her soul was being forced to share a spot with the beginnings of self-doubt. *Do not let him push those buttons. Not again.* She had convinced herself that Luke was most definitely her reward for a life of penance with a man who never really cared about her feelings or truly understood her. But quicker than a snap of her fingers, Howard's words made what she and Luke had shared seem suddenly tawdry, as if she had made a terrible error in judgment.

"You know what, Michelle? Who cares? I don't, though it's still my last name people are going to hear while the gossip mongers are hard at work. If you want to play the whore for the first guy who takes pity on you, have at it, darling."

Luke's screen door rocked back on its hinges, cracking against the wooden siding so sharply that both she and Howard jumped. Luke stepped onto the porch and with slow, measured movements brought his big body to within two feet of Howard's.

"Mr. Latimer," Luke said, his tone clipped, his eyes icy.

"It's *Doctor* Latimer," Howard corrected, raising his chin in an arrogant way that proved totally ineffective against Luke's towering height.

"Whatever," Luke said, purposely ignoring him. He snaked a hand around Shelly's waist and she tried not to stiffen at the accusing gaze Howard was giving them. A tiny burst of air whooshed past her lips when Luke pulled her tight against his side.

"Mmmm," he said, sticking his nose in her hair and running it along the shell of her ear. "You smell good enough to eat. But let's start with a kiss," he whispered and then trapped her face between his hands and kissed her as if he hadn't seen her in a month.

Her emotions teetered between annoyance and longing. Had they been alone, she'd have thought nothing of his caress. But with her ex an arm's length away and Luke knowing that Howard could hear every whispered word, the blatant display of masculine possession was enough to set her on edge.

"Could you be more juvenile?" Howard said in a disgusted tone, crossing his arms over his slight chest.

"Probably," Luke said. He draped his arm casually over her shoulder and gave Howard a knowing look. "I could get caught parking at the levy at two in the morning and have the cops find a Fourth Avenue hooker trying to give my limp dick the breath of life."

Shelly looked at Howard's suddenly pale face. She shared his shock.

"Does your girlfriend know? Rumor has it that happened less than a month ago. If anyone's acting juvenile...I don't know, man. You want to be the pot or the kettle?"

"I don't concern myself with innuendo or veiled threats."

Shelly watched them glare at each other and the silence stretched.

"Well how about not-so-veiled threats?" Luke asked, his voice getting dangerously low. "Get your pansy ass off this porch, Howie. And don't you ever...*ever*...talk to her like that again unless you want to see what else I can do with my grimy hands."

"God, Michelle. I can't believe this is what attracts you now. Before long you'll be getting matching tattoos and hanging out at the local pool hall."

She opened her mouth to respond but Luke interrupted.

"At least that's legal. We won't be dodging arrest or paying a thousand dollar fine for a little ink and the occasional sinking of the cue ball."

"You're a cocky bastard, aren't you?" Howard said, taking a step back. "I hope you enjoy whatever she's giving you now, because I can guarantee it's not going to last."

"And you," Howard glanced at Shelly with a look of pure abhorrence before walking down the stairs and calling over his shoulder. "Enjoy your Anne Bancroft moment, Michelle, because once he gets bored with you and trades you in for his usual pussy *du jour*, then you will be well and truly fucked, my dear."

\* \* \* \* \*

Shelly took another bite of the tenderloin and chewed thoughtfully, unable to taste the perfectly cooked meat. She and Luke had tried making small talk but the silence had stretched to the point that it might as well have been a roar.

He tossed his fork onto his plate and the clatter made her look up. "Are you pissed that I kissed you in front of him?" Luke asked, studying her face.

"Yes." It had been pretty Neanderthal but that wasn't what bothered her the most. "Why didn't you tell me about him and the hooker?" she asked.

"I didn't think it was that big of a deal, plus I heard it straight from a trooper who had already received the word the whole thing wasn't to be publicized. Apparently your ex has friends in high places."

"Why did the officer tell you? How did he know you'd be interested?" Shelly asked. She stared at him, trying to keep the accusation from her eyes.

"He'd heard I was seeing you. Thought if the shit hit the fan I'd like a heads up.

"So you could protect me from yet another blow where Howard is concerned."

"Something like that."

"Is there anyone you haven't told about us?" she asked, the tone of her voice rising.

"Unlike you, Shelly, I'm not ashamed that we're together."

"That's so far from the truth."

"Bullshit! It's taken you all this time to tell a handful of your friends and now that your peers know, you're getting all pissy with me."

"I'm not getting pissy and I'm not ashamed."

"Well that's the vibe I'm getting now. I should have realized it before but it came through loud and clear when your ex was spouting all his lunatic opinions and you did absolutely nothing but listen to his shit."

"Why would I argue with Howard over something that's none of his concern?"

"Maybe so you could tell him that his less-than-subtle mind fuck wasn't going to work. That you wouldn't let him put you right back in the center of doubt where we're concerned."

"Lower your voice, Luke. I'm not about to sit here and have you yell at me."

"Yell at you? This is far from yelling."

"Howard never raised his voice to me."

"Maybe that's because Howard never really cared for you," Luke said, his voice dropping in pitch. "I've busted my ass these past weeks trying to undo the damage that cocksucker did to your psyche."

Shelly's entire body went cold. It was just as she'd thought—the pity factor revealed.

"I didn't realize you thought I was so hopelessly fucked up." She pushed her chair back and stalked out of the kitchen, heading toward the front room, hoping she could reach the stairs that led to her bedroom before the dam of emotion she was trying to hold in place broke free.

"I didn't say that," he replied, following in her wake.

"You didn't have to. I might be a jumble of low self-esteem but my intelligence is the one thing I'm pretty confident of."

"Really? Well, you're acting pretty damn stupid right now."

"*What?*" She spun around, unable to believe his words.

"You heard me," he said, stuffing his hands in his front pockets. "You're not even trying to see the big picture, Shelly. Take off the fuckin' blinders."

She watched his features, drawn tight with anger, and felt the ache in her heart implode. This was exactly what she had feared, the moment she'd known was bound to come.

"I think you should leave," she said, clenching her jaw to keep her emotions at bay.

"Leave? Just like that? No more talking?" He sounded totally surprised and she walked slowly to the front door.

"I think we've said enough." She grabbed the knob and pulled the door open.

"I'm giving you my opinion and you just fuckin' decide when the conversation's over? You didn't shut old Howie down mid-thought. I wish the hell you had."

"This isn't going to work, Luke."

He walked forward and stood before her, toe-to-toe, not saying a word until she looked up and into his eyes. She saw it all, everything he was feeling. Shock, hurt and a look that closely resembled desperation.

"Don't do this, Shelly." He reached for her shoulders and she backed away. If he touched her she'd crumble—physically and emotionally. He'd affected way more than just her body.

"Just leave, Luke. Just go."

# Chapter Five

ഇ

"What are you doing here?" Tom's voice was loud and sharp and Luke pulled his body out of the slumped position it had drifted into and sat up straighter in the recliner.

"Drinking all your beer. What time is it?"

"It's eleven forty-five. When did you get here?"

"Right after dinner." Luke watched his eldest brother take in the number of empty beer bottles on the coffee and end tables and knew he was calculating. "Where've you been, bro? Wait, don't tell me. You should have taken a shower after banging your beloved. Her scent's a little stronger than I remember," Luke said, purposely ignoring the long-silent understanding that the night they could have possibly shared Tom's now fiancée would never be discussed.

"Are you trying to make me beat the shit out of you?" Tom asked, plopping down in the matching recliner.

"Actually...yes. I'm looking for a thorough thrashing and thought 'which one of my brothers could help me out?' Andy's too laid back, Jason's the king of the two-fingers-to-the-chest jab. What the fuck good would that do me? Matt and Sammy aren't even an option because with their twin-lepathy they could join forces and probably kill me, and I'm not looking to be dead, just numbed to the point of I-don't-give-a-fuck. So, who better than Tommy Boy to help me out? You nearly choked me to death on that 'night that won't be mentioned'. I'm pretty certain you're the sibling for the job."

"What the hell did you do, Luke?"

"I fucked up."

"You always fuck up."

"Fuckin' right," Luke admitted, trying to snag a beer. Once…twice…a third time.

"Give me that," Tom said and Luke watched the bottle move far from his reach. "What's up?"

"I told her she was stupid."

"Who?"

"The Professor. Shelly."

"Christ, you are a dumbass. What's she got, like a dozen degrees?"

"Yeah. One in everything except reality."

"Is that a reality forged from copious quantities of Labatt Blue?"

"No. It's the reality of her not being smart enough to realize what we have going is special. That it doesn't have a fuckin' thing to do with age and it's not as simple as two consenting adults scratching an itch."

"You sure about that? 'Cause I know that's how it's been with nearly every woman you've hooked up with over the past…what…eighteen years?"

Luke sat and gave that some thought. Tom was right. But he didn't want to admit it.

"Don't make me out to be some sort of prick. That shit works both ways, Tommy. You haven't been gone out of the game so long that you don't remember what those chicks are like, how they've changed."

"I know what you're saying. But you fucked them and left them, pal. We all did. You've just had that epiphany of realizing what a worthless horn dog you were."

"Epiphany?"

"Yeah, the one brought on by finally being with someone who's turned the tables on you," Tom said. "It's fuckin' scary, huh, pal?"

"Petrifying," Luke admitted softly. "It's never been like this with anyone else."

"You need to tell her that, dumbass."

Luke sat and stared at his brother's amused face. He didn't see a damn thing remotely funny.

"I can't tell her that. She's fresh off the divorce. She's not ready for another round of commitment and I would never want to pressure her."

"You don't know that. Maybe she just needs a little indication on your part that you're content to be with her and no one else. That you aren't looking to possess her. Strong women don't like that shit."

Luke snorted. "Fuck up number two. Her asshole ex-husband showed up and got her thinking I'm going to dump her for some young ditz and that she's making a fool out of herself for being with a younger guy and I sort of went all Flintstones on her."

"Shit."

"Yeah. Marked my territory with a big wet one, brought his puny dick into the equation and threatened to go after him with my bare hands."

"You are one pathetic piece of work *and* you're a chickenshit."

"Fuck you, Tom."

"No. Fuck you. And get your head out of your ass before it's too late."

"You're supposed to be imparting some words of comfort and wisdom, big brother."

"I'm trying, shit for brains. Open up your ears and listen."

"How the hell am I going to fix this? I'm not the perfect man. Not like you and Jay and Andy—"

"We're far from perfect, especially where our women are concerned. You don't have a freakin' clue."

"No? Well I know I want what you fuckers have. What Mom and Dad have," he said, clearing his throat when it cracked with emotion. "Is that too fuckin' much to ask?"

"I swear to god, Luke. If you start crying, I'm going to beat you sober." Luke looked at his brother and saw his eyes turning misty.

"Christ, Tommy," Luke said on a low moan, pushing his hands through his hair, pulling so tight his scalp hurt. "I love her."

"I know you do, you stupid fuck."

"One month and I don't even want to think about being without her."

"What makes you think you have to?"

"She doesn't want to see me."

"Good thing," Tom laughed. "Cause you look like shit."

"She all but told me to go fuck myself," Luke admitted, pushing the footrest of the recliner closed.

"And you, the brother who never hesitated to tell us to go for what we wanted, are just going to curl into a ball and lick your fuckin' wounds?"

"What else can I do?" Luke said, watching Tom get up.

"Right now?" Tom offered Luke a hand and helped him to his feet. "You're going to head toward the guest room and spend the night. We'll figure it out tomorrow when your head's clear."

"Thanks, man." Luke closed his eyes and fought to swallow the lump in his throat. "I owe you."

"No you don't, asshole. We're even."

Tom pulled him forward and gave him a brotherly hug, thumping his back before letting him go. "If it weren't for you making that play for Tessa, then passing out when you did, we might have never gotten together."

Luke made his way down the hall and staggered into the bedroom, Tom close behind. "That's bullshit, Tommy. I predicted you were the one she lusted after all along."

"You did at that, Nostradamus."

Luke pulled his shirt over his head and tossed it onto a chair. He unzipped his pants and let them fall to the floor, his mind racing.

"You and Tessa going to have kids?"

"It's a fuckin' scary thought, but yeah. We'll give it a go sometime down the road."

"Shelly can't have kids. They tried, did the testing, didn't use any sort of contraception."

"You guys have already talked about this shit?" Tom asked, picking up his jeans and tossing them over the shirt.

"It came up during one of many condom discussions." He plopped down on top of the comforter and pulled the lightweight blanket at the bottom of the bed over his body. "Jason was a great teacher when it came to responsibility and protection, wasn't he?"

"Yeah. Trojan Man has nothing on him," Tom laughed.

"She begs me to ride bare," Luke said, watching the smile slide from Tom's face. "I haven't…but I sure as fuck want to. She swears it'll be fine. What do you think?"

"Jesus, why are you asking me?"

"Because you've never steered me wrong. Not once," Luke said softly.

"She's definitely not what you're used to."

"That's what I love about her most," Luke admitted.

"She's not out fuckin' around," Tom said.

"One guy the last twenty years," Luke replied.

"She's not looking to trap you."

"No fuckin' way. She's her own person. Through and through," Luke said.

"If there isn't any risk," Tom said, looking him square in the eye. "You ought to give her what she wants."

His lids were heavy and he fought to stay awake and since Tom was being so helpful, maybe ask another question. "But what if I've got some sort of extra-potent sperm?"

"Christ, you are fuckin' gone," Tom replied. "Years of being the one all the girls wanted has dulled your cognitive skills, asswipe. Do you honestly believe you're so goddamn special you possess some form of miracle jizz?"

When he said it like that it sounded pretty ridiculous. "Maybe."

Tom laughed and Luke gave him a little smile as he teetered on the brink of slumber. But he heard Tom's final words, delivered in a tone that was pure brotherly comfort.

"Go to sleep, super dick. We'll talk in the morning."

\* \* \* \* \*

"C'mon, sleepy-time Shelly. Up and at 'em, girlie."

Shelly moaned, pulling a pillow over her head, wondering what had compelled her to ever give her best friend a key to the house. "Shut those freakin' blinds, Tilly."

"No way, birthday babe. Get your fanny up and in the shower. The self-imposed Howard Hughes act is over. Starting now."

"Fuck you."

"Oh real nice, Professor Latimer. Wouldn't your students just like to know the extent of your knowledge of the English language?"

"Leave me alone. If I want to wallow in my own stench, I should be allowed."

"Oh, boo-hoo."

"Go home, Tilly."

"Not going to happen. I've put too much time and effort into making this the happiest forty-fifth birthday a woman could ever hope for. Now get up and get washed. It's two

271

o'clock in the afternoon and the party starts in less than five hours. We need to decorate and hit the market."

"Why do you do these things?" Shelly groaned, rolling out of the bed and heading to the bathroom. There was no use arguing with the woman.

"Because you're my best friend and I care a great deal about your happiness and I'm probably not the only one."

"Stop, that wasn't even a decent segue."

"Fine. Just get in the damn shower and make yourself presentable in case tall, blond and dreamy shows up."

"That's not going to happen."

"Why? Because you're hiding in your room and can't hear if the doorbell rings?"

Tilly was partially correct but Shelly wasn't about to admit that fact. She'd convinced herself she had taken two sick days because of some viral infection had ravished her system. She was still trying to figure out an explanation of how it had hit her heart instead of her stomach.

"Because that was three days ago and I told him to leave."

"And he did. A man who listens — now there's an oddity."

"You're coming to his defense?" Shelly couldn't believe it.

"Didn't it feel good when he came to your defense?"

"No."

"Your heart didn't just surge a little when he got all possessive?"

"No."

"Liar."

"Real men don't threaten to kick someone's ass, Tilly."

"Passionate ones do. What real men don't do is undermine their ex-wife's happiness. They don't fall back on the same mentally abusive ploys they used for years to make her think she's deficient in one way or another and they don't throw caustic remarks over their shoulders as they walk away. That's the shit cowards are made of."

"You'll never understand, Tilly," Shelly said dejectedly, plopping down on the edge of the tub.

"How many times have you uttered those words to me over the past eighteen years?" she asked, perching alongside Shelly and taking her hand. "Give me your hypothesis and let me prove it or dispel it."

"Spoken like a true Physics teacher," Shelly mumbled. Tilly sat patiently waiting and Shelly said, "He could have any woman he wants."

"And he's told you he wants you."

"Look at me, Tilly!" Shelly yelled, spreading her arms wide.

Tilly swatted her arms down. "No! You look at you, you idiot. What are you worried about, a few little wrinkles? Tough shit. They make lift serums for that or haven't you walked past a cosmetic counter in the last four years? Your skin is all but flawless, your hair has enough body you don't have to do a damn thing with it and you're not going to need collagen injections in those made-to-suck-dick lips anytime soon.

"And don't you dare say a word about him finding something wrong with your body. You made the mistake of talking to me the day after he first screwed you into the magical land of multiple orgasms and just about every time since. You've already told me how he loves the fact he can't get his giant hands around your boobs, despite the fact he tries and tries. And any man who truly didn't love the width of your ass wouldn't wax poetic about it every time he's had you on all fours.

"So you don't have a twenty-six inch waist. When you're our age—unless you're committed to worshiping at the altar of Precor—who the hell does?"

She stopped for breath and Shelly wrenched the conversation from her grasp and blurted the truth. "I don't want to make another mistake."

"A *mistake*? You're kidding me? Not being with that man, not giving it a fair try—one that doesn't allow thoughts of what anyone thinks about the relationship except the two of you—that would be a mistake, Shelly. And you know what I think?"

"Keep going. Don't stop now," Shelly said with a wave of her hand.

"I think your inner critic is getting the best of you. There's no reason why this relationship shouldn't work. You guys share the same interests. You have the same intensity. You didn't have that with Howard. You conformed to the things he liked. I remember when you were a ball of fire, queen of the flaming Bacardi shots. Remember when Rod Hampton singed his eyelashes going head-to-head with you?"

"Proud moments," Shelly said with a snort.

"The best," Tilly said, missing the sarcasm. "Then slowly, year after year, your asshole of a husband wore you down until you were doing what he wanted and not a damn thing for yourself. You'd forgotten how to live. You'd all but lost your confidence. Until four weeks ago."

"I don't like arguing."

"Oh, please. The unhealthiest thing in the world was the fact you and Howard never once got into a real fight. Your whole take on confrontation is skewed. If you and Luke would have kept at it a few nights ago, you'd have gotten everything ironed out and probably had the best make-up sex ever."

Shelly stared at the small octagonal floor tiles and reached for Tilly's hand again. "I'm scared."

"Of course you're scared," Tilly's voice softened and a second later Shelly was wrapped in her best friend's embrace. "But buck up, girlie. You might never get another shot like this. And if it doesn't work out, you can send him my way.

How's that sound? I tend to like them tall and lean but to have a guy who would venerate the size of my ass, I can overlook the bulkiness."

"I'm going to have to apologize," Shelly whispered against her friend's shoulder.

"Yeah. That's going to suck. No one likes admitting they overreacted. But you've got other things to worry about right now. Saying sorry to sex-on-two-legs can be your first official duty as a forty-five year old. Presently, it's time to party and there's a tiara waiting downstairs with your name on it!"

\* \* \* \* \*

Luke listened to the thumping bass and hoped Shelly's party wouldn't go on into the wee hours of the morning. He needed to see her, needed to apologize for being an idiot. *Gonna tell her you love her?* He didn't have an answer for that question. Yet.

He turned the three-by-three square box over in his hands, wishing he had stopped and picked up some wrapping paper. He'd been in such a hurry to get home from his shop it had never crossed his mind until he'd peeked out his window and seen the brightly colored gift bags and presents her guests carried into her house.

There had to be something lying around he could use. He got out of his chair and headed to the kitchen. Nothing. He walked into his garage and saw the recycle bin. In no time flat he was back in the kitchen and had her present decently wrapped in last Sunday's comics.

"Luke?"

"Dude, where are you?"

"Kitchen," he called, wondering what the twins were doing at his place at nine o'clock on a Saturday night.

"We're in possible deep shit," Matt said without preamble, spinning a kitchen chair around and straddling it.

"Fuckin' understatement," Sam replied.

Luke looked up at Matt and shook his head. "Village People called...said they're missing their construction worker."

"Real funny, dickhead. I'm a damn cable guy. Why the hell would I dress like I'm in the family business. That's not right."

"Why are you dressed up at all? Sammy's not."

"Yes, I am," Sam said. "I'm one of the Geek Squad."

"Real stretch," Luke laughed, smoothing the final piece of tape on Shelly's gift. "Where's the party?"

They stared at him, their matching hazel eyes widening as they answered as one. "Where the fuck do you think?"

Then Luke remembered. The talk about some lady seeing them at the bachelor auction and wanting them to dance at her friend's *birthday* party.

"No way," Luke said, shaking his head. "No fuckin' way."

"We thought you'd say that. But dude, you have no idea how much Mrs. Wakeford is paying us," Matt said.

"Whatever it is, I'll double it," Luke said.

"Fine. Eight large," Matt said, sticking out his hand.

"You're getting four hundred bucks?" Luke asked incredulously. "What the fuck did she hire you to do? Christ, don't tell me you two are supporting your computer and clubbing addictions by turning into man whores."

"She wants dancers, Luke. It's the easiest thing in the world. Just put on the right kind of music, sway and rock, peel off the clothes nice and slow, stop when you get down to the banana hammock. Simple as that," Sam replied. "We really can't bail on her. That's not right and we'd get a bad rep."

"Why the hell didn't you call and have her hire someone else when you found out it was Shelly's party?" Luke's head was starting to throb.

"We didn't get the address until this morning. It was too late to cancel. Plus…"

"Plus what?" Luke demanded.

"Plus, we heard you and the Professor sort of weren't together anymore," Sam said. "So we thought maybe you wouldn't care."

"You didn't think I'd care if my brothers made a stripper sandwich out of the woman I've been seeing for the past month?"

"We were ever hopeful," Matt said.

"Even though we're aware that's about twenty-eight days longer than your usual relationships," Sam added.

"But then Tom called us on the way over and said not to do anything to fuck up your plans," Matt said. "What the hell *are* your plans?"

"My plans," Luke said through gritted teeth, "are to get everyone—including the Professor—to realize that Shelly and I most definitely belong together."

"We are so screwed," the twins said in unison again.

"Come on." Luke walked to the front door, his brothers close behind. "We'll settle this right now."

They walked up to Shelly's screen door and Luke was about to ring the bell when a tall woman decked out in leopard print, from her spiked heels to the pair of glasses perched on her nose, turned the corner and saw them.

"Oh my god, you're early. We're nowhere near ready for you yet, and as scrumptious as your point man looks, I'm only paying for two of you. That was the deal."

"Mrs. Wakeford." Sam shouldered Luke out of the way and pulled the screen door open. He grabbed the plus-size cat woman by the wrist and pulled her onto the porch. She tiptoed across the planks and then teetered into Sam in such an overt manner, Luke had to laugh.

"Let me guess, you must be Tilly," Luke said. He'd never met Shelly's best friend but he'd heard all the outrageous stories.

"I am, gorgeous. And you are?"

"I'm Shelly's neighbor." *The man she's been screwing like a nympho for the past month. The man she's afraid to talk about. The man who can't live without her.* "Luke."

"Oh," she said offhandedly, still sizing Sam up. "Oh! Luke. Oh my god…you're here…you're back."

"I really never left."

"I know. I heard. Okay, listen. We've got to keep you two out of sight," she said, herding Matt and Sam away from the door and farther down the porch before turning back to Luke. "And you—"

"Tilly? Where are you?" They froze when Shelly's voice drifted out the door.

Luke looked through the screen and there she was, standing in the middle of the hallway, looking like a freakin' angel, a small tiara sparkling on top of her head, a look of worrisome surprise on her face.

"Luke?" she said softly, coming nearer.

"Go inside before she sees us," Tilly frantically whispered.

"Happy birthday." Not waiting for an invitation, he opened the door and stepped inside. He took his time and looked her over from head to toe. She was ten times more gorgeous than she'd been just days before. He looked at the uncharacteristically tight T-shirt she wore, the graphic of pins and a rolling ball proclaiming THAT'S HOW I BOWL.

"Nice shirt," he said with a tiny smile.

"No shit," he heard Matt whisper.

"Like a dead heat in a zeppelin race," Sam said a little softer but not quiet low enough that Shelly didn't peer around Luke's frame.

"Hey," they greeted her.

She looked slowly from them to him and Luke wiped his palms against his jeans and closed the distance between them, the lines he'd practiced and rehearsed that afternoon evaporating the minute she walked forward and wrapped her arms around him.

Shelly had a moment of utter fear when he didn't move, when his arms hung useless at his sides. But then he engulfed her, slid his massive arms around her back and her waist and hugged her in a way that matched the desperation she'd felt.

"I'm sorry," she said, tilting her head back, waiting, hoping for his kiss.

"We need to talk," he said in a thick voice. "Alone."

She turned her head and saw Tilly and his brothers standing on the other side of the screen, two of them with identical smiles on their faces while the third was moving her eyes in exaggerated movements from center to upper right, clearly trying to tell Shelly to get her ass in Luke's bed as fast as humanly possible.

"I don't think we do," Shelly said, threading her fingers through his soft hair and pulling his mouth down. She traced the kissable fullness of his lips over and over with the tip of her tongue until he quit holding back and melded their mouths together in a tongue-stroking dual that had Shelly's mind whirling.

She wrapped her arms around his neck and pulled herself higher. She wanted to simply crawl inside his strong, hot body and never return. She'd show him—show him how wrong she'd been, how badly she'd missed him. How much she needed him. The man inside the sent-from-heaven body. The man who'd made her see things clearer than she had in years.

The tension twisting her muscles into tight knots cleared in a rush when he spanned the center of her ass with one big hand and pulled her against his thighs. He was hard and ready and she wanted to feel more.

She broke the kiss but wiggled her hips tighter against him. "I think that pretty much says it all, don't you, Scooter?"

"Not even close," he said, his eyes promising a great deal more. "I didn't mean to crash your party." He loosened his hold and let her drop to her feet while his fingers blazed a trail up and down her spine.

"Screw the party," Tilly said, flinging the door open and rushing to their side. "It's clear something better has...come up."

Shelly inwardly groaned at the way her friend's gaze had flicked to Luke's crotch.

"And, since you're unable to fulfill your duties as the birthday girl, the responsibility falls to me as first runner-up." Tilly reached over and pulled the tiara off her head. She twirled the rhinestone-studded crown around with two fingers. "I will carry out your duties in your absence to the best of my abilities." She turned toward Sam and Matt and gave them a feline smile "Gentlemen...I've got the crown."

They walked forward, each of them giving Luke a flat-handed pat to the chest before they flanked Tilly and moved their bodies in close enough that Shelly watched her friend's eyebrows arch.

"That's perfect, Mrs. Wakeford," Matt said, taking the tiara from her hands and setting it on top her flaming red head.

"Mmm-hmm," Sam agreed. "'Cause we brought the scepters."

"Oh," Tilly all but purred. "Yum."

Luke groaned and pulled Shelly out the door.

\* \* \* \* \*

"Were you that confident that I'd throw myself at you and we'd end up back here, right where it started?" Shelly asked, tracing the cute little dot on his chest that hadn't been the drop of chocolate she'd hoped it was several weeks before. But here she was, sitting naked on his lap, thinking about leaning down and kissing it...and a great deal more.

"It?" He trapped her hand and brought her knuckles to his mouth, running each bump between his lips.

"This. Us."

"Us. That has a good ring to it but no, I was scared shitless that you'd slam the door in my face and break my fuckin' heart."

"Luke—"

"No...listen. I intended to say a whole lot more than 'I need to be inside you right now'. That was pretty pathetic."

"It was pretty effective," Shelly teased.

"But I wasn't shooting for words that would lure you into bed," he said, his eyes all seriousness. Then she saw the twinkle. "I could have just offered to let you play with my ass and got the same result."

"I do not lust after your butt," she said, without of drop of forcefulness. She was surprised when he let that remark slide.

"I had an entire speech planned, starting with an apology for impugning your intelligence."

"I was being ridiculous. It was stupid."

"No, it was your opinion but may I point out, it was wrong?" he said with a tiny smile. "You're entitled to what you want to believe. I don't want to change that, Shelly. I just want us to work through our issues in the future. We're probably going to argue from time to time. People who are strong willed do that sort of thing. It's totally normal and it doesn't mean they love each other any less."

Shelly's eyes snapped to his and her heart did a forward roll in her chest.

"But we have to trust what's between us and if it feels right to you and me, and you know for a fact it sure as hell does, then we focus on that and give the narrow-minded detractors a big 'fuck you'."

*Dear god!* Did he even realize what he'd said? He was on such a roll she doubted it.

"This can be the best thing that's ever happened to either of us," he said softly. The rest of his sentence was left unspoken but she read it loud and clear in the depths of his dark eyes.

*If you let it.*

He eased her off his lap and onto the mattress. "Wait here. I'll be right back."

She watched him pad down the staircase that led directly to his kitchen, her heart thundering as she tried to push her churning thoughts aside. She didn't want to be naïve and think it was possible to fall head over heels for someone so quickly. She wasn't even sure it was healthy to do so. *It's not as if Howard left one day and you jumped Luke's bones the next.*

She had tried to convince herself it was his body that was still the main attraction but that was a complete and utter lie. It would have been so much easier to have him prove he was the lothario his reputation alluded to. But that wasn't the case. Not at all.

He reached the top of the steps and walked to the bed, a small package in his hand.

"Happy Birthday, Shelly."

"Not Professor?" she asked, smiling at his choice of gift wrap as she took the present from his hand.

"No," he said, sliding onto the bed and taking a cross-legged pose in front of her. "This is for the woman behind the brains, the one inside the killer body that drives me wild every time I see it naked and most times when it's fully clothed. The woman who's made me realize how damn lucky I finally am."

Shelly looked down at the box and swallowed against the lump in her throat. She had no intention of dissolving into a puddle of tears. She had been overly emotional lately. Maybe it was just the hormones. *Bullshit!* She undid the comic wrapping and read the box.

"Serrated Hex Flange Screws/Steel/Black Oxide." She tilted her head to the side and gave him an indulgent smile. "Thank you, Luke. They're just what I wanted."

"We don't all shop where they give you little aqua-colored packages. Open it up, funny woman." He rested his elbows on his knees and let his hands fall between his legs, summarily blocking the tantalizing view of his own package.

Shelly opened the lid and pulled a crumpled paper towel out of the way. Lying on another layer of towel was a dark necklace, the chain mounded over the pendant. She pulled the links upward, the box falling from her hands when she looked at the design.

The heart was hand forged from a solid length of metal but instead of the bottom ending in a neat little point, the craftsman—and there was little doubt who he was—had extended the ends and twisted them three times around each other before melding the design closed.

"Twisted steel," she said softly, her eyes misting.

"Yeah. And from now on, you're going to be the sex appeal part of that phrase. Here, let me help you." He took the necklace out her hands and slid it over her head. "I hope it's the right length. I didn't have time to make a chain, a friend of mine had that one in his shop."

"When did you do this?" Shelly asked, no longer caring that his gaze was following the tear rolling over her cheekbone.

"The day after I acted like a royal asshole," he said, leaning forward and brushing the wetness off her face with the pad of his thumb. "I hope those are tears of happiness and not the kind that leak out when you're faced with the dilemma of wearing something you don't like because you don't want to hurt the gift giver's feelings."

"Oh my god, you're an idiot," she said, looking down at the pendant, the forged bottom resting just above her cleavage.

"I will defer to your superior intellect," he said, leaning forward and kissing her other tear away.

"It's perfect. It's beautiful...one of a kind," she said, taking his handsome face between her hands.

"Just like you," they said together, the meeting of their lips cutting off their shared laughter.

His kiss was slow, tender and she wondered how someone so massively large and undoubtedly strong could be so gentle.

"Come here," he whispered, urging her forward until her knees were on either side of his hips and his cock was proudly erect between their bodies.

She watched him reach down and pick up the metal heart and run his thumb over the design. The chain tugged against her neck as he shifted the pendant to her left breast and held it over her heart.

"Is it too early to tell you how I feel?" he asked, pressing the metal hard against her skin, not to the point of pain but with enough force that when he let it drop the outline of the pendant was clearly visible.

Shelly didn't want to have to jump up and run from the room in fear that things were going too fast. She wasn't going to screw this up. They had all the time in the world. "It probably is," she answered.

He traced the indentation against her skin with two fingers and she closed her eyes and embraced the rush of desire starting to build.

"When do you think you'll be ready to hear that I'm in love with you?" He leaned forward and kissed the open area inside the heart, his warm lips lingering against her flesh a very long time.

"Luke…" she hesitated, not knowing what to say.

"Tell you what, how about I ask again in a month? One month, Professor. How's that sound?"

She looked into his eyes and smiled. "One month seems to be our magic number," she said, unable to refrain from touching him a minute longer. Shelly ran her hands down his chest and over his stomach until she reached his cock. She fingered the vein pulsing along his length and he grabbed her hips and urged her upward.

"Guide me," he gently ordered.

"I want to touch you first…feel that hardness. This is twisting steel in its truest form," she said, gripping him loosely and rotating her wrist back and forth as she worked her way up and down his shaft.

"You can touch me anytime," he said, the centers of his eyes quickly dilating. "But right now, I want to feel your pussy when you sink onto me, nice and slow with nothing between us. Just my dick stroking away while your hot walls grip me."

Shelly's eyes widened. "Luke…before? Oh my god, I was so desperate…it was so fast…I didn't even realize you weren't covered."

"Yeah, it's not how I imagined my first time would be, either. I needed you so badly, my mind caught bits and pieces of how good it felt but it was my heart that was on overload."

"Your first time?"

"I told you I didn't go without protection. I never have."

"Ever?" she asked incredulously.

"Never."

She felt his hands close around her hips and squeeze and she rose up and pressed his cock head against her wet folds. Eyes locked, he helped her slide slowly downward, their mutual groans long and loud.

"Oh my god, Luke." She loved that as wild and experienced as he was, there was something special that only they shared.

"That's fuckin' heaven, honey. Just stay still for a while. Let me take it all in. It's soft as silk...and hotter than lava."

Shelly gave her inner muscles a little squeeze and he moaned louder.

"Do that again," he said, moving his hands to her ass and spreading the soft globes so he was a little deeper. "It's so much different than when you're spasming, when you're just about to come."

"Better?" she asked, squeezing him again and loving the way his beautiful features tensed.

"Hell no, that's the best, Professor." He gave her that lopsided smile, the one that was his and his alone. "But I want to feel a little more of this. Wrap your legs behind me."

Shelly slid one leg and then the other around his back, the action forcing his cock deeper and her clit flush against his pubic bone.

He used his hands and rocked her hips in movements so slight Shelly couldn't believe the erotic effects he created. With each rotation her clit barely bumped his body while his cock pulsed inside her. Over and over until she gripped his shoulders, prepared to help increase the speed. He grabbed the globes of her ass in a forceful grip and stopped her.

"Let me. Just let me guide your sweet pussy around the way I want. I'll never be able to describe how amazing this is. I wouldn't want it to be with anyone but you."

The raw honesty in his intent gaze shook her.

"Is that an unmanly thing to admit?" He uncrossed his legs and slid them straight, the new position filling her aching pussy to the max.

"Oh my god," she moaned, sinking her nails into his shoulders at the previously untried position. "There isn't anything unmanly about it—or you.

He arched a brow and slid his hands between their bodies to palm her ass.

"Tell me again," he ordered sexily, biceps bunching as he lifted her upward until only the tip of his cock was still inside her and his warm breath was caressing the center of her chest.

"You're the manliest man on Earth," she said, holding his gaze.

He lowered her, his cock stroking her channel with slow, torturous friction before raising her up again and asking, "Is that all?"

"I love how you make me feel sexy," she added hopefully.

"I'm trying to make you feel something a little more intense than 'sexy'," he deadpanned.

Shelly disguised her smile by biting her lip as he eased her downward again, using a snail-like pace.

"I love all the things you do to me with your lips and your fingers."

He lifted her a third time and held her poised and her pussy clenched as she thought of her next words.

"I love your cock and all the ways you love my body with it."

"Shelly," he growled, guiding her downward so quickly she gasped. "You make me so hard and hot—with a glance, with your words. Lean back and let me feel all of you. Let me love you deep and hard until we both explode."

Shelly let go of his shoulders and relaxed her upper body, grabbing his legs just below his knees. He worked her body up and down his steely cock, their position allowing his shaft to stroke the engorged zone along the front of her vagina and she felt the first deep little roll of orgasmic promise.

He had spoiled her. His unending quest to locate each and every spot on her body that brought her pleasure, to shower them with his undivided focus until she screamed his name, had ruined her for life.

She felt the heat blossom in her core, flames licking outward until her entire body was encompassed, until her skin prickled and moisture broke out upon the surface.

"So hot," she moaned, closing her eyes as the pressure increased and her body tensed.

"So good," he added, the sound of his rasping breath echoing around her.

She dug her heels into his back, toes curling into the mattress as the long, rolling waves began.

"Open your eyes. Watch us come."

Shelly forced her lids open. His features were taut, his nostrils flared as he fought for control.

Desire tumbled through her body and her breathing turned harsh. This time she wouldn't go off with a blinding array of lights dancing behind her eyelids. This release would come with the muted haze that she'd learned—at the end of his extremely skilled fingers—accompanied the G-spot orgasms that racked her body minute upon minute.

"Oh my god, Luke. It's starting." He was bringing her along with nothing other than his cock's steady rhythm and she fought to embrace the sensation as he had taught her.

"Your walls are rippling. Rollin' against me every time I reach deeper. I love it, Shelly. I fuckin' love how you respond for me."

As if in tune to his words, a long contraction gripped her. She gasped as others followed in it wake, the exquisitely rolling waves allowing her to barely catch her breath as her heart rate drummed out of control. Part of her longed to scream "faster" while another part—the part that was enjoying the singular sensation of having her desire milked out of her in long, slow twists—begged her to keep quiet.

"Yes." It was barely a sob, not at all indicative of the maelstrom of feeling assaulting her inner walls. And then her release was fully upon her and she went off calling his name over and over, no longer hesitant to tell him what he was making her feel or how very much she adored him.

Luke crushed her to his chest, burying his hand into the hair at the nape of her neck as he took two final pumps before his scorching release shot deep into her quivering center, his jumbled words of love filling her ears.

She wrapped her arms around his back, exhaling one last wavering breath before her breathing slowed. His breathing remained erratic and she tightened her arms, reveling in the way his heart was hammering against her right breast. She loved knowing they had the same effect on each other.

Luke gently maneuvered her onto her back and pulled his semi-soft cock free, leaving a thin trail of their combined desire along her thigh as she slid her legs leisurely down his body as a familiar euphoria began creeping into her bones.

"Mmmm," he hummed, draping his satiated self halfway across her body. He blinked his eyes open, his expression so blissful she had to smile. *Too gorgeous for words and all yours — every last inch.*

"What made you finally relent?" she asked softly, dampening the pad of her thumb with her tongue before reaching between them and carefully bathing the tip of his cock.

His long fingers encompassed her wrist and he slowly brought her hand to his mouth, shocking her nearly senseless when he sucked her thumb between his lips. "Mmmm. We taste good together, Professor."

"Oh my god," she groaned. "Don't try to distract me with your brazenness. I'd like to know."

He snorted, his big chest sending a spiral of warmth through her as he pressed against her breast

"I gave in to the lure of ditching the raingear because I have no willpower," he said, reaching up and pushing some wayward strands of hair behind her ear.

"Bullshit," she uttered, her inflection so similar to his he laughed aloud. "Truth and honesty, Scooter."

"I relented," he said, touching his forehead to hers, "because I want to meet each and every one of your sexual demands, Professor…and the not-so-sexual ones as well. I want to do whatever it takes to keep you right here in my arms. Forever. And a very wise man told me the best way to do that was to simply give the learned Professor Shelly Latimer what she wants."

Shelly's heart swelled as she stared into his teasingly dark gaze. Forever. With a man who valued her as a person, desired her as a woman, and had no intention of ever trying to change her. Forever sounded heavenly.

"Well, next time you run into that learned man, thank him for me, because I have exactly what I want, Luke Henderson. I have you."

# *Also by M.A. Ellis*

**ဢ**

Love's Choice
Seducing the Siren


# *About the Author*

**ဢ**

M.A. Ellis is a firm believer that everyone should pursue their dreams…no matter how long it takes to achieve them. She wrote her first short story, What I Want To Be When I Grow Up, more than a few decades ago. It was read by a total of seven people. (For those who are interested, the answer to that intriguing statement was a toss-up between a veterinarian and a nun.)

Thanks to the encouragement of a creative writing guru at Northern Kentucky University, she stepped out of her neat little writing boundaries and penned an erotic poem, which ultimately led her to the vastly stimulating world of erotic romance. It's a vocation she truly loves — equally as rewarding as furry, four-legged creatures and a heck of a lot more entertaining than Friday nights at the nunnery.

When not devoting her time to crafting tales of hot encounters and steamy romances that always have a happy ending, M.A. concentrates on the delightful task of honing her master baking skills, eagerly focusing on the realms of cheesecake and chocolate which are, in her humble opinion, the only 'c' words that matter.

She lives in northwestern Pennsylvania where temperatures rival those of Ice Station Zebra a good portion of the year—making it the perfect arena for devising stories where one spark can ignite a welcomed inferno.

M.A. Ellis welcomes comments from readers. You can find her website and email address on her author bio page at www.ellorascave.com.

### Tell Us What You Think
We appreciate hearing reader opinions about our books. You can email us at Comments@EllorasCave.com.

# Why an electronic book?

We live in the Information Age—an exciting time in the history of human civilization, in which technology rules supreme and continues to progress in leaps and bounds every minute of every day. For a multitude of reasons, more and more avid literary fans are opting to purchase e-books instead of paper books. The question from those not yet initiated into the world of electronic reading is simply: *Why?*

1. ***Price.*** An electronic title at Ellora's Cave Publishing and Cerridwen Press runs anywhere from 40% to 75% less than the cover price of the exact same title in paperback format. Why? Basic mathematics and cost. It is less expensive to publish an e-book (no paper and printing, no warehousing and shipping) than it is to publish a paperback, so the savings are passed along to the consumer.

2. ***Space.*** Running out of room in your house for your books? That is one worry you will never have with electronic books. For a low one-time cost, you can purchase a handheld device specifically designed for e-reading. Many e-readers have large, convenient screens for viewing. Better yet, hundreds of titles can be stored within your new library—on a single microchip. There are a variety of e-readers from different manufacturers. You can also read e-books on your PC or laptop computer. (Please note that Ellora's Cave does not endorse any specific brands.

You can check our websites at www.ellorascave.com or www.cerridwenpress.com for information we make available to new consumers.)

3. *Mobility.* Because your new e-library consists of only a microchip within a small, easily transportable e-reader, your entire cache of books can be taken with you wherever you go.

4. *Personal Viewing Preferences.* Are the words you are currently reading too small? Too large? Too… ANNOYING? Paperback books cannot be modified according to personal preferences, but e-books can.

5. *Instant Gratification.* Is it the middle of the night and all the bookstores near you are closed? Are you tired of waiting days, sometimes weeks, for bookstores to ship the novels you bought? Ellora's Cave Publishing sells instantaneous downloads twenty-four hours a day, seven days a week, every day of the year. Our webstore is never closed. Our e-book delivery system is 100% automated, meaning your order is filled as soon as you pay for it.

Those are a few of the top reasons why electronic books are replacing paperbacks for many avid readers.

As always, Ellora's Cave and Cerridwen Press welcome your questions and comments. We invite you to email us at Comments@ellorascave.com or write to us directly at Ellora's Cave Publishing Inc., 1056 Home Avenue, Akron, OH 44310-3502.

erridwen, the Celtic Goddess of wisdom, was the muse who brought inspiration to story-tellers and those in the creative arts. Cerridwen Press encompasses the best and most innovative stories in all genres of today's fiction. Visit our site and discover the newest titles by talented authors who still get inspired - much like the ancient storytellers did, once upon a time.

CERRIOWEN PRESS

www.cerriowenpress.com